I0818053

The System Apocalypse

Short Story Anthology Volume 2

With Stories By…

D. J. Rezlaw
InkWitch
Craig Hamilton
Andrew Tarkin Coleman
Mike Parsons
Nick Steele
Chelsea Luckritz
David R. Packer
Corwyn Callahan
E. C. Godhand
Jason J. Willis

and

Tao Wong

Copyright

The System Apocalypse Short Story Anthology Volume 2

A Starlit Publishing Book
Published by Starlit Publishing
PO Box 30035
High Park PO
Toronto, ON
M6P 3K0
Canada

www.starlitpublishing.com

Ebook ISBN: 9781778551055
Paperback ISBN: 9781778551062
Hardcover ISBN: 9781778551079

Books in the System Apocalypse Universe

Main Storyline (complete series with 12 books)

Life in the North

Redeemer of the Dead

The Cost of Survival

Cities in Chains

Coast on Fire

World Unbound

Stars Awoken

Rebel Star

Stars Asunder

Broken Council

Forbidden Zone

System Finale

System Apocalypse – Relentless

A Fist Full of Credits

Dungeon World Drifter

Apocalypse Grit

System Apocalypse: Australia

Town Under

Flat Out

Bloody Oath

Anthologies and Short stories

System Apocalypse Short Story Anthology Volume 1

System Apocalypse Short Story Anthology Volume 2

Valentines in an Apocalypse

A New Script

Daily Jobs, Coffee and an Awfully Big Adventure

Adventures in Clothing

Questing for Titles

Blue Screens of Death

My Grandmother's Tea Club

The Great Black Sea

Growing Up – Apocalypse Style

A Game of Koopash (Newsletter exclusive)

Lana's story (Newsletter exclusive)

Debts and Dances (Newsletter exclusive)

A Tense Meeting (Newsletter exclusive)

Comic Series

The System Apocalypse Comics (7 Issues)

The System Apocalypse Graphic Novel: Issues 1-7

(Limited hardcover edition)

Contents

Welcome to the Human History Forum

Welcome, Galactics!

The Human History Forum is the premier forum for the galaxy's favorite new entrants from the thirteenth Dungeon World—Humans! Love them, hate them, hunt them; you'll find stories about their greatest heroes and their most worthless zeroes.

Before you go any further, please note the following rules:

1. No Spam, Advertising, Self-promotion, or Skill Use on the Forums

While we are a gathering of enthusiasts, these forums are a no spam or advertising location. Understand that we have employed the latest technology to hunt down those breaking our rules and will impose a System-fine on rule-breakers.

Repeated rule-breakers will be referred to the Forum Judges. You do not want them to come for you. Or do. They pay us a portion of their earnings when they impose their Credit penalties on you.

You have been warned.

2. Do not post System-restricted material

Your System-restricted material will be deleted. You will be reported to the appropriate authorities. We are not your monster to call for freedom of information or other arbitrary plans. Deal with it yourself. Acquire your information legally via the System and then post it.

3. Postings that might be offensive, abusive, harassment, or otherwise are done at your own risk

Remember, if you post anything that might be offensive or which might constitute defamation, harassment, or abuse, it is entirely at your own risk. Remember, we have Crusaders, Justicars, and Master Classes who visit this forum.

Use common sense while posting. This is a site for serious historians, not childish insults. We do not utilize any security or obscuring Skills.

4. Post in the Correct Forum

Please refrain from posting the same story, article, or treatise in several forums. If in doubt, ask the moderators. They will allocate your story to the correct forum. Remember, we have sections for System-verified, verified, speculative, and "slash" fiction. Make use of it properly.

All moderator decisions are final.

5. Remain respectful. Or don't. Just don't blame us.

Strive to be professional and courteous. You have every right to disagree, but do so courteously. Again, remember, Trolls, Justicars, and Forum-Seekers are all prowling this forum. As one of the fastest-growing interest groups, we attract a lot of attention.

It is not our job to keep you safe. It is yours to be respectful.

6. Retaliation for no good reason will result in bannings and outings

Yes. In contradiction to point five (5) above, we do want lively disagreements. If you choose to undertake retaliatory attacks for professional and courteous disagreements, we will ban you and out all such interactions to appropriate parties.

And the final rule,

7. Have fun!

We are all here because of our shared love of human history and stories. So have fun. Enjoy yourselves! And don't wander into the slash sections unless you know exactly what you're getting into.

Human and Galactic Interactions – Positive Bent

All right, you goblin-loving sacks of shit (respectfully!), I'm halfway done with my thesis about human and galactic interaction. Starting from, of course, the most famous of all beginnings, to current crises caused by humanity's "Champions."

However, my thesis advisor says I'm being very one-sided in my current dissertation. So I need more stories to showcase more positive Galactic interactions. You know my preferences and what I'm looking for, you ingrates.

As always, I've got recordings of the latest XC Arena Fights, the Mona X-45 Sub-Light Asteroid Runs, and the JK Monsterpede Works in trade and rewards.

Show me what you got, you ingrates.
---- SharkEater_Gss-9811

CorruptQuestor42 – Formation of the X-People Guild by humans and miscellaneous immigrant aliens in Sao Paulo

SharkEater_Gss-9811 – Boring! Do better.

XanBRedMage-Crystal44 – How about this? First ever alien and human dungeon run in Bangui. Anomalous dungeon creation due to a fluctuating Mana wave formed a dungeon well ahead of the curve and nearly saw the destruction of the entire city.

SharkEater_Gss-9811 – More like it. Keep it coming.

JoeDak_asp_DD – This work? A little more tame, but it's a positive interaction. Non-combat classer too, which is rare, right?

SharkEater_Gss-9811 – Sounds boring, but let's see what you got. It'll probably tickle my professor's junk. And he's got four.

After Party

by D.J. Rezlaw

I'm Dave, and I like to party.

At least, that was my slogan back when I was a party planner in the big city. You know, before the System happened. Before we all got Classes and Skills, and ninety percent of us died. I'd probably be dead too, if I hadn't come back to my hometown in middle-of-nowhere Texas to plan a friend's bachelor party. The city I'd lived in didn't fare too well. Lots of dead people.

So I got lucky, in a way. I lived. Most of my family lived. The surrounding countryside started out fairly low-leveled, which made surviving easier, if not easy.

I got unlucky, however, in other ways. For example, I was *very* drunk when I made my Class choice. Remember the bachelor party? It went on into the early hours of the morning and looked as though it might keep going… until we all started seeing blue screens in front of our faces.

I've sworn off alcohol since then actually. Thanks to that stuff, and my stupidity, I'm now a level 40 Party Planner. Yes, that's my Class. And yes, it's been *very* hard to level. The apocalypse started nearly two years ago, and this is as far as I've been able to get. And that's with working my rear off every day. Us "non-combat" classes gain experience, and thus Levels and power, by completing quests tied to our class's goal. A crafter class has quests to craft things. A lawyer has quests to… sue people? I don't really know how a lawyer levels, or if any even survived the System.

But a Party Planner? Turns out that I *drastically* overestimated the demands for parties in the apocalypse when I chose this Class. Not much to celebrate, what with all the monsters and death. No parties mean I can't complete my Class quests, which means no access to easy, safe experience.

Instead, I've had to go out with the combat Classes to fight the mutated animals and brand-new monsters that roam the plains around our small town. My Class doesn't come with any offensive abilities, but I grew up hunting with my dad and friends. Now, the things we hunt are much more likely to hunt us back, but still, I'm familiar with the concept. I purchased some combat spells from the Shop, and I have my Party Hard buff, so I'm not completely useless. Not nearly as useful as I'd like to be, but I don't slow people down too much.

Several of my friends, on the other hand, chose *actually* useful Classes.

"Look out!" Marsha calls as she tackles me to the side.

A red, slimy rope as thick as my arm misses us by inches as we fall, before slurping back into the mouth of the horse-sized bullfrog hiding in the tall grass near the trail. It's big, ugly, and has an extra pair of legs. A glance is all it takes for my Level 1 *Identify* skill to trigger.

Grey-Bellied Groggert (Level 53)

Even before we stop moving, green is leaching from the plants around us and forming a ghostly shell around Marsha. She's a level 45 Plant Warden and the tank for our regular group. That Plant's Gift shield of hers can really take a beating—as long as she's around living green things. Which is good, because from the chorus of earth-shaking croaks coming from farther in the grass, I can tell this groggert isn't alone.

But that's okay—neither are we.

"Yeehaw!" The pounding of hooves on the hard trail almost drowns out Connor's shout as he gallops around the corner. Before his horse even slides to a stop, Connor raised his rifle and fired five times, all the shots slamming into the groggert's massive forehead. Each bullet glows white with the power of his Wild Blast skill.

I've gotten up by this point, but before I can use a single Skill or fire my beam pistol, Marsha has stabbed the wounded monster twice with her sword, killing it.

As I said, I'm not completely useless out here, just mostly.

I activate my group buff, Party Hard, which gives a 10% increase to Stamina, Health, and Mana Regeneration to friendlies around me. Like most of my abilities, it's more powerful if I apply it to an event I've planned, but it still has some effect when I use it to boost my hunting group. That's all I have time for before two more groggerts hop onto the trail, their grey-green bulk shaking the ground as they land.

I raise my beam pistol, a Mark V Humbolt Special that I've been carrying, and upgrading, for the last year. As I fire off a quick blast, I duck back behind Marsha. Two years ago, hiding behind the five-foot-nothing former cheerleader would have seemed nuts. Now, thanks to our different stats and Skills, Marsha probably has three times my Health. And that's without considering her shield. I've been putting most of my free attribute points into Constitution, but I still only have 510 Health. I'd be crazy not to hide behind the slim blonde.

My first shot hits one groggert on its fleshy mouth, leaving a single mark but not doing much damage. Okay, straight energy blasts don't seem to be the ticket. Time to try out my gun's newest upgrade. The Mana Attunement Module, and its associated user manual download, wasn't cheap, but if it does what the salesman said it would…

My Mana drops as I fire my next blast, this one tinged a pulsing red. My aim stays true, and the shot goes straight into the groggert's open mouth as it prepares to unleash its tongue. When the beam impacts the back of the demon frog's throat, an explosion of flame and force sends the groggert flying onto its back.

"Yes!" I yell, before glancing at the indicator on my gun.

That one shot took a quarter of the battery on my pistol, but the effect was definitely worth it. The Mana Attunement Module lets me channel compatible offensive spells into the pistol's beam, overcharging the spell at the expense of the battery and delivering it with pinpoint accuracy. Luckily for me, Firebolt, an upgraded version of my first Store-bought spell, Spark, is compatible with the gun.

With one groggert on its back and half of its Health gone, the rest of the battle ends quickly. I keep the inverted groggert busy with regular casts of Firebolt, mixed with a few blasts from my pistol, while Conner and Marsha take down the other one before turning on mine. Soon we're left with three steaming, horse-sized toad corpses. Which, conveniently, is exactly why we're out here.

Conner swings down from the saddle and laughs as he claps me on the shoulder. "Great job, Dave! Brilliant! I wouldn't have thought to pretend to be so helpless that the groggerts we were hunting would hunt *you* instead! You saved us tons of time!"

He has a big grin and uses the same tone of voice he always does when he's messing with me. It's good to hear him laugh again. We've grown distant recently, but it's easy to forget that in the afterglow of battle.

I wince and rub my shoulder, letting out a little chuckle of my own. Connor's an Advanced Class—only level 1, but that means he has 50 levels of Basic class under his belt. His Basic class, Cowboy, gave him plenty of points in strength, as my complaining shoulder attests. I don't know much about his new class, Monster Rancher, but it must be a lot more difficult to Level. He got the class during the Big Raid a few months back, but hasn't Leveled since then, even though he's been out grinding for experience every day. He told me he's still figuring out what the Class can do, and he'd show me once he did.

"Yeah, playing bait is what I do best." I stored the first of the corpses in my Party Prep expanded inventory. It's the Class Skill I use the most, letting me transport the bodies of edible monsters and making hunting as a team much more efficient. It can also be used for carrying other party-related items, but it's mostly just to let me be more useful on hunts.

"No, pack-mule is definitely your role." Marsha grins.

I laugh even as I know she isn't wrong. I don't really mind. Lugging these behemoth frogs back with us would have been a major chore, even with our enhanced strength and Connor's horse Silver. Instead, for the low price of three Skill points and losing 15 mana regeneration per minute, I can store all three corpses with plenty of room to spare.

"Is that it?" Connor shifts in his saddle. I can tell he remembers he didn't want to come on this errand in the first place and is anxious to get back to town.

To check, I pull up my personal quest list. The self-assigned tasks don't give any System rewards like experience for completing them, but this is far more convenient than scribbling notes on random scraps of paper. I scanned through the list, noting that everything has been marked complete.

"We're set!" I dismiss the translucent blue screen from my vision with a thought, my mind already moving to everything else I have to get done before tonight.

Connor whistles, and Silver trots up from where she has been munching on the grass. He places one hand on the horn of the saddle before swinging nimbly onto his seat. Looking down at me, his expression changes, moving from the levity of a moment ago to the almost permanent scowl I've seen on his face for the past two months. "I still don't see why you want to serve roast groggert at this thing. Only people that will eat it are those damn Furries, and we shouldn't even be inviting them."

I sigh as I look at the trampled grass where the bodies had just been. This again. Glancing at Marsha, I see her looking worriedly between the two of us. She's heard this argument more than once, and not just between Connor and me. She doesn't approve of my plan either, but she isn't as… outspoken as Connor is. I can understand how they feel, even if I don't agree with it. Change is hard, and letting go of old grudges is even harder.

I try humor at first. "Roast groggert is actually pretty good once you get used to it! Kind of fishy, but…" Connor's scowl deepens, and I sigh again. "Look, I get it. The *Hrugther*"—I stress their real name— "aren't from around here. We've had our differences, but—"

"They didn't take your home!" Connor almost yells, before he takes a deep breath. "They're invaders," he says more calmly. "This is our land, not theirs."

"They're refugees," I say, already tired of the argument we've had so many times over the last few months, since I started to actually get to know our neighbors. "And we would have been dead a hundred times by now if they hadn't—"

"Stop. Just stop." Connor's voice is flat. "I came out here because you're my friend, and I'll come to your little party, but don't ever ask me to like those dog-headed freaks."

His horse stomps on the ground, perhaps sensing her rider's anger. Looking down at Marsha, he holds out a hand. Marsha gives me a quick, apologetic look before swinging up behind Connor.

"Are you going to be okay out here?" she asks, indecision on her face. They know that my next stop is the Hrugther, but Marsha is too much the tank of our group not to worry about leaving me alone out here.

I give her a brief smile and a wave, and that's all Connor needs before he takes off back down the trail toward our home. Honestly, I'd been surprised the two of them agreed to come with me on this hunting trip, given everything. Connor hasn't even been hunting with our regular party recently, preferring to go out with some others who share his feelings.

I guess I'd better explain what that's all about. You see, Blue Screens, Levels, Classes, and monsters spawning to eat us aren't the only changes that came with the apocalypse. We also got new neighbors. Our town has always, technically, been two separate entities divided by a river. More of a large creek, really, but it was enough. We'd even had two different mayors, one for each half, although I think only the mayors cared. Most of us just considered it one medium-sized town.

And then the Hrugther appeared on the other side of the river. They said they had purchased that part of the town, our town, from the System. The same System none of us had asked for or wanted, and that had been doing its best to kill us.

It didn't go well, and most of that was on us. If the Hrugther hadn't been significantly more powerful than us, and if they hadn't had a code of honor that stopped them from doing more than defending themselves from our attacks, it would have gone far worse.

I know, I know. What kind of savages attack another group of sentients unprovoked? Well, you have to understand that until a few days prior, none of us had ever met an alien. We had just survived the start of the apocalypse and had been fighting nonstop against monsters and mutant animals to *keep* surviving. And then these aliens that look as if they came straight from a furry convention showed up? And they were part of this System that was destroying our world?

Yeah, we attacked. Not all of us, but I was there. Looking back, it was stupid. I mean, our highest leveled fighter, Connor, was only level 4 at that point, and most of us were level 1 or 2. On the Hrugther side? They had two Advanced Class fighters, and most of their *kids*, at least ones old enough to have a Class, were at higher levels than us. We couldn't even hurt them, but we were too new to the System to understand how it worked or how outclassed we were.

Luckily for us, one Roar of Dominance from their leader was enough to force us to our knees, the Charisma-based ability too much for our low Willpower to resist. That meant they didn't need to use actual violence to defend against our attack. Equally lucky—they let us live. Even if they kicked all the humans out, forcing them to what is now our side of the river. As long as we stayed on our side, they stayed on theirs, even though they could have wiped us out.

That confused me, but as I've learned more about our neighbors since then, it makes sense. Once part of a powerful empire of warriors, the Hrugther have been on the losing side of one too many wars.

They really are refugees, as I told Connor, a scattered people looking for a home. This group saw a chance for that home when Earth became a Dungeon World, and they pooled their resources to purchase half of a little town in the middle of Texas. Despite fighting for scraps for generations, their pride and their honor remain strong, which is one reason they let us go.

As one gruff Hrugther told me later, "If we killed every pup who tried to bite us, no pups would grow to be warriors!"

The other reason they let us live was more practical, and one that the cooler heads on our side eventually came to realize as well—Dungeon Worlds are dangerous, and there is safety in numbers.

By sending out every person who is willing to fight, even non-combat classers like me, we have managed, barely, to keep up with the monsters spawning in the plains on our side of the river.

If we had to cover both sides? This new world would have wiped us off the map by the end of the first winter. And that isn't counting the timely advice we've received from the Hrugther, like when they warned us to look out for Alpha and Boss monsters. Maybe they just helped us so they didn't have to worry about a monster swarm hitting them in the back, but we appreciated the aid anyway.

Or at least some of us did.

A distressing percentage still resent the Hrugther for taking over part of our town. Some are like Connor, who had lived on the other side of the river and so felt personally robbed. Others just need someone to blame for the System, and our neighbors are the closest target for their hate.

And as often happens, that anger and distrust has been met with anger and distrust from some of the Hrugther as well. All in all, we haven't had the easiest relationship with them, but it mostly stayed civil as long as we both stayed on our respective sides.

Until the Fire Ants, that is. About a year into the apocalypse, we started seeing giant, mutated Fire Ants wandering around on our side of the river. As much of a pain as the little guys had been, these big ones were way worse.

Little known fact about the pre-System fire ant—their venom is so potent that if one the size of a tarantula bit a regular pre-System human, it would be fatal. These guys? Bigger than cows, and they had more than their venom to fight with. I guess the System took their name seriously, because we're talking literal flames from these bad boys.

We tracked the ants back to their nest, which at the time was just a Monster Lair. Its entrance was right next to our side of the river, about two miles south of town. As we had done hundreds of times, we sent in our best hunter team to destroy the nest. They didn't invite me of course, but Connor had complained loud and long about finding "those damn Furries!" inside the nest already. Turned out the ants had built their monster den tunneling *under* the river, with entrances on both sides.

That was the closest we came to open conflict, at least since that first day. Both us and the Hrugther claimed the nest, so neither of us cleared it, neither side wanting to break the uneasy peace.

We would kill anything that came out of the entrance on our side, like our neighbors did on theirs. Most people actually forgot about the ants, except when complaining about the Hrugther, especially when the ants stopped coming out. The only ones who really noticed were the hunters, and they were just glad for the break from fighting the flaming bugs.

Everything was quiet for about a month… until wave after wave of ants came pouring out of the entrances. We'd let the monster den fester for too long, and it had turned into a full-blown dungeon. And then when we didn't clear it… well, it did what dungeons do when no one bothers to take care of them. We had a full monster horde on our hands, flaming ants flooding from both sides of the river.

If we hadn't had sentries at the nest, the bugs would have caught us completely unaware. As it was, we lost too many good people that night, the worst casualties since the early days. We fought back, and that time we actually worked *with* the Hrugther. Together, we beat back the horde and eventually cleared the Dungeon.

I actually helped with that. We all did, on both sides, those of us who could fight or provide buffs.

I won't say our two races became best friends overnight, but the battle helped us see each other in a new light, at least a bit. The Hrugther saw that we had grown strong and were worthy of respect, and we saw that the Hrugther would sacrifice to save their town, their people, and us.

It didn't fix things, but it gave us a chance. An opening. A victory worth celebrating. And what better way to bring people together than a party? It took some doing, but I convinced both sides that our peoples deserved to celebrate our triumph and remember the lives we had lost. I've been planning and preparing for that celebration since then.

And that party is in—I look at the System clock in the lower left of my vision—ten hours, forty minutes, give or take a few seconds.

I've been working on this party nonstop for two months, and there is still so much to do! I walk toward the nearby river and the bridge. I'm not too worried about being attacked on my way because groggert are territorial, known for eating any monster smaller than them and running from anything larger.

The fact that we had killed those three meant I should be clear at least to the water, and the Hrugther keep their side of the river well-patrolled. Still, I activate my Store-bought stealth ability, Quiet Steps, just in case. Even though I want to hurry, I move slowly, trusting my Skill and skill to keep my noise down. I won't be able to finish my massive to-do list if I get eaten by a monster.

While I move through the tall grass, I pull up the notifications from our brief fight earlier.

3 X Groggert (Level 61, 63, and 64) Slain!

Your share of the experience: 2,186

Level Up!

You have reached level 41 as a Party Planner. Stat Points automatically distributed.

You have 2 Free Attributes to distribute.

1 Class Skill Point available to be distributed.

I pause when I see the Level up notification, feeling a surge of satisfaction. I'd been stuck at Level 40 for a month, and my experience gain had slowed to a crawl as I'd had to focus on the party instead of hunting.

Finally! I put my free points into Constitution, my go-to stat since I really enjoy being alive, and pull up my new Skill options. I'm tempted to put the skill point into my Party Hard buff, even though it's a lower tier, because it's one of my few Class Skills that is useful in combat. I've placed six points into it already, and I hope a few more will let it evolve into an even more useful skill.

Still, level 41 means I've finally unlocked the highest tier skills my class offers, and it doesn't hurt to look at what they are. I pull up their descriptions.

Customize

The Party Planner can access a limited Shop interface to customize a typical Event Material, changing it to another Material of the same Event category (food, drink, decorations, etc). Base Material must be System-registered. Tier of Material can be upgraded for additional cost. Choices in Customize interface based on Skill level and recipes known.

Cost: 100 Mana per kilogram changed. Additional cost for upgrading Tier of material.

Party Stamina

Passive: The Party Planner gains 5% additional Constitution.

Active: The Party Planner emits an aura that gives all friendlies at the party 5% additional Constitution while at the party. Buff limited to 5% of Party Planner's Constitution.

Cost: Passive: Permanently reduces Mana regeneration by 5 mana per minute.

Active: 5 Mana per minute

Bounce

The Party Planner gains final say over who may remain at their Event. The Party Planner can target one System-registered guest to the Event and Bounce them. Targeted guest must have violated an official Event Rule as defined by the Party Planner at Event Registration. Targeted guest is stunned and loses access to System skills and abilities for two minutes. Effect modified by Level and tier difference between target and Skill tier.

Cost: 500 Mana

I realize I'd started walking faster as I read through those, and I force myself to move more cautiously again, but it's hard. These are surprisingly good! Or at least the first two are.

Customize could let me make a tidy profit, if I'm reading the description right, by buying low tier materials and upgrading them to a higher tier. Basically, I could turn Mana into credits, which would be very nice. And Party Stamina would give me effectively 10% more health while in combat, not to mention the boost to my team.

Bounce seems pretty niche, so I set that one aside. If I were running Events as a business, it would make sense, but I need Skills that can give me an edge in my day-to-day life.

I'm really torn on the other two, however. One gives direct benefit in combat, while the other means a steady source of Credits that I could use to buy better equipment or new Skills.

As I'm deliberating, I hear a slight rustle in the grass behind me and I realize I'm being stalked. Allowing myself to be so distracted while out in the wilds is a rookie move. I passed over the bridge while reading the Skill options and I'm now approaching the Hrugther side of the town, the tall wall they built visible from here. I steady my breathing and do my best to keep my footsteps consistent. Another rustle.

Almost…

There!

I spin around and catch the black fuzzball that comes hurtling out of the tall grass toward me. Stepping backward to absorb the impact, I feel sharp claws skitter over the armor on my chest. I spin to the side and, with a brief surge of strength, push my attacker to arm's length.

"Ah! No fair!" Agalder, the aforementioned fuzzball, whines as I hold him up before me. "You promised! You have to let me pounce you!"

He's about the size of a three-year-old human, and just as wiggly. He squirms, trying to get free. Some things are consistent between our two species, and the energy level of young kids is one of them.

Of course, we rarely let *our* kids out to play with the monsters spawning outside of town, but the Hrugther have a different view on child endangerment than we do. Part of that is probably due to having been in the System for so long, but part of it is just their culture. They value safety a lot less than we do. Although even they don't usually let their young out unsupervised…

Laughing, I set down the squirming kid. "I said I'd let you *try*." I try to keep my perception open, searching for any sign of the caretaker I know is out there. "Stay away from the dry grass when you stalk. It makes too much noise—"

Cold steel presses against my neck and I freeze on instinct. A moment later, a throaty chuckle comes from right next to my ear and the knife blade withdraws as if it had never been there. Agalder, below me, has what passes for a smug grin on his furry, doglike face. I shake my head as I turn, a wry smile on my face, already knowing who I'll see.

A tawny figure stands a few feet behind me, her large, expressive eyes laughing as she twirls a dark steel blade in one hand. Esslin is the much older sister of the pup at my feet, and also my best friend among the Hrugther. Her body, under the armored tan suit she wears, looks surprisingly human. If you ignore the sleek fur that covers the rest of her and her almost canine face and tail, you'd think she was a twenty-something human woman. A very fit, dangerous-looking woman who's still pointing a knife at me and has definitely noticed me checking her out.

Again.

I really need to get a girlfriend. Maybe if I increase my Charisma…

"You said you were going to pounce him, Lin!" a piping voice says from behind me.

Esslin's eyes widen in panic. Hrugther do not blush, but thanks to the body language knowledge I downloaded from the Shop, I can read her embarrassment in the slight droop of her tail and flattening of her pointed ears. I'm struggling with the direction of my own thoughts as well, and I'm really glad my tanned skin hides the heat I feel coming to my cheeks.

"I said I would 'get him' if you failed, little one," Esslin says hurriedly as she makes her knife disappear. "And I did." This last is said with another laughing glance at me, her voice deeper than a human woman's.

I snort. She and I both know I hadn't stood a chance against her. She's a level 5 Lone Stalker, an Advanced Class that specializes in stealth, for crying out loud.

"Yeah, good job picking on the non-combat Basic Class, Esslin." She lets out her own snort of laughter before I continue. "Now, I'd love to stick around and play training dummy, but I have a delivery for your father. Is he in his shop?"

"Did you get them? We have seen none on our side of the river in ages…" Esslin says, her voice eager.

Instead of answering, I drop one of the groggert corpses onto the ground next to us, flattening a large circle of grass. The two Hrugther don't even flinch, used to the magic tricks of the System, but they showcase their canine grins at the sight.

"Yep, and I have two more like that in my bag." I touch the cold flesh of the massive amphibian and pull it back into my Party Prep storage. "But I really have to hurry, so…"

"Of course. Father actually sent us to look for you." She scoops up her brother and turns back toward the gate into the town. "He said something about groggert needing at least eight hours to roast properly and…"

Esslin laughs as I sprint past her. I was cutting my delivery too close!

I only slow down when she admits to stretching the truth—because of her father's class as High Pack Chef, he only needs six hours to turn the carcasses into the fully prepared dishes I'm planning on serving at the party. She just wanted to see me run, the b—I stop myself. Somehow, calling her a female dog seems like a cheap shot, even in my head.

As we walk, still at a good pace but no longer running, Esslin grills me on the plans for the event. She's been my main cultural liaison during the preparations, and I've relied on her to make certain I understand the critical elements of a party from her culture. Mostly that boils down to lots of traditional dishes, but there are important dances and music as well. Working together, we've planned an event that should be a celebration of both of our cultures.

"And you will have the bars of candy?" Agalder asks from his perch on Esslin's shoulders. It's the third time he's asked, and the third time I've reassured him we will. What is it with kids and candy?

"Have you even ever tried a candy bar?" I smile at him, amused.

"No…" He looks sad, then brightens. "But my friend, Peggy-Lynn, says she has! I can't wait to try one!"

I chuckle, making a mental note to stop by the Store for a few more bags of chocolate. It's a small price to pay to encourage the young friendships I've seen crop up between the children of our two people.

This side of town is so familiar, yet very changed. The Hrugther have kept most of the building exteriors, but seeing aliens walking down the street still gives me a strange sort of vertigo. And it isn't just the Hrugther. A menagerie of beasts and monsters walk, crawl, or fly through the town, from mutated, giant bobcats to strange creatures I don't have a name for. For whatever reason, about half of Esslin's people have Beast Tamer type classes, and their varied pets and companions add to the oddness of the scene.

It doesn't take long to make it to Esslin's father's store, built in an old Whataburger. He greets me warmly with a traditional arm clasp as we walk in but hurries us out after I drop off the meat. The roast isn't the only dish he's preparing for tonight, and even with his Skills and skill, he has to hurry to get everything done.

He isn't the only one, and I head quickly toward the human half of town. Esslin comes with me, having dropped off her brother to "help" in the kitchen. I still need to meet with the baker about the pies and cake, and Maria about her more traditional Mexican dishes, and I need to make certain the tables are—

My first sign of trouble is Esslin disappearing. I don't see the clawed hand that grabs my shirt until I'm already slammed up against a wall. My ribs creak as they grind together, and my health drops by fifteen points from the impact. I look up to see my least favorite Hrugther.

"Hi, Lanfrig. Could we not today?" I wheeze out, doing my best to stay calm. I don't make eye contact, knowing from experience that he views it as a challenge. It grates, not being able to stand up to him, but this is an unfortunate reality of the System that I've learned to deal with. Lanfrig is a level 3 Fanged Warrior, an Advanced Class, and he could squash me like a bug. "Big party to throw, and—"

"I told you to stay away from my sister, Human." Lanfrig growls. "You might have fooled her, but I know what you cowardly humans really are."

I look around exaggeratedly. "I don't see your sister here, do you?"

He looks around the street, and I watch as he notices the other Hrugther staring at him, an Advanced Class warrior, as he holds a non-combat Basic Classer up against a wall. None of them are a match for him in a fight, but they don't have to be—it's his pride, not his health he's worried about.

He lets me go with a growl, stalking off through the crowd. After a few glances, the rest of the Hrugther ignore me, and I head toward the bridge again.

Esslin joins me a few minutes later. Her tail is lashing, and the fur on the back of her neck bristles.

I glance at her. "Thanks. I know—"

"Don't," she snaps, then takes a deep breath. "I'm going to break his arm next time he touches you. *I* get to decide who I'm friends with, not Lanfrig."

I nod but stay silent. Lanfrig lost a close friend in the Fire Ant attack and has made it very clear to me he blames humans for it. I've asked Esslin to let me handle the situation. It isn't a macho thing—I've long since grown used to the idea of powerful women stepping in to save my bacon from danger—but it's all about results. I want to bring our communities together, and I feel that violence, especially between brother and sister, is the last thing we need. Maybe I'm wrong, as I'm not an expert on their culture, but that's how I feel.

After a few minutes of walking in silence, we cross into the human town. There, Esslin opens up again as she gets lost in her curiosity. She's been a regular visitor here for several months, and still, she has questions. I answer as best I can as we rush about, getting everything ready for the party.

Several hours later, I'm standing at the top of the stands of the local high school football stadium. The football field is one of the few places large enough to hold the celebration and, being nestled close to the center of town and the river, it makes for a safe and neutral location.

I look out over everything one last time. The grass has been freshly cut. Rows of tables, covered in delicious-looking food and drinks, line both sides of the field. I'm too far away to smell the apple pie I can see on the nearest table, but I can already taste it in my mind. A large central area has been reserved for dancing, and rings of smaller tables surround it for mingling and eating.

I couldn't get a live band, but upgrading the music system in the stadium hadn't been terribly expensive. Fairy lights, which have a totally different meaning now that magic is real, hang above and light the entire scene with their ever-shifting glow.

It's ready, or as ready as it will be. I glance at the clock. Five minutes until go time.

With a thought, I activate the button in the air before me, the one that reads "Start Party." It's not the first time I've pressed it of course, but that was always for little after-hunt celebrations or birthday get-togethers. Then, the Skill had boosted my party-related Class Skills, and I don't expect anything different now.

Inviting two entire towns must have crossed some threshold, however, because this time, a new screen pops up, asking for parameters. I hadn't expected there to be paperwork involved, and I glance at the clock nervously as I read quickly, making selections as I go. Type of celebration, Victory. Cultures involved, Human (Texan), Hrugther (Bone Claw). Rules… I enter the only one I can think of, "No violence, except in self-defense." Hopefully I'm filling this out correctly. I really wish my Class had come with a manual. I rush through the rest of the selections and finish as the clock rolls to the top of the hour.

As I select "Approve," a wave of Mana rolls out of me, followed by a steady drain as the auras I've selected activate. They should help everyone enjoy themselves tonight, keeping them full of health and stamina while also helping people relax. The cost to keep them up will be manageable, with the occasional Mana potion, but I will want to prioritize my Mana regeneration rate if I want to do this often.

A notification goes out to those on my invite list, which is everyone in both towns, as soon as the party opens, thanks to my Class Skill Party Invite. I never thought I would actually get to use that Skill, but I had to get it in order to unlock some more useful Skills in my Class Skill tree.

I'm alone at first, Esslin having gone home to get ready for the party, but it isn't long before the first people arrive. Soon the place is… well, not packed, given how many we've lost, but we comfortably fill the space. The music, right now a piece from the Hrugther that sounds surprisingly like country music, is playing over the sound system.

At first, the two species stay mostly apart, standing with their own kind. And then there is a laugh as a little human girl, maybe four years old, pulls Agalder onto the dance floor, followed shortly by more kids of both species. That's all it takes to break the ice, and everyone mingles. I'm still getting used to using my Class Skill Host's Insight on such a large group, but everyone I check seems to be enjoying themselves.

Maria, the level 35 Abuela, looks as though she's thirty-five years old again, even with her still-grey hair, as she dances with a grizzled older Hrugther. The gene treatments she bought from the Store, along with her increased stats, have done wonders for her. And she definitely deserves the fun, as she's outdone herself making the tamales I'm currently munching on. Her food is *literally* magic.

Then there's Darryl, the large Armorer who used to be the town's auto mechanic. He's the leader of the Artisan classers and has stepped naturally into the role of Settlement Owner after the previous Owner, the Mayor, fell to the Ants. He's been one of my largest supporters in getting this party approved and planned, at least from the human side. Darryl's sitting at a table near the dance floor, a wide smile on his face as he watches the crowd.

For the second time that day, I'm surprised by the clawed hand that grabs me by the shirt, but this time I don't mind nearly as much. Esslin drags me onto the dance floor. I try to protest, but she doesn't listen. I don't protest too hard…

The party will run fine without me for at least one dance. "Cotton-Eye Joe" plays as we make it to the middle of the floor, and I'm amused to find that the Hrugther have their own version of line dancing. The humans on the floor quickly pick up the new steps, and the mixture of the two cultures makes me laugh as we dance.

Swinging to the left, I see Lanfrig glaring at me, but his father has a hand on the tall warrior's shoulder. I'm certain we'll have words later, but for now, I'm just glad he's come to the party.

The dance turns us again, and I catch sight of Connor standing with his new crowd, the most vocal of the anti-alien humans, over near the food. My enhanced Perception lets me clearly see the disgust on his face as he watches the dance. I'm still hopeful that those like Connor and Lanfrig, people on both sides most resistant to change, will see the good that can come from this. At least most of those hard cases are here tonight, which is a good sign.

Before I can snoop more, the song ends and we walk, laughing, to an empty table near Darryl. Esslin leaves to get us some food, and I settle in to people-watch.

As I'm thinking how well the party is going, better than I ever hoped for, I notice that the ground is shaking, rattling the table, even though the dance floor is temporarily empty. I look to the center in time to see large red mandibles burst through the grass, followed quickly by something out of my nightmares.

Fire Ant Soldier (Level 55)

Condition: Boosted

There are screams from the crowd as the ant pushes itself all the way out of the earth, dirt cascading from its back. And it isn't alone.

Already I see more mandibles poking from the earth as ants dig free. Many of the humans and Hrugther pull back to their own sides, the memory of the Raid still clear in their minds. I back away from the dance floor to a space midway between the two sides and stare in shock.

What in the world is going on? We killed all the ants and wiped out their Dungeon. And what does that "Boosted" status mean? It's almost like a class skill a Beast Tamer could use to enhance their pet, and I didn't see anything like it on the ants in the past. I don't have time to worry about that mystery, as the first ant is already heading toward the human half of the party

"The Hrugther are attacking us!" an angry voice yells from the far side of the field us. Connor, surrounded by many of the other die-hard anti-alien humans, is pointing at the Hrugther. "Those beast lovers must have raised up an army of ants in secret!"

My old friend is shaking with rage, and some in the crowd repeat his cry. Combat Classers step forward to protect the defenseless in the crowd, but more ants are pushing from the earth. Are we facing another horde?

Looking at the Hrugther, I see anger, but also confusion and fear. I sweep Host's Insight over them. I'm not certain what I'm looking for, but whatever it is, I don't find it. Could the Hrugther really be attacking us? Why? With my Skill still active, I look over the humans. More fear, more anger, more confusion.

I freeze when I reach Connor and his new friends. There, I feel anger, but no fear or confusion. I feel anger… and satisfaction. I see a blinking notification in the upper right of my vision, and I open it, already knowing what it will say.

An Attendee (Connor Blake) at your Event has broken the Rules.

Time seems to freeze as I take in the situation. Humans who had just been dancing with Hrugther are now pointing weapons at them. The furred aliens are raising weapons in return. There are more ants, always more ants, crawling over each other, skittering from that blasted hole. Crashing my party.

And Connor, my oldest friend, is the one who, somehow, sent the ants, destroying any hope of peace between our two peoples. I stare at him and he notices, looking at me with a smirk and a half shrug.

I feel rage as I slam open my Skill tree and slot my one remaining skill point into Bounce, the skill I'd earlier dismissed as useless. Then I select Connor, pointing one finger at him. He looks confused for a split second before Bounce triggers. Mana rushes into the skill, and a bright flash of light goes off around his head. When it clears, he's on the grass. His companions look stunned as well, many of them slumping to the ground and the rest swaying on their feet or holding their heads.

I don't have time to worry about that, because the ants go berserk with their handlers taken out. Now, instead of heading toward the heavily armored human defensive line, ants are scattering everywhere, looking for the easiest prey. An ant heads toward me, mandibles clicking, and I back up, pulling my gun out of my inventory. Before I take too many steps, however, there is a high-pitched yowl and a higher-pitched scream as Agalder darts out from under a table near the ant, his little human friend hot on his heels.

If they had stayed quiet, maybe the ant wouldn't have noticed them, but they didn't, and it did. The red ant charges after them, and I don't even think as I race forward. The kids are too close for me to risk using my gun, but they won't stand a chance against the eight-foot-long monstrosity if I do nothing.

As the ant lunges forward, mandibles wide, I slide between it and its young prey, gun raised. I get off one shot, just one, the slug bouncing off the creature's hard shell, before it crunches down on my ribs. If it weren't for the armored skin suit I'm wearing under my party duds, I would have been sliced in half. After two years of fighting, I feel naked without it, and now I'm very glad I didn't take it off. Even with it, I lose half my hit points from the attack, and I scream in pain.

My ribs break and grind together as the monster bites down, but I manage to raise my gun, even as I'm losing health by the second. I'd like to say I aim carefully, but hey, I'm being eaten by a giant ant.

Somehow, I get off one more shot, this one Empowered with my Ice Lance spell. The last of my Mana floods into the blast, which drills into the creature's brain from point blank range. As my vision goes dark, my Mana gone and my health ticking away, I feel myself drop to the ground. The ant falls limply next to me.

***

Surprising myself, I wake up sometime later, lying on a cot someone set up on the side of the field. Well, that's unexpected. Welcome, but unexpected. I really thought I had bought the farm there.

A soft, furred hand is brushing my hair, and I look up to see Esslin. She's sitting next to me, looking over the football field. It's dotted with corpses, but luckily all the ones I see are giant ants.

"We won?" I croak, then wince at my voice.

She looks down with a smile. "You definitely know how to throw a celebration, Dave Carver."

I snort as I stand from the cot, my health no longer dangerously low. "Some party all right." I look out over the carnage. "We were so close. And then Connor's darn ants ruined everything. Do you think our two people will—"

She laughs. "Ruined? You didn't see the rest of the party."

Then she explains. Apparently when I expelled Connor from the party, I had selected the "Notify Other Guests" option, and everyone saw the message. The humans had quickly captured Connor and his cronies, then worked together with the Hrugther to kill the rest of the ants. It hadn't been hard for them, especially once the Boosted status wore off of the bugs with Connor knocked out.

A few minutes with the town's old sheriff, a level 46 Texas Ranger, got the truth out of Connor. His class, Monster Rancher, apparently let him raise and breed monsters, like the ant eggs he had taken from the nest before we'd wiped it out. The Class also gave him the ability to give others the temporary Title of Ranch Hand, which let the Ranch Hand help raise the Monster Rancher's horde. Together, he and his cronies had been funneling all their experience into quickly growing their little army, getting ready for the false flag attack they had planned for the party.

"His plan almost worked." I look out over where we had just been partying not long before. "He almost drove us all apart again."

"But he didn't," a gruff voice says, and I turn to see Lanfrig walking up, his habitual glower missing. Esslin bristles beside me, but he raises a hand. "Peace, sister. I haven't come to harass your human… friend." Looking at me, he says, "I've come to thank you. I saw the ant that nearly killed my little brother, and I saw you, a non-combat Class human, stand in front of the beast. I was too far away to save him, but you stood in my place." He puts a large, clawed hand on my shoulder, his eyes serious. "I owe you a life debt." He looks slyly out the corner of his eyes at Esslin. "I've decided that you may court my sister."

My eyes go wide as Esslin lashes out with an embarrassed, outraged growl, Lanfrig dancing backward with a belly laugh. His laughter ends with a cough as her kick catches him in the chest, sending him flying backward into the bleachers, where he lands in a cloud of dust. The humans nearby look startled, but the Hrugther shake their heads, used to the antics of the Advanced Class siblings.

I watch as humans and Hrugther work together to clean up the mess, two peoples coming together in the aftermath of a tragedy closely averted. In the center of the field, Darryl, our town's acting mayor, is talking to a greying Hrugther I recognize as their Clan Leader. They clasp forearms, as if they have reached some kind of agreement.

Instantly, a notification pops up in front of my face.

Hidden Quest Completed!

A party you have planned and hosted has been the catalyst for ending a multi-year cold war between two different species. Not bad for your first real party.

Reward: 10,000 XP, Title Gained: Peace Partier. All Fame gained from Events planned by you increased by 10%.

Congratulations!

For achieving your first title, you receive a bonus +5,000 XP

I smile as I wave away the prompt. All in all, this wasn't the worst party I've thrown, and I know it won't be my last. There really is still plenty to celebrate, even in this new world.

Looking for Australian Survival Stories Please!

I luv, luv reading about Australian ~~horror~~ survival stories. Does anyone have any more?

---CoyoteMutant9882

Kanundraspies981 – Have you tried the Kira and family stories (see System Apocalypse: Australia thread).

CoyoteMutant9882 – Yes! Love them. I need more!

Bla's8kkm – Australia is the most boring continent for works. It's all "Death here. Death there." By the time you get to liking the humans, they're dead. Why bother?

CDeantheBeard887 – I like the misery. Anyone got more of the face-eating dingo stories?

CoyoteMutant9882 – Please, not on my thread. So sad. :(

RedspearsseestheMoonintheGreenGradient – How about this one? School teacher and kids. I pulled it while searching for… other things.

Daisy's Preschool for Little Adventurers

By InkWitch

At story time, the children sit on the floor in a half moon around their Guardian, Daisy. Smallest at the front, bigger ones behind. Daisy perches on a metal bar stool and holds the book high, so everyone can see the pictures. At first glance you might think she was a kid herself: small, hair in pigtails, and wearing shorts over flower-print leggings.

Fifteen kids come to preschool in the corporate box of the Cake Tin—the local name for Wellington's stadium back when it was used for rugby and sometimes international concerts. Even then, New Zealand was a long way from anywhere else.

Daisy didn't have much interest in rugby, but she's passionate about the small team in front of her. She can see what used to be the pitch through the wall of windows. The field is now mostly turned over to growing vegetables, but one square is a training ground for hunters. The kids copy the hunters' moves when they play.

But right now, the kids are focused on a picture book she's made.

"'Kiwi finds her food at night. She stays safe from daytime predators. Here comes a possum. What will kiwi do?'" She looks up, waiting for suggestions.

"Stab with her beak!" says Murphy, eyes bright.

"She does have a quick, sharp beak." Daisy grins.

"Call for her friends," Xenon muses, looking at the others around him to see if they agree. When his classmates nod, he relaxes. How could she could build his confidence?

"Kiwi could run to her hidey hole," four-year-old Lily says softly. Her mother leaves her most days now, before going fishing in the harbor. The youngster is coming out of her shell and enjoying herself. Daisy gives Lily a thumbs-up and the little girl grins.

"Before we find out," Daisy says, "who can show us a letter from their name?"

Six-year-old Kastor scrambles over protesting legs and arms to come up front and point out a capital K and a lower case k on the page. She hears his knives clinking in his pockets as he squirms under Daisy's stool. He circles to the back of the room, then he clambers onto what used to be the bar.

Meanwhile, Murphy has found them at the end of possum and helped William find half his name.

"Okay, little adventurers, let's find out what kiwi does!"

Daisy turns the page.

Kiwi stabs! Kiwi runs! Kiwi hides!

"You were right!"

Daisy is quite pleased with her next illustration. Before the System apocalypse, she was studying animation. It's nice to have a Class where she can still use her art, and she has an appreciative audience.

The kids suck in their breath in delight when they see Daisy's tui. Little fingers point at feathers, beak, and claws. You wouldn't get that reaction from a client in an advertising agency. This is the tui they commonly see outside the stadium and along the waterfront. The birds work with the community as scouts and enjoy safe nesting in return.

It helps that a few Beast Tamers keep them in line.

She lets the kids stroke the inky-green feathers and thinks about selling pictures to the System Shop—would there be a market? Maybe art from a Guardian in Aotearoa would have some value. Then she could buy more art supplies.

With his teacher lost in thought, impatient Kastor reads the page aloud from his perch at the bar. He leans forward, balancing on his toes and flapping imaginary wings. Back in the day, a preschool teacher would have called his climbing dangerous, but the System fixes kids and they're far more athletic and coordinated.

"Tui finds food in… fuff …fow?"

She lets him keep working on the word, remembering her own joy in cracking the reading code.

"Flowers!"

"Great job, Kastor! Yes, tui are nectar-feeders. Do you want to try the next sentence?"

Encouraged, Kastor keeps going.

"How does tui stay safe from… monsters!" Kastor ad libs the last word.

Well, that works. No reason to pull him up on missing "predator." The kids throw out more ideas.

"Flying fast! Tui flies fast! Zip zip!" says Murphy.

"Tui calls to the Hunters."

As if on cue, a tui calls out an urgent set of whistles and caws.

Shadows fall across the classroom. Murphy's face goes from excitement to fear as a throbbing formation of giant wasps drop into the open arena. The last wasp, the length of a two-seater couch, breaks off from the squadron and hovers outside their windows, scanning the room.

"Get back from the windows. Take cover or take off!" Daisy hears herself saying, in a voice that is calmer than she feels.

She watches the wasp as some kids scamper through the heavy fire doors to the concourse beyond. She casts Shield of Protection to give the hiders more cover. Adrenaline sizzles through her body. If the wasp gets in, she'll have to fend it off before anyone else gets here. They've already got a swarm to deal with down on the pitch. Keep calm. Think. Think. Where would it be most vulnerable?

The wasp smacks into the main middle window and bounces back, as though it hadn't known the barrier was there. Giant faceted eyes stare inside.

Behind her, the fire door thuds shut. Inside the corporate box, the remaining kids rustle under cover then go quiet.

The wasp thuds unsuccessfully against the window again, then turns away. Just as she thinks it has given up, it returns at speed. Shards of glass and masonry spray inward, then the creature is inside. It looks even bigger as it slowly rotates, deciding where to strike. The air is charged with a tang like burnt sugar and blood.

The Guardian doesn't wait; she runs forward and vaults onto the wasp. If she can take away its height advantage, she might overpower it. She clamps her arms tightly and brings her legs down to bash at the wings. They move and spring back like high-tensile steel. Okay then, let's try something different. She locks her legs around the thorax and hangs on for a bumpy ride.

The wasp bucks and lumbers, off-kilter from her weight and the unexpected attack. She grapples forward, calling on Arms of Protection for extra strength and courage, and goes for an eye with her fist. There's a satisfying crunch.

Still airborne, they reach the bar where Kastor peeks out from a high cupboard. As soon as they're in range, he slams the door against the wasp like a shield. The wasp turns away as Kastor comes out with a knife in one hand like a demented Jack-in-the-box. She lands another Guardian-fueled punch as Kastor jumps up behind her. Kastor grunts and the wasp jolts; whatever he's doing back there is damaging the insect.

The wasp bangs against a wall, trying to lose them, its whine a keening sound now. They clip a trophy case, which keels over and blocks the fire door, trapping everyone inside.

She has to make the kill before one of her kids is hurt, or worse. She fights against panic, clamping her knee-hold tighter as the predator surges toward the ceiling. She ducks in time to take the blow to her back rather than her head, and it rains ceiling tiles.

Daisy swings a looping roundhouse punch, the strike breaking part of an enormous compound eye. She pounds the same spot until her arm sinks elbow-deep in yellow gore. Another punch and part of the head drops to the floor. Meanwhile, its long legs twitch, moving cushions. It's still hunting.

A child stands up from where she's been uncovered. The wasp makes a slow turn back, mandibles open, ready to rush in and take a Lily-sized bite. Daisy's left arm is punching now, battering the other eye. Panic gives her more urgency. But the wasp is still moving toward her littlest charge.

Lily holds the reading stool feet-out in front of her like a lion tamer.

"Eat this, bitch!" the little girl shouts, ramming the stool into the wasp's snapping venomous mouth and nimbly stepping to one side.

The wasp slams into the floor, the metal bar stool imbedding farther into its maw, smashing the pharynx.

Daisy gets up, arms sticky with ichor, as the monster makes its final twitches. Kastor dances around, brandishing the stinger.

The classroom is destroyed. Kids crawl out of hiding spaces and examine the carcass laid out on the reading mat. She can show them how to loot it.

"Miss Daisy?"

Lily pulls on Daisy's sticky leg. She's holding the picture book—it's a little banged up, but it'll make it. Lily looks worried. "You won't tell my mummy I said a bad word, will you? It just came out!"

Daisy, trembling now it's over, gives Lily's small body a hug. "I'm going to tell your mummy what a brave little adventurer you were today."

She sets Lily on the bar, legs swinging over the edge, and works on levering the fallen display case clear of the doors. The trophy cabinet crashes clear and its contents roll out, clanking like a cutlery draw. Kids on the other side pour back in to look at the dead wasp.

Daisy picks up a cup. *Player of the day* is etched on one dented side. She scoops up more trophies and calls for everyone to line up.

The first adults arrive at the corporate box just in time for prize-giving.

Love for the Shorties?

Any fellow shorty lovers here? I got a dozen stories about Pooskeens—including that terrorist "Redeemer of the Dead's" attack on the Calgary enclave. But I'm looking for more stories, ass-over-tea-kettle numbers really. Putting together an anthology showing the continued oppression of the vertically challenged. Gimsar, Pooskeen, even Pharyleri. Give it to me.
---- J-EdgeHunter_Gates11

Kuiooaasss18882 – I got some short lover erotica. Pooskeen, Gimsar, even Goblin and Pooskeen. You want it, I have it. Real, mod, AI overlay, and sense stand-in. You want it, I got it.

YunnaWurtzKS_11 – Damn it. Can someone delete the spammer?

McGregor_mod_Hunterzone111 – I got it. I've already started a Prey-Predator search on him. He's using a Second Front Class Skill, but it's only at the Advanced Level. Idiot.

J-EdgeHunter_Gates11 – Pervert, you mean.

McGregor_mod_Hunterzone111 – You're right. I also put a System lock on him so he can't access the forum.

J-EdgeHunter_Gates11 – Still need stories, aliens.

CoyoteMutant9882 – The Gimsar have taken over the salt mines down near Krakow. Changed the name to some fictional place too, just because they thought it was cool. Got some really cool videos in there, including a full documentary by a reporting team. Only negative is, it's recorded in another language – Polish.

J-EdgeHunter_Gates11 – I'll read it. I got an AI that can handle basic translations. I'll set it on translation right now and check it over later.

YellowSub_xxs118.471 – Came across this while doing my research on underwater dungeons. Merfolk and water gremlins spawning within the same dungeon. That work?

J-EdgeHunter_Gates11 – Gremlins aren't of interest. Sorry.

YellowSub_xxs118.471 – Gremlins are people too!

McGregor_mod_Hunterzone111 – Reminder, keep it civil. Gremlin and sapience arguments are never civil once they get going. I've already started one hunt, don't make me work overtime here, people.

XanBRedMage-Crystal44 – I got something from my orbital scanners. It's an entry by a group of Pharyleri, headed to that starport in the American continent.

J-EdgeHunter_Gates11 – Interesting. Let me take a look.

Ground Control

by Craig Hamilton

The freighter didn't have an observation lounge, or even any windows at all. With limited living space for crew, the vessel didn't have passenger accommodations either.

From the nearly empty cargo hold of the *Starlit Voidhauler*, Zejyc Galeblast could only tap into the craft's external sensor feed from where he sat on a pile of crates strapped to the evenly spaced clamps set into the floor of the cavernous bay. The feed showed a distant blue speck that soon grew close enough to reveal green and brown land masses throughout the ocean-covered world, all wrapped in layers of wispy white clouds.

Earth. The Galactic Council's thirteenth Dungeon World.

By now, most of those who cared about such things knew the toll the System integration had taken on the planet and its native population of sapient bipedal mammalians. Though more than ninety percent of the human species had died off during the assimilation process, a surprising number of the more resilient survivors now combatted the Galactic settlers across the available territories on the planet, hindering interstellar immigration.

Sight of the distant world brought with it a glimmer of hope that pierced through the oppressing malaise that had plagued Zejyc in the months of the long journey. The promise of a fresh start lay within reach.

The pre-System borders were being redrawn by the combination of Galactic colonization, native conflicts, the development of new dungeons, and the ever-increasing Mana density that led to stronger monsters. All of which spelled opportunity for those willing to take the risks.

Sometimes such gambles paid off, such as the Sprocketsworth Clan's development of a high traffic starport. Other times they failed horribly, as with Clan Steamspanner's disastrous attempt at developing their own intergalactic hub.

Dragons cared not for the plans of mere mortals.

Zejyc sighed, brushing a hand through his mop of forest-green hair. Unlike most Pharyleri, who often sported their natural bright neon colors, Zejyc kept his hair dyed more subdued tones. There was no sense in making an easy target for enemies to sight in ranged attacks if not wearing a helmet.

A firm hand clapped down on the Pharyleri's shoulder and pulled his attention from the sensor feed.

"Why so glum? The trip is almost over."

Zejyc looked at the hand resting on his shoulder, then up at the gnome who stood above him.

"Less than a platoon left out of a battalion, Byruc," Zejyc said. "That's how many walked away from our last contract."

Byruc Wingbrake shook his head. "Not your fault. Your da put us in that situation when he signed that contract with poor terms. You got us out when it all went sideways and the contract failed." The older, gray-haired gnome gave Zejyc's shoulder a squeeze before dropping his arm.

"I know. The old man was such a big part of my life that it just feels empty with him being gone." Zejyc trailed off at the thought of his father. His fists clenched in the lingering pain of loss and the frustration of how the failed contract had left the company with a broken reputation and empty accounts. Only selling off the last of the vehicles and heavy equipment had provided enough Credits to fund this trip, with just enough left over to provide housing for the rest of the survivors until word was sent of a place to relocate.

"You've grieved for your da and your fallen friends, so cut the shit and stop feeling sorry for yourself. Despite everything, you stepped up. You made a solid plan, and you got the command squad to make this trip. We all agreed to this. Maybe we're not much of a mercenary corp anymore. Maybe it's a long shot to find acceptance in one of the big Clans. Even if the Sprocketsworth won't recruit us, there's still a chance with the Steamspanner Clan after their losses. You've kept us together, and that makes you a true leader."

"Thanks for the dose of reality and the kick in the ass."

"You know I'll always shoot straight with you. Besides, this plan beats joining some old guild as lone Adventurers."

Zejyc chuckled. "Mandatory Quests? Quotas for Dungeon runs? No thanks."

The intercom in the corner of the bay crackled, interrupting the conversation. "All hands. Brace for turbulence and stand by for atmospheric entry."

Zejyc glanced around. Besides the crates, there wasn't much of any place to find support for the handful of Pharyleri in the cavernous compartment.

"Gear up," Zejyc ordered the other gnomes. "Clamp in with your magboots and seal your vacsuits."

"You really expecting trouble, boss?"

Zejyc looked at the speaker and scowled. Vek Thunderspark, the youngest member of what remained of the Galeblast Mercenary Corp command squad, winced at the expression.

Zejyc started to growl and cut himself short. Tensions had run high after their last disastrous contract, and tempers had only grown shorter over the lengthy journey. "Vek, it's a Dungeon World."

The young Pharyleri rolled his eyes but joined the others in swapping out equipment from their Inventory. "Whatever. Maybe we'll finally get to kill something."

Zejyc ignored Vek's muttered response and changed into his own battle gear. The youngster did have a point. It would be good for the squad to burn off some of their frustrations in a little conflict.

The helmet raised up from the suit collar and the transparent visor snapped down over Zejyc's face to seal the battle suit. The seal cut off external sounds and left Zejyc within a momentary bubble of silence as his Neural Link connected with the suit.

The suit sensors came online within a fraction of a second, and a translucent display projected the suit status onto the visor as the internal computer ran a status check on the rest of his equipment. The audio pickups caught inane chatter from the ship's crew over the intercom, which the captain had left online.

A glance at Vek showed the young gnome rolling his eyes again but remaining silent now that everyone was suited up. Comm discipline was the mark of a professional organization, and the Galeblast Mercenary Corp were nothing if not professional.

The sleek suits worn by each gnome were covered in individualized patterns customized to fit their personal fighting styles, but all currently sported gray, blue, and white aerial camouflage.

Zejyc's suit checklist came up green within a few seconds, the queue fading away to be replaced with a list of the squad around the hold. Each name on the list blinked green as their suits reported online and linked them in shared battlefield data-net.

Vibrations ran through the floor of the hold as the freighter entered the outer reaches of the planet's atmosphere. The external visual sensors dropped, blinded by the extreme heat of the atmospheric entry.

The crew on the ship's bridge chattered through the routine descent for several minutes, mostly about plans for shore leave while the freighter was loaded for the return leg of the trip. The turbulence gradually settled down as the vessel ventured farther into Earth's atmosphere.

Just when it seemed that it would be a smooth landing, the pitch of the voices increased. Zejyc recognized the tone and shared a glance with the gnomes around him as they all reached the same conclusion. Something was wrong.

The sounds over the intercom were of a crew in panic.

"Where did they come from? The sensors should have picked them up!"

Something pinged the outside of the freighter, followed by several more ringing impacts. Then a long squeal sounded through the cargo hold as something outside scraped along the armor protecting the cargo bay doors.

The clomp of Zejyc's magboots echoed across the hold as he stomped over to the speaker and pressed the intercom.

"What's the problem?" The gnome's commanding tone cut into the garbled voices on the comm.

"Harpy swarm!" Zejyc recognized the frantic voice of Captain Hrug. "Harpies everywhere. They're tearing into the ship!"

Another screech of rending metal echoed through the empty hold, emphasizing the captain's claim.

"Levels and numbers?" Zejyc asked. The mercenary commander's calm stood in stark contrast to the distressed freighter captain.

"40s and 50s," Hrug replied. "Probably about a hundred of the suckers out there though."

A semblance of sanity found its way into the captain's voice during the report, but the lower Leveled monsters didn't give Zejyc much pause. Not when every member of the command squad held an upper tier Advanced Class.

"Will you help?" A glimmer of hope filled Hrug's voice.

"What's it worth to you?"

Hrug gasped. "You'd refuse to aid us?"

Zejyc snorted. "You charged us through the nose for passage, only to stick us in a barren cargo hold for months."

"Fine," Hrug growled. "I'll refund your payment."

"Plus thirty percent," Zejyc replied as another tremor from the monster attacks shook the vessel.

"Ten percent."

"Twenty."

"Bah, fine." Hrug spat. "Take your blood money and save my ship."

"Pleasure doing business with you, Captain."

The Captain's growl cut off as Zejyc shut off the intercom and faced his crew, smiling as a notification informed the gnome that a tidy sum of Credits had poured into his account. "We've got a job."

The hungry expressions on the team revealed through their translucent visors that they'd all been listening to the conversation.

Zejyc moved to bay door controls mounted next to the intercom system. Then he slapped the door controls. Of course, the panel didn't open on the first touch. It required a second press while holding an override button, due to the default lockout in place to prevent the hold from being accidentally vented into vacuum while the freighter traveled between planets.

The roar of rushing air filled the hold as the bay door cracked open. Several shadows from the monsters outside flickered past the widening gap. The Pharyleri squad marched toward the ramp and weapons appeared from Inventories as they prepared for battle.

A shape darted into the opening, revealing one of the monsters to the team.

It was roughly humanoid in form with a pair of thin, bird legs and feathered wings in place of arms. The monster's limbs ended in sharp talons that tore rents into the bay door as the creature scraped through the gap. It pulled itself forward with claw-like hands at the ends of the wings. The foot talons were significantly larger and carved furrows into the ramp beneath it as the opening lowered far enough for the monster to stand upright.

Crimson beams lanced from the mercenary squad and cut into the harpy. The avian beast threw back its beaked head and let out a shrill cry.

Zejyc barely glanced at the warning that flashed on the heads-up-display of his visor, the notification announcing the sonic affliction automatically dampened by the armor. Instead, the gnome activated a Class Skill to analyze the monster and pass the information to his squad.

Harpy Scout (Level 44)

HP: 459/840

Another barrage of energy beams cooked the monster and it collapsed on the ramp, one wing flopping over the edge. The air rushing past the opening caught the appendage and spun the carcass around as it was yanked out of the doorway.

"That's why I prefer melee," Byruc grumbled. "Now I've got to catch up to it and snag the loot."

The grizzled gnome continued mumbling as he threw himself out of the cargo hold.

Zejyc followed, launching himself into the open sky. He shot through the cloud of harpies that swarmed the freighter as he fell.

For a moment, he marveled at the view. The dark blue-black of space overhead. The brightness of the sun beyond the atmosphere. The noticeable curvature of the horizon. The fluffy banks of the cloud layer, hiding the dark green forests and fields far below.

Despite the picturesque vista, Zejyc focused on the red dots swirling across the display of his visor. Each crimson indicator marked an enemy picked up by his suit sensors and was a target to be engaged.

Deploying into hostile airspace was tricky business for the uninitiated, but for the Pharyleri jumping from the cargo bay, it was just another day on the job. Glide wings deployed from the booster pack on Zejyc's back and the thrust units in his boots engaged, the brief freefall becoming a glide before he pulled up in a tight climb and turned back toward the descending freighter.

A trio of harpies had pursued as he fell away from the vessel, and Zejyc angled to meet them. Keeping his arms tight to keep his flight profile steady, Zejyc opened fire with a beam pistol, using the integrated sight built into his suit display. The visor's reticle followed the aim point of the weapon and kept the stream of energy focused as it burned into the closest harpy.

The rays carved deep furrows into the creature's flesh until its health bar emptied and the body lost the sleek profile of a diving raptor. Zejyc shifted his aim to the second of the trio as he slipped up under the falling carcass. By the time he reached the dead harpy and looted it with a touch, the second was also falling limply.

Kicking off the first carcass pushed it into the flight path of the third creature and propelled Zejyc toward the second dead avian. The gnome rolled onto one side and tagged the body with his free hand to loot it as it fell past. Continuing the roll onto his back, Zejyc resumed firing at the final harpy as he allowed himself to fall after the plummeting carcasses.

The creature dove toward Zejyc with talons extended, and he throttled up to pull beyond the descending monster's reach. Another barrage of energy beams tore the creature apart, and Zejyc looted it before resuming his flight back toward the embattled freighter.

The black mass of harpies still surrounded the large vessel, but clumps of the swarming monsters showed where the rest of the Pharyleri were engaged. Zejyc angled toward the nearest cluster. Occasional flashes of metallic blades glinted within the clump, identifying Byruc engaging in his preferred form of combat. Zejyc fired into the thickest point of the melee as he closed in, knowing the energy beams wouldn't hurt too much even if they managed to punch through to the armored gnome buried somewhere in the midst of the monsters.

Bodies of the flying creatures fell away from the scrum as Zejyc banked around the mob. His attacks drew the attention of the greater swarm, and a dozen peeled off from attacking the freighter to follow him.

Leading the monsters a short distance, Zejyc activated Solar Starburst and a series of tiny lights streaked out in an arc behind him. The small flares, no larger than a pea, grew to the size of a fist as the harpies bypassed them unnoticed before the radiant bursts detonated in a brilliant flash amongst the creatures.

Zejyc cut his thrusters and flipped head over heels before reengaging the boosters to rocket back toward the blinded monsters. Beam pistols in each hand raked energy rays over the shrieking creatures, burning away feathers and flesh.

The multitude of dying harpies finally overwhelmed Zejyc's ability to loot them all, falling out of reach as the gnome focused on taking out as many as possible while they were dazzled from the Skill. The mercenary growled in frustration at the lost Credits those unlooted kills represented.

Beyond Zejyc's current opponents, the scrum of harpies surrounding Byruc exploded in swirling steel as he carved free of the mob. Lengthy punch daggers extended from each arm and gleaming metallic talons extended from each boot, tearing harpies into bloody chunks.

Across the sky, dead and dying avian monsters cascaded in a gory rain as the remaining Pharyleri mercenaries employed Skills, spells, and weapons to cut through the swarm. The final handful of harpies sensed their demise and attempted to flee, banking away and splitting up to evade their pursuers. Even those that had burrowed into the freighter crawled out of the holes and scattered across the sky. The fleeing monsters were quickly brought down, their wings lacking the raw acceleration of the Galeblast mercenaries' thrusters and jetpacks.

The mercenaries formed up and glided after the still-descending freighter. The vessel showed numerous gouges in its armor and trailed smoke in several places where the harpies had burrowed inside, but it clearly remained flightworthy and under control.

Zejyc signaled the freighter over his helmet's communicator, but the channel remained silent. The Captain might have paid the Credits for the ship's defense but was clearly still unhappy about it.

"Seems Captain Hrug might be holding a bit of a grudge," Byruc said as the group leveled off alongside the freighter and found the cargo hold doors sealed shut, apparently having been closed after the team's departure. "That's not very polite, seeing how we saved his freighter."

"No, it's not," Zejyc replied. "We're still going to make sure the ship gets to the ground in one piece."

"Do we have to, boss?" Vek whined.

Zejyc kept himself from rolling his eyes. Barely. "If we weren't on the starport sensors before the harpy attack, we certainly are now. We wanted to make a good impression when we got here, and this is our chance."

Vek sighed dramatically.

"Lock it up, Thunderspark," Byruc barked. "We only get one shot at this, and we need to make it count for the rest of the platoon."

A new voice cut into the conversation, overriding the inter-squad channel. "Unidentified individuals in flight around the *Starlit Voidhauler*, contact Starport Ground Control on this channel."

Zejyc accepted the connection and responded. "Copy, Starport Ground Control. This is Galeblast Actual of the Galeblast Mercenary Corp with a flight of six, inbound after completion of short-term contract to the *Starlit Voidhauler* to clear away their little monster problem."

The frequency went silent for a moment as traffic control evaluated the response.

"Roger, Galeblast Actual. Our scopes show clear skies around the *Starlit Voidhauler*, but you can follow them down to complete your contract. At one thousand meters, break off and land your flight at transponder Six-Delta."

Zejyc repeated the instructions back to the traffic controller, confirming the accuracy of the guidance received.

Breaking through the final layer of clouds revealed the sprawling complex of the starport below. Even from altitude, the different sections for varying sized craft were clearly delineated.

The *Starlit Voidhauler* dropped toward one of the larger berths that currently sat empty, a lengthy and wide support structure for the largest of freighters. It didn't take long for the freighter to descend past one thousand meters, and Zejyc guided his team onto a separate flight path that followed a series of waypoints indicated by following the Six-Delta beacon.

Surprisingly, the course didn't head toward the smaller berths used by passenger transports. Instead, the transponder led them in a curving flight around the traffic control tower. Zejyc caught sight of several smaller automated anti-personnel cannons cautiously tracking their movements, but the massive Icarus cannon on top of the tower held the Pharyleri's attention until he dropped below the tower's height.

The beacon led the flight to an open section of tarmac outside the primary administration building at the base of the tower where a pair of Pharyleri waited for the Galeblasts' arrival.

Zejyc glided down to hover in front of the two gnomes before retracting his thrust units into the armor of his boots and his glide wings, dropping him to land lightly in front of them. The rest of the mercenary unit landed smartly behind him in an evenly spaced V-formation.

Zejyc's helmet collapsed back into his collar with a command from his Neural Link and allowed fresh air to flow over him as a warm breeze blew steadily from the west.

The first waiting gnome, magenta hair slicked back into a mullet that hung over the collar of a pressed set of khaki coveralls, looked up from a tablet and looked at Zejyc with a puzzled expression. "Are you the leader of the Galeblast Mercenary Corp?"

Zejyc stepped forward. "Zejyc Galeblast. My father was killed on our last contract and I'm in command now."

"I'm sorry for your loss," the gnome replied. "I'm Fonbin Springporter, special assistant to Clan Leader Sprocketsworth. The Clan Leader would like to meet with you, if you're available?"

Despite being phrased as a question, Zejyc knew that the request was nothing less than an illusion of choice. "I'd be delighted to join the Clan Leader."

Fonbin smiled warmly. "Fantastic. My sister, Glemi, here will see to your troops and provide refreshments during your discussion."

Zejyc glanced at Byruc and nodded, leaving the older gnome in charge of the squad. Then he followed Fonbin toward the building beyond the landing pad. A pair of heavily armed mech suits with multiple weapons packages mounted on their limbs and shoulders stood on either side of the doorway into the building.

After the doors closed behind them, Zejyc said, "Pretty heavy armaments."

Fonbin shrugged. "The Clan Leader will provide an explanation, but things have gotten a little tense around here lately."

Fonbin remained silent for the rest of the short walk up a flight of stairs and down a lengthy hall before ending in a lounge with an empty reception desk. The double doors leading into the Clan Leader's office door were open, and Fonbin led Zejyc inside.

"Clan Leader Borgym Sprocketsworth, Pharyleri Clan Elder and Prime Administrator," Fonbin announced as Zejyc stepped into the room. "Clan Leader Zejyc Galeblast, Commander of the Galeblast Mercenary Corp."

A gray-haired gnome sat behind a large desk that dominated the back of the room, his hands steepled under his chin. A bank of monitors made up one wall and showed an active command center, tiered rows of workstations filled with Pharyleri hunched over their consoles.

Zejyc followed Fonbin's guidance to one of the chairs in front of the desk and sank into the brown leather seat as the assistant left the room and closed the doors. The comfortable chair conformed to the mercenary's body, and he looked up to find Borgym's gaze fixed upon him.

"I was really expecting your father, Commander," the Clan Leader said, dropping his hands to rest on the desk.

"You knew my father?" Zejyc asked.

Borgym nodded. "I hired him for a contract shortly after he took over from your grandfather. What happened to him?"

"Things fell apart on our last mission. Most of the Corp didn't make it out, my father included."

"I'm sorry for your loss," Borgym said. "Not just for your father but for all of those no longer with us."

"Thank you for your sympathies, Clan Leader. The journey here was long enough that the feelings are no longer so raw, but we're trying to get on with our lives."

"Understandable. What brings you to Earth then? Another contract?"

Zejyc sighed. "With the way things ended on our last contract, the Galeblast reputation isn't worth much. We're not really looking for a job so much as we're looking for a home."

Borgym sat back in his chair as he considered the mercenary. "And the word is out that the Sprocketsworth Clan is expanding."

It was a statement instead of a question, but Zejyc still nodded.

Borgym let the silence grow, taking the measure of the mercenary. Finally, the Clan Leader leaned forward and folded his hands on the desk. "I'll be upfront with you, Commander. Conflict is brewing across this Dungeon World. The Sects, Guilds, and Factions are making moves against each other, while the human natives are finding allies and attempting to reclaim their cities.

"The Clan is forming our own alliance to push back against those encroaching on what we've built here. Trained mercenaries with Combat Classes and experience in battle are sorely needed. Your fight on the descent was impressive, but if you and your troops join us, then it won't just be monsters you battle."

"I appreciate your honesty, Clan Leader. We're prepared to fight for our place here."

"All right then. I'm willing to offer you and your troops probationary membership in the Sprocketsworth Clan, though you will each need to individually make a System-bound loyalty agreement to become a member."

Zejyc nodded. "That is more than understandable for a Clan in conflict. For myself, I agree to those terms, and I imagine the others will as well."

Borgym smiled and stood, coming around from behind the desk to greet his new probationary Clan member. "You must be hungry after that fight on your arrival. Let's go find your troops and get you some food. We'll sort everything out after you've eaten."

***

The sun dipped toward the horizon as Zejyc watched from the upper level of the starport control tower. The loyalty agreements had been sorted, along with a fantastic dinner, and now the mercenary stood on duty for the first time as part of the Sprocketsworth Clan.

The panoramic view that looked out in all directions through armored windows from the control tower was a long way from the cramped hold of the freighter. Fortunately, the passage booked for the rest of the Galeblast Mercenary Corp—who were now on their way—was a little less spartan.

One of the air traffic controllers looked up from their console. "Commander, looks like there are a couple griffins harassing inbound craft to the northwest at an altitude of four thousand meters."

Zejyc glanced at Byruc and Vek, the two Pharyleri already moving toward the access hatch that led to a newly installed launch pad designed to help the aerial combatants reach altitude quickly.

The former mercenary, and now Commander of the Sprocketsworth Defense Force, looked back at the ATC technician. "We're on it, Ground Control."

Magical mysteries of Musical Talent (Or Humanity's Lack Thereof)

Seriously, what happened to most of humanity's musical talent? It seems like ever since the Dungeon World came about, anyone with any talent is dead. You'd think they'd have figured out how to make use of their non-Combat Class abilities to help them survive like other groups, but outside of a few notable exceptions, they haven't.

And worse, the musical Classes who have survived are mediocre talents at best. And some of their greatest talents are already dead. Couldn't we have started the System, like, a few decades ago? We could have saved so many of them then.

Anyway, anyone have any links to decent human musicians?

- AintGonnaLetYouDown001A

*%22^^KilltheBuzz – You talk about good music and you use that as your username? I smell troll.

AintGonnaLetYouDown001A – Nah, man. I just really like that music. Here, see. This is why.

*%22^^KilltheBuzz – As if I'll fall for that.

IntheWebNoOneCanHearYouScream_02 – I have the GaGa Diaries. It's all *tied up*.

AintGonnaLetYouDown001A – We know. Everyone knows. What you did is close to outright slavery, coming in at the last moment to take them. And drop the web-based puns. It's not funny.

IntheWebNoOneCanHearYouScream_02 – Says you. I *spi* others who are cackling.

AintGonnaLetYouDown001A – Moving on.

Daiyu_Frass-singer0991 – How about Tagaq and the Hu? You can't say they aren't good at what they do.

AintGonnaLetYouDown001A – I'll give you them. But they were in the right place at the right time to get support – or support one another. You open to a swap?

Daiyu_Frass-singer0991 – Always.

AintGonnaLetYouDown001A – Anyone else?

Pedromannana-vass91 – I got the ends of all the big players if you want. I've been collecting recordings of it for the human celebrity machines, including some of these reality show stars.

AintGonnaLetYouDown001A – Not interested. Looking for living musicians.

DeBruyn_Collapse211not – How about a failed singer made good? Prime 5D sense immersion material here. I've been mining it for a show I'm trying to pitch. This one's got a decent ending, but I'm not sure my financers are up for it. Give me your real thoughts, I'll pass it on for free.

AintGonnaLetYouDown001A – Another no-name? Whatever. Forum's dead today. Wonder what's going on. Let me take a peek.

DeBruyn_Collapse211not – Some people have no manners. Whatever.

Song of Whispers

By Andrew Tarkin Coleman

♫Boring work. Boring work. Boring work. Hate this job. Better than fighting. Monsters worse. And I get Credits. So I can eat. Hate this job. Hate this job. ♫ I finish emptying the urea tank into the barrel and unlock the wheels on the dolly under it. After an hour at work, I no longer smell it—I half expect to see a blue box granting me Urine Smell Immunity. Of course, other people still smell it. No matter how careful I am, some always gets on me. I dump the barrel into the vat and start loading pig hides into the vat.

I stop singing under my breath as Bob approaches.

He says, "We need to talk."

Crap, did he hear me? I look at Bob, dreading the next words. In a small town surrounded by deadly monsters, any job is hard to find.

"I have to let you go, Donna. It's not just your slow performance; whatever squad I put you in performs worse. I'll pay you for the full day, but you have to go now."

Before I know it, I'm gone. Firing got a lot simpler after monsters killed ninety percent of the world. No one really cares about paperwork anymore.

I head over to the clinic because, well, there's always work at the clinic—it's the single worst job around.

I sing "Mad World" by Gary Jules as I walk. It's a nice day, but it's hard to be happy when you get fired.

Doctor Zach seems glad to see me, even for a half day. Healer Zach now. They pawn off the hardest task on me—taking care of the three catatonic patients: Greg, Sarita, and Ethyl.

This job requires physical strength and a willingness to deal with bodily fluids. Particularly the harsh, uric acid smell of pee. It's also mentally taxing dealing with patients this badly damaged. They made it through Hell Night, survived the monsters, and made it back to our little Safe Zone. Physically.

Mentally, I'm not sure where they are, but they aren't in Cardee, Kansas. They probably would have died by now, except little Sarita is Mayor Garcia's young daughter. The Mayor pays for the clinic out of his own profits. Should call him Adventurer Garcia now, since he hunts down monsters most days. With a particular hard-on for the fish folk that held Sarita for two days. Haven't seen any of them near us for over a year.

The clinic is always short of workers. Not just because feeding, bathing, and otherwise taking care of the "sleepers" is a hard job. Dirt, poo, sweat, spit, snot are all things I can deal with. But they're a constant reminder of the worst side of this hellhole I call Dungeon Earth.

Speaking of which, a few points in Strength has made it a lot easier for me to move unresponsive bodies around. I think I'll increase my Stamina next time. Whatever job I do tends to be physically taxing. Also helps my singing—don't want to run out of juice halfway through an imaginary concert at the Hollywood Bowl.

Physical wounds can be healed by any Healer. Usually the System ameliorates mental trauma, but the fish folk have a spell that the system does not heal. It requires more specialized abilities to undo the trauma it causes. Unfortunately, Cardee doesn't yet have those services. Working with the mentally unstable is, ironically, depressing.

I silently sing a little bit as I work. Technically I'm using my Sub-vocalize Class Skill. It lets me sing unheard by most. But my mood sneaks into the songs. I improvise a bit, riffing off Harry Chapin's "Cat's in the Cradle." A song about a son and a father never getting to spend time together reminds me of Sarita and her father.

I hate working at the clinic and avoid it as much as possible. But it'll take a week or two to convince someone to give me even a menial job. I've got some cash, but every Credit counts. When you're living hand to mouth in the middle of the Dungeon Earth, as a *Singer* for God's sake, you take what you can get.

I still regret taking Singer as my class. Worst possible class for a Dungeon World. Understandable why I didn't take a combat class, but couldn't I at least have chosen a crafting class? Even a portrait painter makes something they can sell.

No, I had to follow my dream, and when those evil little blue boxes offered me Singer, I snapped it up faster than a mark betting on Three Card Monte. I was never practical. I guess anyone who tries to make a living in the arts is a bit of a dreamer, even before Hell Night.

Now, however, I have become practical. Necessary in a small town on a Dungeon World. We don't even get many aliens way out here. Too weak a zone, thank God, to interest most.

Which is why I sing whenever I can. I have three ranks in Sub-vocalize, my highest Skill, because it lets me sing without disturbing others. Few people realize what I'm doing. While singing doesn't improve my Class Skill, practice still makes me a better singer. People are so obsessed with gaining Class Skills, they sometimes forget you can still learn things the old-fashioned way.

Who knows, maybe I'll be offered an Advanced Singer combat class. Bards are things, right? Maybe I could end up as a Siren?

Yes, and God is about to turn me into an Archangel and "Quest" me to destroy the System. At my current rate, I should hit Advanced Class in about two hundred years. But honestly, my dreams may be the only things keeping me from ending up next to Sarita, being fed pudding by someone who made as many bad choices as I have.

I sing a bit of Jim Croce's "Operator." I'm over all my ex-boyfriends, but the self-denial fits my mood better than anything else.

After work, I go to the diner. The smell is practically intoxicating: delicious meat, fresh baked bread, and a hint of sugary goodness. Mrs. Patel still runs it, but not many people eat here.

"Hello, Mrs. Patel. I was wondering if you could use a busboy. Well, busgirl."

"Sorry, Donna, I wish I could. Even before the monsters, we weren't doing so well. Once we got a System Shop, the Mayor bought pallets of MREs for emergencies. Cheap and tastes like it, but still. Most of my customers are adventurers, and they pay with monster steaks as often as Credits. They know I can grant some buffs, but they can get more options from the Shop."

"I could work for food. I'm sleeping at the rec center." A lot of us non-combatants are still doing that. Tight, but they got water, lights, and no monsters can spawn there.

"Honey, that's the deal I have with my daughter. I wish I could support two of you, but I can't. Not now."

"Thanks, Mrs. Patel. Think of me if things change."

"Will do. Here, take a pork kebab to go," she says with a bit of pity.

The pork kebab is delicious. It helps that I'm hungry. Good food always tastes heavenly when your body craves it. Why anyone would prefer the alien crap, I do not know.

I go to the next place on my list, without too much hope. I've already worked for too many people. In a small town, not only are there few jobs for unskilled labor, but word gets around. The more you get turned down, the harder it gets. And I get turned down a lot.

I work hard, keeping positive and singing some "Tubthumper." On Dungeon Earth, you have to get back up again or the monsters eat you.

By the end of the day, I suspect that Bob has spread rumors about me being a bad luck charm. No one wants to hire me for any task. The best I'm offered is lumberjill while Adventurers guard us.

No thanks. That's a quick way to get eaten.

I'm near the gate when there's a huge commotion. People shouting, metal locks clanging shut, the scrape of things being dragged. I join the crowd and see Mayor Garcia's party come in, all bloody. Literally—it stains the dirt where they stand. Wait, I thought his party had six…

Everyone gathers around and listens to the Mayor.

After he gathers his breath, he says, "It's the octohogs."

Cardee had one of those giant industrial swine farm-factories before Hell Night. A multi-national corporation kept hundreds of thousands of pigs in warehouses. They outnumbered us from day one.

Of course, many of them died on Hell Night too, or we would all be dead. So we've been farming the resulting monstrous swine for the past two years. It's an important job, providing food and keeping the swine from overrunning us. There are three main groups: the huge ogre hogs, the poisonous spitting hogs, and the octohogs.

The octohogs have two tusks, four normal legs, and two octopus-like clawed tentacles coming from their back. They have thick brown fur—even on the tentacles—that makes for toasty warm jackets, if a bit scratchy. Also, octohogs are pretty territorial, even compared to the other hogs.

"They've changed. They threw rocks at us. They're living in nests, and worst of all, they have plans." He looks at Mrs. Larna. "They killed Muddy."

Mrs. Larna cries. Muddy, Muhammad Larna, was her son and our best close combat fighter.

"What are we gonna do?" someone shouts.

Murmurs spread through the crowd. I use my Class Skill Read the Crowd, and I'm not surprised that people are scared with some pockets of grief (hmmm, didn't know Muddy and Christina were so close), but mostly anxious for the future.

Someone asks, "What's so bad about planning?"

My old boss Bob replies, "That's mankind's advantage. How we killed dire wolves, saber-tooth tigers, giant sloths, etc. Why we rule the world instead of bears. The System can be thought of as instant evolution. If the octohogs are becoming more intelligent, they'll become the dominant monster in Kansas and could wipe us all out. Just like we became the dominant species on Earth and wiped out dire wolves, saber-tooth tigers, and giant sloths."

"No. We're going to wipe *them* out," shouts the Mayor. "They're beginning to become smart, but we've been intelligent for millennia. Real weapons, books, even fire still exceeds their limits. But not ours. We'll gather all our adventurers and split into three parts. Our stealthiest will lead the hogs into the higher zones to the west. Our fastest will lead them toward the fish men to the north. The rest will wait and attack the young and females that remain in their nests."

The crowd cheers a bit halfheartedly. Most of the fear has been downgraded to anxiety. Seeing his success, the Mayor and the other community leaders go off to plan.

A couple of stanzas from The Beatles's "Being for the Benefit of Mr. Kite" flash through my mind into my mouth and I almost forget to Subvocalize the song.

***

Come morning, I try to raise my own spirits. During my morning ablutions, I sing very loudly. Rodgers and Hammerstein's "I'm Gonna Wash that Man Right Outa My Hair" is my favorite bathing song. The water relaxes my mind with warm memories of softer times as it cleanses my body.

A blue box appears

Congratulations!

Through diligent effort and singing almost loud enough for monsters to hear miles away, you have gained a Level!

Congratulations on reaching level 19!

You have gained 2 free Attribute points and 1 free Skill Point!

I look over my options one more time and make my selections. The free attribute points go into Stamina. My available Class Skills are Sub-vocalize, Sing it LOUD!, Background Instruments, Read the Crowd, Jazz it Up, and Emotive Singing. I have ranks in all except the last. It's time to see exactly what Emotive Singing does.

You have selected Emotive Singing. Sing your heart out!

You now have 1 rank in Emotive Singing.

I activate the Skill and belt out some of Shania Twain's "Man! I feel like a Woman!," but I don't notice anything different. I'm sure I'll eventually figure out what it does. Just have to keep using it.

Breakfast, walk to the Clinic, then work.

I start with a sponge bath for the sleepers. Oh God, the smell. Worse than the pee. Other's people poo always smells worse than your own. I clean up the bathroom mistake while mentally cursing. Can you call it a mistake if it happens multiple times a week?

I brush some hair. Least bad part of this job and kind of satisfying. Dealing with pretty soft hair is an easy task. So I Sub-vocalize Lizzo's "Good as Hell" as I do Ethyl's hair, because who doesn't like a hair flip?

Next up is Greg. I think his head is actually bobbing to the music. Strange, sub-vocalize should prevent everyone from hearing me. Also, a little bit annoying while I try to brush his hair. Catatonic isn't comatose. They can get agitated; I've seen Greg punch someone who pushed him. He can even speak—if you count repeating what you just said as speaking. Sarita and Ethyl, on the other hand, haven't spoken a word since Hell Night.

Come lunch time, the Mayor visits Sarita with presents in tow—it's her birthday. He hands out ice cream to all the patients and staff. I have the feeling he wants one more good day with Sarita before he fights a death match with the octohogs. I put my ice cream in my Inventory and prepare to feed Sarita first. The Mayor gives me a cup of chocolate ice cream with sprinkles for her, and I sit next to Sarita.

"♫Happy birthday to you. Happy birthday to you. Happy birthday, dear Sarita. Happy birthday to you, ♫" I sing as I feed Sarita.

"Good friends and true," says Ethyl.

We all turn and stare. Ethyl hasn't said anything since the monsters came.

Healer Zachary comes over. "Did Ethyl just talk?"

Mayor Garcia says, "She said 'good friends and true' when Donna sang the 'Happy Birthday' song."

We all look at Ethyl, but she doesn't say anything more.

Zach says, "She used to work at a restaurant that sang as they gave you a cake on your birthday. Donna, please sing again."

I rack my brain for the original version. It had the "good friends and true" line, but most people just use the "How old are you now?" chorus. "♫Happy birthday to you. Happy birthday to you. Happy birthday, dear Sarita. Happy birthday to you. ♫"

"From good friends and true," adds Ethyl.

"♫From old friends and new, ♫" I continue.

"♫May good luck go with you! ♫" sings Ethyl with actual rhythm.

I add, "♫And happiness too. ♫ "

Ethyl finishes off with the standard chorus, ending with, "♫How old are you? ♫"

They all break out clapping. Finishing a song isn't repeating someone else's words. This is the first sign of life Ethyl has shown in years! I ignore some notifications for now and clap with everyone else.

Zach asks, "Ethyl, would you like some chocolate ice cream?"

For one second it looks as if Ethyl isn't going to speak, but she says, "Vanilla."

Zach gets some vanilla ice cream and feeds her. I note he takes care to put Ethyl's hand on the spoon as she eats, encouraging her to feed herself.

"What happened?" asks the Mayor.

"I got a new Skill, Emotive Singing."

With a broken voice and with actual tears leaking from his eyes, he asks, "Do-do you think it might help… Sarita?"

I can't give him hope. Hope is an evil little bastard that likes murder suicide. I reply, "I was feeding her when I sang 'Happy Birthday.' She didn't respond."

"We sang the Spanish version most of the time. Sarita rarely sang that version. But she annoyed the crap out of everyone with the movie *Frozen*. Could you sing 'Let It Go' for us?"

Could be worse. At least it's not "Baby Shark."

I renew Emotive Singing, add in Background Instruments for good measure, and grab a spoon-slash-pretend-microphone. As invisible instruments start up, I belt out "Let It Go." Sarita doesn't react, so I keep singing. When I get to the title lyric, I extend the pause more than Idina Menzel did, Sub-vocalize it, and point the "microphone" at Sarita.

"Let it go," comes out in a bare whisper. That tiniest of whispers, just above my own sub-vocalized voice, but it rings louder than all the other sounds in the world.

I continue singing the rest of the song. Each time I get to the title part, Sarita sings it a little bit louder. By the time I finish, people are cheering and I'm in the Metropolitan Opera House, singing to a packed crowd. At least in my mind.

Once it's over, I go through my notifications. '+5 happiness buff for two hours to all, +5 hopeful buff for two hours to Sarita, +10 sanity buff 10 minute for all, catatonia debuff permanently reduced by -1 for Ethyl and Sarita'.

Zachary confirms it, "My Examine Patient says she has cured a tiny part of the catatonia. It will take multiple treatments, but I think we can get Sarita back. I think we get all of them back!"

I smile. "I think we can negotiate something."

That's when they realize they want a minimum wage employee to use rare Skills. I see a flash of annoyance on Zach's face. He didn't really need to hire me, and he thinks I am going to gouge the Mayor. Except for major emergencies, magical healing keeps this place from being too busy. Obviously, he employed me to help me, as much as to avoid doing the less pleasant jobs here. A wave of gratitude swells from within me. It isn't the first time—people keep surprising me with hidden kindness. I heard all those stories about disaster bringing out the worst in people, but all I have is a long list of people to repay.

Mayor Garcia says, "I'll give you anything. I'll give you everything!"

"You misunderstand me, Mayor Garcia. You will pay me nothing. The city, however, will pay me a reasonable fee to visit the clinic every day at noon for personal treatments for those who need my Skills. Not just the sleepers. It's better to cure PTSD, especially in adventurers, before it gets too bad."

"I'll pay for extra treatments all day for Sarita."

"I can't do that, Mayor. In the mornings, I gotta sing for the adventurers. Probably at Mrs. Patel's place." Combine her cooking buffs with my singing and who knows what can happen.

"Won't they need individual songs? It's clear not every song works with every audience."

I activate Jazz it Up, the System sends a suggestion for modifying some lyrics, and I smile and sing some Beastie Boys, but switch the famous drawn-out lyric to "♫CAAAARDEE♫" Nice bit of improvisation. I add "Some things are more universal."

***

Executing my plan isn't quite as easy as I thought it would be. Mayor Garcia spreads the word and come morning, a lot of people are in Mrs. Patel's restaurant, but they're standing, not eating.

I go to the bar, activate Sing It LOUD!, and shout over everyone, "Today's an experiment. First one's free and all that. Tomorrow, if you want in, there will be a cover charge and you *will* buy breakfast. Cover charge to be determined by Mayor Garcia for the first week; after that, by me and Mrs. Patel."

I see a couple of people wise up, take a seat and order some breakfast. I shine a smile at them, and guess who I focus on as I begin the show? Read the Crowd. Background Instruments. Jazz it Up. Emotive Singing.

I start with Kelly Clarkson's "Stronger," with some minor changes. Because that's what we need to do—get stronger. Some great lines in that song about other people underestimating women aren't hard to modify to refer to the aliens underestimating Earth. Even the loneliness works with some minor modifications.

I finish up and reactivate Read the Crowd. Half the people here have a +1 Morale Bonus, lasting for hours. Not bad for one song. My first song. Let's try some more…

***

Forty minutes later, we know it works. I gave some +10 bonuses. In fact, it works too well.

"We need you on the hog hunt," says Mayor Garcia.

I stand there shocked. The ancient curse of your dreams coming true is nasty. "I am *not* a Bard! I have low Health and Mana, not to mention a total of *zero* spells, combat gear, of offensive capabilities."

"We know, we know. There's a fort with running water that we're going to use as a forward base camp. We want you to stay there. Sing some songs before we split up. You stay with the third group and wait until the rest draw off the majority of attackers. Give the last group one last boost before they go. The camp is pretty nice actually, with strong walls. It's about two-thirds of the way to the octohogs. When the last group leaves, Johnny—and his truck—will remain as your bodyguard. After we take out the piglets and sows, Johnny and his family will take you home."

Johnny is twenty-three years old, a moderate level Ranger type. Not bad-looking either. Spending some hours with him won't be unpleasant. But I would prefer someone a bit more powerful if we have to run back to Cardee by ourselves. His father, mother, and two sisters make for a solid team to take me back to Cardee, but they can only do that if they survive the battle.

The Mayor continues. "Look, I need you alive for Sarita. I wouldn't ask if we didn't also need you for the hunt. You could make a real difference. We, um, sighted smoke coming from the octohogs. I think they're experimenting with fire. We have to take them out soon."

You have been offered a Quest!

Help wipe out the dreaded Octohogs before they outsmart you and wipe out the lonesome town of Cardee.

Rewards: Experience, Credits, and the respect of the Town of Cardee.

Do you accept?

In the end, I agree to go—after I negotiate a good price. Mayor Garcia agrees to give me a double share of any Credits we bring in. While my money problems may go away if we can turn the Patel place into a buff factory, that takes time. Who knows, it might not work; or I might need to build a stage. If I'm going to risk my life outside a Safe Zone, I'm gonna get paid and paid well.

The next morning, we all meet up by the Patel place. She's got three coolers set up labeled "High Zone," "Fish Folk," and "Sows." Everyone is lined up, getting two prepared meals, two drinks, and a snack.

A huge sign above them says, "PLACE IN INVENTORY. Eat meal 'one' only after you are told to at the Fort. Save the first drink for just before you leave. Eat the snack if you need some healing. Save meal 'two' and the other drink for an emergency."

Mrs. Patel and her daughter are telling everyone the same thing as they hand out meals.

Mayor Garcia waves me over and hands me a set of food and a potion vial, which I put in my Inventory. Johnny does the same.

"The potion grants invisibility and should last an hour," Mayor Garcia says. "Save them for an emergency. If we don't come back, take the truck and go. Only use the potion if you have to leave the truck. Hopefully you can keep them for another day."

The trip out is uneventful, but I'm pretty tense with worry. I haven't been this far from a safe zone since Hell Night. I obsessively look out the truck window even though I'm in an entire convoy of adventurers who can protect us. I don't see any monsters, but what about when we aren't surrounded by an army?

By the time we get to the fort, my hands hurt from clenching so long. The fort is nice. It still has the old Godmat sign. It used to be a restaurant that served this incredible flatbread called *lefse.* It tasted like a hearty kiss on the tastebuds. One more thing I miss. Maybe I can get Mrs. Patel to make some. I think it's just naan with some potato in the dough. Now I'm hungry, but I shouldn't eat until after the show.

While everyone else sets up camp and eats, I figure out where to do the show. No one ever accused Kansas of being hilly, so I climb onto the fort wall. It's wide enough that I don't have to worry about falling off.

I prep the area with a tiny table off to the side with some water, a chair for some of the slower songs, and I'm ready. I activate my Skills again: Read the Crowd. Sing it LOUD! Background Instruments. Jazz it Up. Emotive Singing.

"YOU GUYS READY TO ROCK?"

***

I finish my version of "Mama Said Knock You Out" by LL Cool J and the crowd is really into it. Some people are using minor fire spells or abilities like they used to use lighters. I even got some people singing along with me, once they learned my version of the chorus. I revel in the acclaim and hope I never get used to it. Then I see Mayor Garcia in the corner, shaking his head and giving me a hand sign to finish.

"I'd love to keep singing, but Donna says it's time to KNOCK THE HOGS OUT! Mayor Garcia…" I point at the Mayor and climb down the wall.

Johnny has a glass of water waiting for me and I thank him before I gulp it down. I glance over a whole slew of notifications, dismissing them. Nothing important, just experience I earned and buffs I granted.

Johnny says, "You did fantastic. Groups one and two should be gone in ten minutes. Five minutes after that, Act Two starts for group three."

I eat my food and drink my shake (not giving either the attention homemade food deserves), then start the next set. It goes well, since by now, I know what I am doing. I finish the last song of the day, with thanks.

I hope I hit the right balance that will help them kill while letting them ignore the fact that their targets are sows and piglets probably smarter than chimps.

I wonder how common this problem is. We can put points into Intelligence when we Level up. Can monsters do the same? Is there some strange monster somewhere with a high Intelligence but no one to teach it? Worse, are budding geniuses forever imprisoned in fingerless bodies, unable to wield tools or perhaps even communicate? I shudder. Intelligence has its benefits, but it would be hell without the necessary accoutrements.

As I rest, I hear the Mayor giving last commands. "If things go wrong, head *south*. You will *not* lead them back here to Donna and Johnny. You will *not* lead them back to Cardee. Where do you head if things go wrong?"

"South."

"What was that? Louder! If things go wrong, where do you head?" says the Mayor.

"SOUTH!"

They drive off, ready to wipe out the octohogs before they do the same to us. May God have mercy on all our souls.

Johnny pulls out a deck of cards, a cribbage counter, and asks, "How do you feel about cribbage?"

Several games and three hours later, we spot the third group returning. We open the gate and let them drive into the Fort.

They haul in some wounded, but there were no deaths and most came away without a scratch. I hand out water and give the healing snack Mrs. Patel made for me to someone who needs it more. While I do so, I notice Johnny talking to his family.

When they're done, Johnny returns to me. "If it's okay with you, Mom wants to spend a few minutes healing before we go. Some of the wounded should stay here and heal up before heading home." He shakes his head. "They had a rough time doing what had to be done."

I eavesdrop on some of the conversations and can tell it was pretty bad.

"… she was protecting her piglet, just covering it with her own body…"

"… the baby just looked at me with these eyes so big…"

"… the piglet saw me kill the sow and charged me like it could defend her…"

"… my grandfather was called a baby-killer after Vietnam. Now I know…"

"… Mitchell and Webb sketch where they ask, 'Are we the baddies?'…"

Guilt and depression are practically oozing out of them. I feel it fill the room even without Read the Crowd. What I do now will affect these people for the rest of their lives. I have one chance to make a real difference, to help them put to bed some of this pain.

Mentally, I go over a few songs, including Eminem's "Cleaning out my Closet," Phil Collins's "In the Air Tonight," and Rag'n'Bone Man's "Only Human." Then I make up my own song.

When it's all over, I don't actually remember the words—got to get myself a recording device from the Shop. But I'll always remember the topics.

I sang of honesty, pain, and regret. I sang about Hell Night, when we lost the paradise we didn't know we lived in. I admonish them to not forget the deaths of billions.

These hogs had turned feral and killed their keepers. They're now monsters, killing for experience rather than for food. Muddy was just their latest victim; I remember all our dead in song.

I sang of those who survived—how we must protect all people, not just ourselves. I sang of family, friends, and the reasons why we'd done what we did. I proclaimed that I would have killed the octohogs myself if I could have.

We are only human—imperfect, trying our best, never exactly right. Heroism is all too often just men doing a particularly good job of surviving hell. We have the right of self-defense and the right to survive. These

Adventurers need to know they aren't alone, and others feel the same despair and guilt. I ended with a couple verses putting the blame exactly where it belongs—on the System that drives everything here on Dungeon Earth.

I liked the song—apologetic but blaming the System rather than us poor victims. Read the Crowd shows me self-doubt is still there, but I reminded them just a bit about why they'd had to kill the piglets. The System is a cruel mistress—not just to us, but to the poor monsters as well.

Johnny and his family take me home. No one speaks, and we let the noise of the vehicle fill the air, if only to keep our emotions from spilling out. We won this battle, but the war has two more sides and we don't know how they went.

When we get back to Cardee, we wait by the entrance until the others arrive. When the last group comes in, we know we truly won. We lost three adventurers out of over sixty who went out. Plus one for Muddy makes four. Survivable losses, never acceptable.

Most importantly, the octohogs are gone and we remain. Oh, some of them will survive the fish folk and the high-level zone, no doubt. But they're scattered and will have a major problem finding a mate. Should they ever rebuild a herd, someone will hear of them before they Level and evolve into a real threat. We may not have ended them, but the threat is gone.

***

"Those *aren't* the words!!!" Sarita shouts.

It's been two months and Sarita still won't let me Jazz It Up. Duets go well only as long as I stick to the *Frozen* lyrics. She just won't let "Let It Go" go.

Honestly, I don't really care. She's arguing with me, and I treasure every word she says. This is where I belong. Not out there giving minor buffs to adventurers. Here, in a safe zone clinic, making life on Dungeon Earth a bit more bearable for those who are truly in need.

THE BIG APPLE

Putting together a serious documentary about New York right now. Need stories to show how the Big Apple has bounced back and retaken its throne as the city to be in. None of this garbage about the West Coast Vancouver with its weird-ass dungeons or the hyperloop trains coming across the Rockies in the Midwest. The Big Apple has always been the place to be, and this documentary will prove it.

WILLING TO PROVIDE STANDARD GALACTIC RATES for interesting stories about the Big Apple. Human native stories given a 20% signing bonus upon acceptance.

- Larsbeyond_WanderingASMR

McGregor_mod_Hunterzone111 – Mod reminder. Don't use caps unless you intend to shout. Especially don't use them for headings. We have non-visual readers in the group.

ZDan9kmma9NN – What's the big apple?

JumpCordRippedXXL88 – Noob! It's Earth slang for the city formerly known as New York in the Americas.

ZDan9kmma9NN – Who you calling noob, you Goblin-lover? Come say it to my face. I'll rip your intestines out and wear them to my sixth wedding.

JumpCordRippedXXL88 – As though you could find anyone who'd even meet you for a mating flight. You're a dozen tailfeathers short of a flight and diving already.

McGregor_mod_Hunterzone111 – Thread and posters sequestered. I'm letting the children fight it out. Apologies to everyone else.

Kuiooaasss18882 – What is going on today? Solar winds in the zenith or the Mana flows in opposition with the System?

McGregor_mod_Hunterzone111 – Just the usual Irvina quarterly session out. A lot of the regulars are watching the new Council session, so we're getting the mundanes flooding in. I'm the only mod on duty.

SharkEater_Gss-9811 – Ouch!

Larsbeyond_WanderingASMR – Fascinating as this might be, stories?

SharkEater_Gss-9811 – Got nothing. Not my thing, man.

Larsbeyond_WanderingASMR – … Really, people?

SharkEater_Gss-9811 – Try again tomorrow?

Kanundraspies981 – I got one. It's not your usual thing, but it might be interesting. Came across my feed because I have an auto-buy for arena altercations. Never know who's going to get kneecapped within the vicinity, you know?

Larsbeyond_WanderingASMR – I was hoping for more than one…

Kanundraspies981 – Say thank you, or I'll remove it.

Larsbeyond_WanderingASMR – I'm sorry! I didn't mean it that way. Thank you! I'll be happy to read about this.

Kanundraspies981 – Now, was it that hard?

Completely Trashed

by Mike Parsons

Me and Joey, we're layin in our blood outside the Shop again. We got problems, and fucking Big Tony always makes sure we got ten minutes to think about 'em while the System gets us back on our feet. This time, like the last few times, his goons didn't even let us in. Fuckers. I spit some broken teeth onto the pavement and wait.

Me and Joey, we got these Classes. I ain't met nobody else that do what we do. Trash Collector and Driver. Tell you what… gotta collect a shitload of trash to get 44 Levels as a Trash Collector. Lotta trash.

Been over two years since the System arrived and we've battled every day to get where we are. Jokers always tell us "one man's trash is another man's treasure" and all that shit. But we ain't found near enough treasure lately and now we're in trouble. Some people make Credits fighting or fucking or making stuff. We get the trash. System rewards us with more strength, more health, more points to put into Skills to pick up trash better than before.

Joey's got a Truck. He's the Driver and he picked a fucking honest-to-God Soulbound, fully working garbage Truck with a compactor and all that shit. Coulda chose a half decent Class instead. If we'd seen what all those other fuckers with combat Classes can do.

Even before the System, Joey was tough as fucking nails. But he loved drivin the truck and hauling trash 'cause he reckoned it was a good workout and he likes things to get cleaned up real nice. Me, I liked to stop into some shops 'round Brooklyn and Queens to shake 'em down a bit. Fucking cops don't pay much attention to the trash man, unless someone's runnin a big mouth.

I didn't do no better with my Class than Joey. Thought collecting trash was gonna be a sweet gig. You see how much shit got fucking wrecked when the System showed up? Crazy! Car crashes, security systems down, people freakin out, monsters everywhere. I was so sure we'd find shit-tons of loot that people left. We'd sell it and make bank! Crazy bank! Credits pouring out of our fucking pockets. Living like kings. Especially with my Class Skill, Take Out The Trash. A good size separate Inventory for anything the System says got zero durability. Anything that's broken.

First six months we went hard, and it worked out pretty good. Good experience and good Levels from the shit we picked up. Some of the broken shit we got could be fixed up. So we scraped together Credits and Joey bought a Repair Skill from the Shop. Found a Shop guy called Big Tony to use as a Fence.

We rumbled around in our fucking tank of a Truck and compacted non-System stuff to sell as materials. Grabbed System stuff and sold it cheap. Took broken shit and fixed it up real good.

Pure profit, baby.

If the first six months was good, the next couple years after that ain't been as sweet for us. People are getting their shit together. Buyin places from the System and fixing them up. Creating Safe Zones. Havin kids. Shit-tons of kids. Pregnant women all over the fucking place. Pretty sure not too many of them are 'cause of me and Joey. But maybe some. We stick to ourselves and keep moving.

Now things are more sorted, the fucking System picks up its own trash. Cleans its own shit up. We gotta be quick and street smart to find stuff we can do something with. Me and Joey, we thought about doin something else, but this is all we know. Everyone who made it this far is crafting and hunting and getting on with their lives.

So me and Joey, we decided to diversify. Follow some Adventurers that maybe seem a bit too cocky. Pick up some stuff they leave behind when they get smoked by monsters. Hang around monster spawns in case somethin bad happens to someone. Maybe once in a while grab some stuff that ain't ours too. Joey's Truck is like a fucking tank and his Skills protect us pretty good as long as we stay in the Truck and ride things out.

Sometimes, though, monsters or some dickhead Adventurers fuck up the Truck a bit. A couple times quite a lot. We gotta get it fixed up or we ain't got no way to get ahead. The System ain't a good place to be owing nobody Credits, and we got a big debt due real soon to Big Tony for fixin up the Truck. Things are gonna be real bad if we don't pay. The System don't fuck around when it comes to contracts.

But now… now the break we need is close. We know it. I got seven points in my Spring Cleaning Skill. Ain't many good Skills that I can get, but me and Joey, we're bettin the farm on this one. Lets me grab broken stuff out of Inventories. People don't even feel it or nothin, so far at least. Good thing for me and Joey is, most broken stuff people keep in their Inventories is there 'cause it's worth something. Gotta roll the dice on a fucking Evolution and hope the Skill bails us out. Big Tony ain't bein patient no more.

Me and Joey, we both groan 'cause we're almost done getting stitched back together and the System's got us to the point our teeth are growin back. Gimme the snap, crackle, and pop of my ribs or my limbs getting bent back the right way any day. I'm fucking over the System rummaging around in my mouth like a dentist on crack.

Once the System's done patching us up, me and Joey look at each other. We don't even have to say nothing. Gotta take more risks and get that next Level fast, so we head straight for our only real hunting spot. We ain't no combat Classers, but we're from the fucking streets.

So now I'm creepin around in a covered parking lot like a fucking ninja… Fuck! There it is! I fire my shitty half-repaired beam rifle and hit this motherfucking cockroach the size of a dining room table right in the head. I pump it with a couple more shots before the Mana battery I taped on falls right off the fucking rifle.

The job is done though. Cockroach scurries out from under cover off Beach 116th Street and Joey flattens the fucking thing, sending bug juice and bits flying everywhere. Don't care who you are, a twenty-fucking-ton skip bin full of metal dropped right on you is bad news.

"Fucking A!" I holler at Joey, and he punches the air to celebrate.

A notification pops up and even though reading ain't my thing, I know what this one is. Been waiting for it for what seems like forever. We been taking risks, killing some monsters just to get us this next Skill Point.

Level Up!

You have reached Level 45 as a Trash Collector.

Stat Points automatically distributed.

Fuck you, System. No free Stat points to assign when I Level up. Every fucking Level it pisses me off. And I ain't always that calm to begin with.

Unassigned Attributes

You have 1 free Skill point.

Would you like to assign it now?

(Y/N)

Still pissed, I hammer the "N."

This is the fucking ticket. I know it. This Spring Clean Skill is gonna evolve. I can't wait to see what me and Joey can pick up. We need something good, bad.

Feelin good, I hop in Joey's Truck and slump down into my comfy leather seat. My boots hit the dashboard and I look at Joey who gives me raised, scarred eyebrow. I nod and give him a shit-eating grin.

"Done?" he asks.

"Done."

We don't say nothin else and Joey floors it for a few blocks down Beach Channel Drive to a place we're staying. It's only a few houses from the Rockaway Beach boardwalk and our best friend Jimmy's place.

Me and Joey, we never take nothin Jimmy says to heart. But he won't shut the fuck up about Big Tony until we threaten to smack him around a bit. After enough beer to drown an elephant, I'm lying on the couch at Jimmy's place ready to assign this fucking Skill point. I don't read so good, so it takes me a while to make sure I've picked Spring Cleaning. Me and Joey, we've rehearsed this a bunch of times, so I know what Spring Cleaning looks like. I drop it. And the world goes dark.

Soon as I come to, I fight the thunder in my head and open up that fucking notification to see it, expanding it to take up my whole vision. Reading this shit's gonna take forever. But Joey's heard me stir from the La-Z-Boy he's crashed out on over in the corner.

"Hey," he says to me, leaning forward.

I flick the notification over to him.

"Holy fuck!" he says.

"What is it? What's it say?"

Joey clears his throat and rubs his eyes before cracking into it.

"Congratulations! Class Skill Evolved. Spring Clean. Allows the Caster to retrieve items with zero durability from any System inventory within Perception plus Luck/2 feet and place them straight into the Caster's inventory for future disposal. Evolved Skill. In a window between 15 and 60 minutes after any sentient creature's death, the Trash Collector may place all items of any durability worn by the Sentient or in their Inventory straight into the Caster's Inventory for future disposal, as long as the Sentient is within range. The Caster also has a chance to retrieve any Credits accessible by the dead Sentient which are not held at a Registered Secure Deposit Entity. Cost, 50 Mana."

"Holy fuck is right!" I yell and jump up off the couch, pumping my fists.

We thought maybe we'd get some good shit, but this is fucking epic! With this Skill… we might just do okay. Increase our take from killed Adventurers. Maybe this Skill gives us other options we ain't never had before.

I fucking hate doin it 'cause it takes fucking forever, but I check my Status to make sure it's there.

Status Screen			
Name	Frankie Rizzo	Class	Trash Collector
Race	Human (male)	Level	45
Health	590	Stamina	590
Mana	70	Mana Regeneration	13 per minute
Attributes			
Strength	100	Agility	34
Constitution	59	Perception	34
Intelligence	7	Willpower	58
Charisma	12	Luck	33

Class Skills			
Take Out the Trash	6	Sort the Trash	3
Recycle	3	Incinerate	1
Spring Clean	8[e]		

When Joey first told me I could drop points into a Skill called Incinerate after Level 31, I was sure our luck was turning. Pictured myself blastin flames like those mages or the flamethrower on Joey's Truck. But the fucking Skill only burns up broken shit and there ain't even enough heat to get a sunburn. Fuck you, System. But now maybe we really got something.

I eyeball Joey and shrug at him.

"What the fuck do we do now, Joey? You know we gotta go see Big Tony." No matter where we go today, I'll be spamming Spring Cleaning like it's coming out of a machine gun. We gotta get Big Tony his money this week or we're as good as fucking slaves for a century.

He grins at me. "Times fucking Square, Frankie! Whoo! Let's go!"

Fucking joker. Times Square ain't nothing like it used to be. Manhattan neither. New York still ain't that stable. Millions killed, but also millions still around. Big buildings have been big targets. One place is still pumping, and that's Nassau Coliseum in Long Island. Used to be where the Islanders played hockey, but now it's a real fucking Coliseum where there's Arena fights for the crowd like the ancient Roman days. Shitloads of people and their junk are always there. And once in a while we get lucky, you just never know.

"Coliseum, Frankie. And then tail some Adventurers to see if we can get lucky. We better start thinkin about those quests though. Think we're probably gonna have to go out there tomorrow to try 'em."

"We better go see Big Tony first," I tell Joey. "If his goons think we're runnin, it's not gonna be no good. He's got us by the balls."

Joey nods and squints. He knows we got almost no time left and Big Tony's got all the cards. If we don't get something good at the Coliseum, tomorrow we'll be doin some real stupid shit. Me and Joey, we got our eye on a quest to clear out a nest of cockroaches and one to clear out some old subway tunnels. But we ain't no combat Classers and we ain't got high-powered weapons neither.

One day at a time.

We hop in the Truck and rumble past JFK Airport back over to where Costco used to be. Now it's just a giant warehouse that's the main Shop for anyone in Rockaway or Long Beach. JFK is now fully an alien landing pad. Area 51 or 52 or whatever. That kinda shit. Place always got ships zipping straight up or down from space. Bet they have some good trash around there, but security's tighter than a nun's downstairs. Me and Joey, we tried once. Maybe if we get to Master Class. Not before… we got nightmares still from that day.

We see a few monsters on the way and they try it on, but around here's an under Level 20 Zone, so we either run 'em over or just keep rumbling. We ain't got time to waste on monsters that give up no Credits and shitty experience. There's a flamethrower on the Truck but… that's another thing from Big Tony we're still payin off.

The Shop's crowded and our Truck gets a lot of attention, as always. Some punks usually try to break into it if we leave it somewhere. Once a group of combat Classers dragged the fucker away to try to chop it up, or hijack it, or some shit. But since it's Soulbound, Joey can call it back whenever the fuck he wants. I hope it disappeared just right so someone got their nuts chopped off.

People here today are mostly minding their own business though. We see some of Big Tony's goons, but they ain't the ones who beat us down yesterday and they don't look too interested in us. So we head in and touch the Shop crystal.

Always gives me a mental twitch to arrive in some place I wasn't standing in before, but we got no choice. And Big Tony is waitin for me. Me and Joey, we always get split up in the Shop and that ain't no good. Fat fucking Tony knows I ain't too good at buyin and selling, so I don't do it much. When we met Big Tony near the start, it was all smiles fencing for us, all friendly and helpful. But then he fucked us over real good.

"Big Tony." I nod.

No idea if the motherfucker is takin the piss with his name and how he acts, but he's a fat Jabba the fucking Hutt lookalike with gold chains and cigars and wearing a red silk robe. Maybe he got all his human culture downloads from the *Godfather* and *Star Wars*. Whatever.

"Frankie! Good to see you, my boy," he says. "What have you got for me? Oh! And I see you've Leveled quite a bit since last time. You boys were meant to come see me every two weeks and I ain't seen you for months."

He don't say nothin about the fact it's his goons that have stopped us. Big Tony's mouth is smiling, but his eyes are hard. I want to slap that fucking smirk off his fucking face, but that ain't gonna help me and Joey out none. Big Tony's got us right where he wants us. Me and Joey, we're staring down the barrel of a hundred years of being fucking Serfs, doin whatever Big Tony wants if we can't pay him back. Fucker put that part of the deal in the small print. Yeah, I didn't read the big print or the small print. But Joey did.

"Yeah," I agree. "We got a few Levels. Got a new Skill too. Gonna fuck up some rich fuckers. Maybe tell your goons to back off a bit so we can show you."

Big Tony laughs and his greyish-green body rolls in waves. I ain't sure if he's laughin about the thought of callin off his goons, or fucking up some rich fuckers. "Whatcha got for a new Skills, Frankie?"

When he sees I ain't keen to say nothin, he leans forward and opens his big fucking eyes as wide as they go. Big Tony's breath stinks worse than the fucking trash from the meat works.

"Frankie, I ain't trying to fuck you over. I already own your ass. You really think you can pull a fucking rabbit out of the hat? Maybe you should drop a few points into Intelligence first."

Fucker. I snort at him since my Class don't give me no choice where my Stat Points go. Ain't none of them going to Intelligence.

"Whatever," says Big Tony, shrugging. "You boys are almost outta time. I don't even have to slap you around when you miss my payment, the System's gonna do it for me. So let's see what kind of broken down, worthless crap you've got to sell. Maybe I can take a few things. Can't imagine a world where the two of you clowns come up with a couple hundred thousand Credits."

I know from experience most of what I got ain't gonna be of no interest to Big Tony or nobody else. I got a lot of broken stuff stored away in my Trash Inventory because of my Skill. But I picked up and "borrowed" a few special things here and there and put them in my System Inventory, so I dump them out on the table.

"Hey, some of this shit's actually not too bad," he says, eyeing some of the robotic tech I've thrown down. "I'll give you ten thousand Credits, plus I won't tell my guys to break your fucking legs on the way out."

As always, I think this fucker might be screwing me over. A Credit haul of 10k is good. Only a drop in the bucket compared to what me and Joey are on the hook for. But I ain't got a lot of people lining up to buy my stuff, so

I give him a nod. I take the Credits and he waves me a notification. Like all the others, I swipe it away without looking at it.

"Thanks, Big Tony. We'll see you soon."

Big Tony just nods and waves at me to see myself out. Joey's waiting for me when I finish, so we get on the road. The drive to the Coliseum is always crazy and we leave the Truck about a mile away, heading in on foot.

Once aliens and humans start bunchin up to wait, I pop Spring Cleaning. It feels a bit different, like it's searchin for something new. Ain't nobody recently dead in range though, so it's just the regular haul. As usual, Joey's watching all around real close as I do it. We know the day will come that we'll pull some broken shit out of some high-Level fucker's Inventory and they'll feel it.

Not too many people in range, but when it's done searchin, my Skill ripples out and I can feel when stuff's added to my Inventory. The System counts it all up for me and I kinda know most of what's in there if I try real hard. A notification pops up and I wave it to Joey as usual. He raises his eyebrows when he looks.

"Five hundred XP, Frankie."

I almost whoop, but don't wanna attract any attention so I keep it to myself. Just a little fist pump. Me and Joey are always linked up so we split the XP. We don't split it 50:50 'cause it's my Skill, but we split it. That's a good haul. Real good. Seems like nobody noticed nothin either.

"Let's go clean some shit up, Joey."

He chuckles and I give him a grin.

For a bit, we just enjoy bein here. All kinds of creatures floatin and waddling and walkin around, all hyped up waiting for the fights. Lotsa chatter in what sounds like Galactic, but I ain't so good at understanding any. By the time we grab some food and get to our seats, it's a couple bouts in. They got big screens showin the action and there's facts and figures about the fighters. Joey gets into it, but I ain't interested. More interested in what's goin on in the Arena.

I got some specs I put on to see better. Everyone has 20/20 vision now, but we're way up in the cheap seats. For now, it's a three-way knock 'em out between some bruisers. Reminds me and Joey of the playgrounds we grew up on and we laugh about some of the shit we used to get up to before the System. I zoom in with the specs to get a better view. Me and Joey, we enjoy another couple bouts, but now the Arena is full up, we got business to do.

Me and Joey, we stand and make our way a few rows up to the top of the Arena. You can walk right round up here, so we do. Can't go farther down unless we got tickets for those sections though. I pop my Skill every so often and feel it pull a few things into my Inventory. We're up at the top and the rich pricks are down the front where my Skill don't reach, but still, we do pretty good. By the time we sit down again I got a couple notifications to wave over to Joey.

"Another Level for me, but you still got a long way to 46," he tells me, grinning.

I give him the thumbs-up and look to see if there's a way we can get down lower to hit the rest of the crowd. The main event's about to start so now's the time.

"C'mon," I say to Joey. "Let's see if we can get down there from the pisser."

We head down and take a leak then wander around a bit till we get lucky and see a guard who's left his spot to watch the fight. We shuffle through and walk down a bit, playin like we're headed to our seats. I pop off my Skill again and feel a good surge of new stuff. I wish we could go around, but down here, you can only go up or down. This fight must be great because the crowd is going fucking mental and nobody is payin any attention to us.

Me and Joey are still lookin for openings when there's a loud, wet smack and everyone goes silent. You could hear a fucking pin drop. I look up at the screen and see the fucking mage with his head caved in and the warrior lookin like he's in shock. Musta been a major fuck up! Usually the loser's Portaled out at 20% Health. Fucking glass cannons.

"We gotta get down there, Joey!" I hiss. "We gotta be in range. They ain't gonna loot no Arena contestant right away."

"You gotta wait fifteen minutes for Spring Clean, remember Frankie?"

Fuck. He's right. We stand around pretending to be in shock while everyone slowly goes back to talkin and some people leave. We slip into a couple empty seats and wait. Soon, way too soon, they grab the mage and carry him down a tunnel goin under the stands. We can see the shimmer of force fields protecting us from the fights, but we keep waitin and as the Coliseum empties, they wink out. Musta been at least thirty minutes since the fight ended.

Me and Joey, we see the force field drop at the same time and he knows what he's gotta do. We wait for a couple more minutes then head down to the bottom of the section. Some security dickwads come over and ask us to move. We play dumb for a bit, but when they grab us, Joey lunges at the lot of 'em and knocks 'em flyin.

One of the pricks shrugs Joey off and tries to grab me, but I got a strength up at one hundred and know how to use it from a lifetime of haulin trash. He don't got a chance when I shove him, hard. Once I got a few feet of space, I dump maybe a ton of rubble from my Trash Inventory down around me and jump over the railing, landin just outside the tunnel. I want to pop Spring Cleaning, but I ain't got enough Mana to pop it twice, so this is a one-shot deal. Some security goons on this floor have noticed me and pull out all kinds of gear, askin to see my pass.

I can't lose this chance. Desperate, I pull a heap of broken stuff out of my Inventory. It keeps piling up as they keep blastin it away and I turn to sprint down the tunnel. I get maybe thirty or forty feet before I get crunched from behind and lifted into the air. My leg and back both snap and my head hits the ground hard. This is as far as I get!

I strain through the ringing in my ears, tryin to pop Spring Cleaning. It's tough to focus, but I fight and I fight. Me and Joey, we need this. I buck up and down, tryin to knock off the fucker on me, but my legs ain't doin nothing.

Wham! My head's rocked to the left, then the right, and back again over and over. I bring my arms up, but soon as I do they get busted up and dislocated.

My world's on fire and I keep gettin bounced around like I'm in a fucking washing machine. Can't even see nothin through my busted face. Then, for a sweet, golden half second, it stops and I throw everything I got into popping Spring Cleaning. I feel the rush when the Skill reaches out, same as before but different. So, so different. I can feel that dead mage somewhere down the tunnel with my Skill.

I get blasted against the concrete wall. The crack of my fucking skull is loud enough I hear it even through the ringin in my ears. Stars and fucking darkness start closing in, but Frankie fucking Rizzo ain't no quitter. Fuck Big Tony. Fuck everyone. Me and Joey, we need this. I strain and strain, then somethin snaps when my Skill locks onto the dead mage. I pull with everything I got. Pull his stuff and pull his Inventory and pull his Credits.

Got the fucker!

I laugh as the security guards lay into me some more. Feelin too good to feel pain, even as my bones crunch. They pick me up and throw me out of the fucking Coliseum through the nearest door, a broken shell that can't do nothin but gasp for air through a broken face.

Joey's been watchin for me, so he's down beside me in a few seconds. We know we just gotta wait it out while the System puts us back together. He ain't lookin too hot neither, but he plunges our best healing potion into me. I ain't doin so good.

"You get it?" he asks.

I nod and laugh, blood sprayin everywhere. My ribs are grinding and pokin me from the inside, but I don't give a shit and wheeze back at him. "Yeah, I got it. Let's get the fuck outta here in case they can find us."

"Or they get to a Shop and try to buy the information about who took his stuff."

Fuck. I didn't even think of that. Hopefully my Class and Skill protect us from that shit, but I doubt it. Maybe this wasn't as good an idea as we thought. With Big Tony ridin our ass, we ain't got much choice.

Me and Joey, we take a while to get up. Longer to limp to a clear side street a couple blocks away. There's enough space, so Joey summons his Truck. We hop in and he guns it to get a few more blocks away. Joey's drivin ain't too good with him still busted up, so we pull over to wait a few more minutes until the System's finished puttin us back together.

"If those fuckers can find us now, a few more miles won't make any difference," Joey says. "We might as well stay here for now."

I just nod and enjoy breathin again.

"Whatcha get, Frankie?"

I pull stuff out of my Inventory. Stuff that looks expensive and magical. Rings and wands and portable shield generators and shit. We stare at the stuff, not sure what to do.

"You think Big Tony will take this shit?" I ask.

"Fuck. Don't know. Maybe we'll need to spread it around a bit. You get any Credits?"

I check my Credits and startle so hard I bang my head against the window of the Truck. "Holy fuck, Joey! That's a lot of numbers!" I wave the window over to him.

Joey whistles. "That's over a hundred thousand credits, Frankie!"

"Joey, you better not be fucking with me. You serious? We might just make this payment to Big Tony?"

We can't help it. We laugh our fucking asses off.

"Hey," says Joey. "We mighta got a shitload of experience for this."

I nod. Could be a lot. Not sure how the System works, but we get XP for collectin trash, so this could be a lot.

"You better open them notifications, Frankie boy!" Joey hollers.

I laugh. If it sounds a bit crazy, I don't give a fuck. It looks like the worm has finally turned and the System has given a bone to Frankie fucking Rizzo. Just wait until you see what I'm going to do with this new Skill, System.

"Hey Frankie, you okay?" Joey asks.

I look over and can see he's concerned and maybe worried that using this new Skill's changed something about me, or between us. "Yeah Joey—great. Fucking great! Let's go see Big Tony and get this party started."

"What if those goons stop us from seein Big Tony again? We gotta make that payment, Frankie."

"This time we're driving the fucking Truck right up to the Shop and jumpin out. Maybe we can run a few of 'em over."

"Know what, Frankie? You're right. Even if they bash up my Truck on the way in, we're going to pay off Big Tony and never see that fucker again."

"Too fucking right, Joey. Too fucking right."

Me and Joey, we're heading in a new direction. Up.

Naval Stories

It's me. You know what I want. Naval stories. The usual deal. Trade for other stories, reviews of your fan fiction from a proper nautical perspective, or Credits. That's it.

------ OhCaptainmyCaptain_99SO

OhCaptainmyCaptain_99SO – Ping.

OhCaptainmyCaptain_99SO – Ping.

OhCaptainmyCaptain_99SO – Ping again.

OhCaptainmyCaptain_99SO – Really? No one?

OhCaptainmyCaptain_99SO – Ping.

McGregor_mod_Hunterzone111 – Please stop spamming. Only warning.

Bla's8kkm – I got one. Came across my feed. I'll take Credits.

OhCaptainmyCaptain_99SO – Credits transferred. Come aboard, my lovely. Come aboard.

Bla's8kkm – That's still creepy.

Trouble Brewing

by Nick Steele

Hidden Quest Completed!

For cleaning 100 toilets in 25 days, you have received the Skill Unclog. Show those Number Twos you're number one!

"Well fuck me with an anchor. Crime *does* pay!"

Unclog

You have learned a Basic Class Skill outside of your Class.

Effect: Pull organic matter through pipes one meter or under. Continuously channel Mana for increased duration.

"Umm, okay. Would have preferred pretty much anything else. Still, better than nothing."

For acquiring a new Skill, you have received 10 XP.

Go get 'em, big shot.

"Well that's just rubbing it in." If crime does pay, it doesn't pay much. Guess that's what you get for being a sailor in the Australian Navy, not a rich-ass fucking plumber.

That said, 10 XP pretty much doubles what I've made this week. And as for the Skill? I grimace. Well, I do clean the heads. A lot.

My crewmates avoid me as I haul a sloshing bucket up two ladders. *Ungrateful bastards. Price of their moonshine just doubled.*

After my previous confines, the flight deck's sweet, fresh air is heaven. I draw a deep breath, wincing at the stench on my person. *Maybe I can't blame them too much.*

A football field of grey stretches before me. It curves to a ski jump at the port bow. Smaller than an aircraft carrier, but not by much, Australian LHDs are amphibious assault ships—though like all things post-System, she's undergone a few changes.

"Hey, Ivy."

Now you're more likely to find winged beasts on the flight deck than helicopters, for example.

The twelve-foot water drake ignores me, blowing salt from her azure snout. Her musk is a pleasant change from breathing effluent, though in its own way just as overpowering.

Passing the beast, I near the edge of the HMAS *Canberra*. A wide, horizontal net rings the ship instead of railings, and I pour my cargo between two breaks in the mesh. Railings weren't good for helos when we had 'em. Not that good for drakes either, I guess.

When the job is done, I pull a dried herring from my pocket. Ivy instantly becomes friendly.

"Hey, hey, easy girl," I say as she gulps the first then noses me for another. I'm forced to step back toward the edge. "Can't swim, remember?"

I scratch her scales as we gaze out over the water. Well, I gaze at the water. Ivy's just nosing at my pockets. The horizon stretches before us, no land in sight. A convoy follows in our wake. I smile. *Survive. Protect. Defend.* Each ship would be flotsam without us. *Because we're the motherfucking* Canberra. *Pride of the Australian fleet.*

Only remaining warship in the Navy, but hey, who's counting?

Intent on enjoying the salt air, I draw a deep breath. My nose wrinkles at the lingering stench of sewage. Guess there's a less glamorous side to the job, too.

Still, HMAS *Canberra* is a beauty—perhaps even more so for my time spent scrubbing it. And she's home. A floating city—well, technically a village—with control crystal and Shop to prove it...

I love every inch of her, from the four modified 25mm Typhoons on her gun decks to the Atlantean torpedo tubes below. Even before the change, LHDs were hard bastards. Now, with System-upgraded weaponry and reinforced armor, the *Canberra* is a force to behold.

I squint gingerly over the edge, observing her scarred and damaged hull.

At least from a distance. Under-sea defense systems for a ship this size are astronomically expensive. The old girl has some—electronic netting, basic force shields, and the like—but Credits always seem tight.

I look down at my distant bobbing turds and spot blackened metal on the hull. Each dint and mark tell a story—this specific scorch mark came from a narwal attack early in the apocalypse. Some off-duty drunk thought they'd throw napalm over the side. Forgot the only thing that can't dive on this godforsaken ocean is us. Fucking pickled moron.

Ol' Iron Balls had been pissed, and for once the Captain had had good reason—we'd needed to insta-patch the narwal holes or risk napalm burning us from the inside out. Rules got a lot tighter on Shop purchases after that. Hence my bootleg. We also ate narwal stew for a week.

It turns out there's a reason we're always broke. Purchasing hull segments from the System for a city ship gets expensive, and to the plethora of monsters in the ocean, we're floating fast food.

***

My best mate helps with phase two of my cleaning punishment a short time later. As he damn well should, considering he committed the crime in the first place.

Not that the asshole seems the least bit remorseful.

"Bottoms up!" Blue cries before tipping an enamel mug to his lips. It clinks against the twig the redhead constantly chews on.

"For Christ's sake, put that away," I mutter, glancing left and right.

"The twig?"

"The contraband."

"Eh, the only thing watching is Ivy."

We're currently scrubbing the flight deck. Well, *I'm* scrubbing. He pulled a cork-topped jug from his inventory and refilled his cup.

"Join me?"

I shake my head.

Blue's head juts back and forward. "Bock, bock… bock!"

Rolling my eyes, I sigh, take the proffered cup, and down it. He may be an idiot, but Blue does keep life interesting.

"Another?"

I shake my head. If that stuff were any stronger it'd be ethanol. I should know—I distilled it.

Blue's offended reply is interrupted by an azure snout at his shoulder. Liquid splashes as he jumps. "What the hell?"

Behind him, Ivy grunts. Trying not to laugh, I produce a fish from my pocket. *Atta girl. Extra fish for you tomorrow.*

I toss Blue a rag for the stain on his MMPU. Rune-laced nano weave laces the grey-and-blue maritime multi-cam pattern uniform. It's got physical and sonic shielding, fire resistance, and we also get short wave and C-MICT thanks to circuitry in the collar. But even before the apocalypse, they were only so-so water resistant.

As Blue dries himself, I glance at the sun. "Almost midday." I resume my scrubbing. "Be cutting it close if we want to finish before the clear lower deck at 1700."

Blue hesitates, then grabs his mop. *Technically* Blue doesn't have to help. But my ass is grass if the deck ain't sparkling when the Captain arrives, and we both know this was all his fault to begin with.

Four hours later, sweat slicking our foreheads, we're *still* scrubbing. Doesn't help that Ivy seems intent on shitting over everything we've done at regular intervals.

I groan as Ivy plops out another fat one, then point my finger and channel Mana.

Scrub (Level Three)

Scour a surface of dirt, grime and bacteria, polishing until it shines.

Active radius: 10cm

Cost: 5 Mana

Who'd have thought my Bootlegger Class would be helpful on punishment detail? I use the Skill designed to sanitize kegs twice before Ivy's mess is gone.

My "best" friend—and I use the term loosely—arches his back as he takes a break from swabbing.

"What's the deal with you and the dragon, anyway?" he asks, throwing Ivy a glance.

A low rumble sounds from Ivy's throat.

"Drake, not dragon," I say, raising an eyebrow. "And they're intelligent, so watch your words."

Ivy snaps at Blue to make my point. Though Blue dodges easily, his ever-present twig is lost in the process. Without skipping a beat, he draws another from his pocket.

Is his personal inventory full of timber? I wonder. We're in the middle of the fucking ocean!

I pluck a dried herring from my pocket. "You know I can't swim, right?" I say, slipping it to Ivy.

Blue shrugs. "So?"

"So what happens if I fall overboard?"

"We're kilometers from the shore. Doesn't matter if you can or you can't, you're still fucked."

I glance back at Ivy. "Not if something wants to save you."

Blue cocks his head, then bursts out laughing.

"What?" I say, going red. "It's worth a try."

"Sure, sure, you're the great drake whisperer. And for my next trick, ladies and gentlemen, I'll make her breathe fire!"

"Fuck you," I mutter, scrubbing furiously.

Blue's reply is interrupted by a notification.

Quest Completed: Scrub the Decks

Reward: 5 credits per deck. (5 credits received); 100XP per deck (100XP received)

Type: Repeatable

"Join the Navy!" we mutter in unison, quarrel forgotten. "See new lands!"

Tradition honored, Quest achieved, and punishment complete, Blue turns for the hatch. "Just in time. Let's clean up, get ready to muster."

But I'm still staring at the notice. "I love the *Canberra*, you know. Wouldn't trade her for a tropical island. But fuck, the XP is shit."

Blue grunts but keeps walking. "'Least the Coxswain didn't realize his punishment gives us XP." He holds up an index finger. "And with my help, you collected. Reckon that's a beer for the service!"

"*If* he hasn't found the keg in storeroom five," I say, catching up. "Fucker's on a warpath."

Blue punches me gently. "Eh, most of the brass knows, I reckon. They're not stupid—there'd be a revolt if we couldn't enjoy *some* libations. Just got to keep it subtle, that's all."

I sputter to a stop. "You're the one they caught selling it by the bucket! Then you bail, leaving me with the fallout."

Blue shrugs, eyes twinkling. "You know the motto—survive, protect, defend. Thought I'd do the first and let you handle the rest."

I roll my eyes. "Let's see you laughing when I cut you off."

"You wouldn't."

"Try me."

Surprisingly, Blue's eyes turn serious. "You know I was just trying to move your product, right? You're always going on about needing XP."

I sigh. "Yeah, yeah. And I do appreciate it. But… well, subtlety is an art. One you should study."

Blue's smile returns as if it was never gone. "Cheer up, mate. When you sell all those sweet, hoppy bottles in your inventory, the experience will come rolling in. Might even get two, three thousand if we work on it. How much 'til you level?"

I sigh. "19,895."

"Oh."

It's an astronomical number, made worse because my Class is essentially outlawed.

First Unclog this morning, then Scrub. I really should have been a plumber.

***

"Captain on deck!"

I snap to attention—feet together, chest out, back straight, thumbs in line with the seam of my trousers. Beside me, Blue does the same. The other 275 crewmembers of *Canberra* make similar movements around us. A short, no-nonsense woman with greying hair strides forward onto a temporary stage. We remain rigidly at attention.

Captain Jane Rust is dressed in MMPU like the rest of us, with only a rank slide and the gold braid on her cap marking her station. One of two title-bearers currently aboard, she's the Commanding Officer of HMAS *Canberra.* I call up the passives her Legati Legionis Class gives us:

Buff: City defender

+7 to Strength, Perception, and Willpower while behind city walls.

Buff: City militia

+6 to Constitution and Agility while behind city walls. Mana pool and Mana regeneration rate increased by 11%.

Buff: Artillery technician

All projectiles fired from city walls do +22% damage.

Fun fact! Another name for city walls on a ship is hull, meaning we're pretty much always buffed. The Skill feels kinda broken, but no one's complaining—compared to anyone on land, we're seriously under Leveled. It's what you get when you can't leave your house to solo monsters. XP splitting sucks.

That said, I'd like to see those Great Keppel bastards take on a level 100 Swordfish. Naval strength has always been about the team, not the individual sailor. It's why so many officers have Classes which give a buff.

Captain Rust surveys us. She nods to the Executive Officer.

"At ease," the XO barks.

With an echoing *thump,* we relax, hands sliding behind our backs as legs part.

"Right, I'll cut straight to the chase," the Captain says, voice clipped and carrying easily. "Neighborhood Watch is tracking a B.A.M. menacing the area. The mega turtle is growing abnormally fast. We believe it's power leveling on the back of several local dungeons."

I swallow. *B.A.M.* is ship slang for *Big Ass Mutant.* You know, like really big. Kaiju fuckers. We've hit them before—only ones that can—but it ain't fun. Need to keep our distance 'cause even the small ones could capsize us.

"Two hours ago, Drake Team Two scouted what we believe is the B.A.M.'s home location."

That's more like it! Stake it out, fire from the horizon, and soak up that sweet, sweet XP. I could *really* use the Levels.

Beside me, Blue whispers, "Loot!"

Oh yes. And the ship needs a bunch of upgrades. Maybe we'll finally improve hull shielding.

The crew mutters.

"Eyes front, gobs shut!" barks the salty XO.

The Captain continues as if nothing has happened. "The monster's Level is too high for Drake Team to analyze, but we estimate that if it *is* feeding off other monsters, we could be looking at a Heavyweight."

It ain't official—well, not System official—but we categorize monsters. Anything under level 10 we call Soups, 'cause that's what we make them into. Under 20 is Sourdough—slightly tougher—and sub 50 are Turduckens. *Too meaty to eat on your own.*

From there, we leave food behind. Sub 100 is a Heavyweight—that's the turtle—sub 150 is Colossal, and sub 200, should we encounter one, would be a Titan. Yeah, yeah, there's too much slang in the Navy. But sometimes trivializing the big stuff helps.

My eyes drift right, attempting to look at a huge, grizzled scar cutting up the radar platform without actually moving my head. We got that little beauty from a colossal Pelican't. Neptune help us should we ever encounter something higher.

"Dolphins, ma'am?" someone calls, redirecting my attention.

Old Salty barks a reprimand, but the Captain forestalls it.

"Fair question. The B.A.M. is currently circling deep water. We will not be sending dolphin teams at this time—yes, they have better tech, but they also need proximity to analyze. I won't risk the turtle diving, or worse, moving toward island populations. The first we want it to know of us are our torpedoes."

The deck resounds with a cheer. I'm not afraid to say I join them.

The Captain's face remains serious. "We've handled Heavyweights multiple times now, sailors. It's what we do. But if HMAS *Warramunga* taught us anything, rest their souls, it's to never let our guard down." She nods to the XO. "Over to you for the rest of the briefing."

***

It's twenty minutes 'til go time. The civilian fleet now sits over the horizon, their firepower useless in the coming fight—none have the range of our torpedoes and Typhoons, if they have weapons at all. The fishing trawler that supplies my herrings has two shotguns, period.

I'm in full combat gear, including standard issue power gloves and anti-flash hood draped loosely around my neck. Though I'm not expecting to participate in this fight, my gun and knife hang from my cracked leather belt.

I should be below decks, gathered with the other non-combatants at our Damage Control stations. But fuck that—there's plenty of time to stand around in a passageway waiting for a fire or breach that will never come. This is a long-distance battle!

Instead, I lean against the ship's stern, taking turns using Blue's battered old binoculars. From this distance, the turtle looks like an island. When I squint, I swear I can see trees.

"Turtle soup tonight."

"I wish," Blue quips, stick bobbing with the statement. "Bloody sick of fish." He motions for the binoculars.

Reluctantly, I hand them over. Without the device's enlargement, all I see is a lump on the horizon. Ivy is a tiny black speck high above.

"Anything?" I ask.

"Just sitting there." Blue's got a magnification Skill that enhances telescopic items. "Drakes could roost and it wouldn't notice." He frowns. "Something's got its attention underwater, I reckon… or maybe it's, like, doing the fish version of sleepwalking and swimming in circles."

Eager for a second look, I hold out a hand for his binos.

Blue scowls. "Where's yours?"

"Lost 'em."

He rolls his eyes. "You *do* know *Canberra*'s a city ship, right?"

"Village ship. Don't have the population for higher."

"Whatever. Point is, we've got a Shop. Use it." Blue glances sideways, a twinkle in his eyes. "Maybe buy a better belt while you're at it."

"What do you think I'm made of, Credits?"

Fucking shit-stirrer. He knows I'm broke after upgrading my pistol. Laser scope, phase damage, and an overload switch all took their price. I got a nice knife too, which cost a pretty penny.

"Also, fuck you," I say, giving Blue the finger. "This belt's a fucking heirloom."

The item Blue so casually mocks was my grandfather's. It's no fancy-schmancy System-integrated whatzit, but the holster works just fine. My gun and knife hang proudly from it.

Blue laughs. "That belts an heirloom like my dick's a wet paper anchor. Which is to say, one tug away from breaking." He hands back his glasses. "Just take back your money from the Pusser."

I roll my eyes. By common agreement, fifty percent of every sailor's income is held in ship's coffers by the Supply Officer. I *could* buy a new belt if I wanted, but that would mean taking back my Credits. Technically allowed, but Blue knows I'd never do it.

The Pusser has a "hoarder" Skill that gives tiered rewards for wealth accumulated. One of the higher rewards is a buff that improves his vault's defense rating. Not a big deal, you might think. But store enough Credits in the bridge safe and the room's classed as a vault. Thanks to our Credits and the SO's buff, that vault is suddenly armor plated.

The Credits are also a rainy day fund of sorts. In the event of catastrophic damage, the Captain can use them to buy emergency repairs for the ship. I sincerely fucking hope it doesn't come to that, but if it does… well, I don't need a new belt *that* bad. Land is hundreds of kilometers away. Keeping ol' *Canberra* afloat is in my best interests.

"Final bets?" Blue asks. "I'm thinking ninety."

I look into the distance, at the bump on the horizon that is the turtle we're approaching. It's obviously big—maybe the size of our ship—but that doesn't always mean high Levels. "Reckon it's survived so long 'cause of that shell. Less *predator* and more just *nothing can touch it.* My money's on level seventy, tops."

Blue whistles. "Your loss. I look forward to that special brew in your inventory."

I glance at the ship's radar array. "We'll see. Should be almost in range of C-MICT."

System Enhanced Identification works a little differently from monitoring systems of old. Pre-apocalypse, HMAS *Canberra* was fitted with tech that all inevitably boiled down to signals being sent out, bouncing back, and showing as information on a monitor. We still have that, of course. It's what we're using to home in on the turtle. But now we also have a Cerubian Mark IV Combat Targeting system.

Commonly known as C-MICT, this new toy pings the System multiple times a second for basic information on *everything* within five kilometers. The setup cost a packet—rumor has it, more than the ship itself—but it can't be fooled, sees through most cloak or stealth Skills you throw at it, and identifies all System-sanctioned ships and monsters.

Words flick into my vision, aided by the tech in my collar. They hover above the monster.

Armored Kraken (Level 185)

My first thought is: *fuck, that's a lot higher than expected.*

My second is: *holy fuck, that's not a turtle.*

My third thought is interrupted as the tree on its back launches into the air. A living harpoon, it snakes around a drake and pulls it toward the water.

Fuck. Fuck, fuck, fuck. "That's not a palm tree, is it?"

The island-not-an-island spins toward us, ocean foaming. A writhing mass of tentacles breach the surface as deeper C-MICT scans reveal more information.

Armored Kraken (Level 185)

This Elite leviathan has decided that being the biggest bully in the bathtub just isn't enough! Hunting the sea for mineral deposits, ships, and other monsters, it uses the bones, metal, and chitin it finds to create plated armor across its body. This one has recently fused to the shell of a giant turtle.

Note: Conductive metals found while scavenging make armored krakens highly sensitive to magical, psychic, and radio-based scans.

A klaxon blares. Comms and defense systems light up. "Hands to Assault Stations. Assume Damage Control State One, Condition Zulu Alpha."

Shit. *Shit, shit, shit.*

Atlantean torpedoes surge in sleek white lines toward the monster, some detonating but most snatched by fearsome tentacles.

The ship's Typhoons boom next. Though they fire at eleven hundred meters per second, the rounds bounce harmlessly off the creature's shell. The monster surges toward us as I hear the call for armor piercing and explosive rounds to be loaded. This was supposed to be a static target—a big old slow-moving monster taken at range. Not a goddamned armored kraken!

We sprint for the hatch, binoculars forgotten.

***

I wade through water already knee deep, motioning Blue to the other end of a long timber beam. With a heave, we rush it back to where my crewmates are desperately patching a hole as large as my head, water gushing around the plate they're sliding across to shore it up.

It hasn't been five minutes since the armored kraken attacked, but the battle is almost over. Though I can only follow the action by the deep thumps reverberating through our hull and the screams echoing above, *Canberra*'s list and flooding passageways suggest I won't like the victor.

Farther down, a huge tentacle with a surprisingly prehensile tip smashes through metal as if it's a wafer, suckers wrapping an unlucky sailor. It withdraws as fast as it entered.

An officer yells into her collar, requesting assistance, and the tentacle breech is instantly repaired. The team moves to another of the hundred smaller holes still lining this passageway, grabbing metal and timber to patch it manually.

We started the battle repairing everything with store-bought insta-patch kits, but those things are damn expensive. If Command are now only addressing critical damage, we must be almost out of money.

The problem, I think to myself, are the damn spikes. The kraken must have barbs of some sort across its body. Or something. Every so often, the ship will creak and groan as if it's being strangled, then three spines appear, a devil's hole punch that pierces the hull like paper.

The ship thumps and groans, listing further as the battle rages. What I wouldn't give to be up there fighting, instead of patching holes down here. I want to know what's happening!

Occasional chatter over the comms doesn't paint a pretty picture. Two of our four Typhoons are out of action, presumably ripped from their bolts. Torpedoes are useless at close range. Beam cannons don't make a dent, and the laser batteries ain't much better. Our shielding went down within the first minute.

Another thump, this time closer. *Fuck, I recognize that sound.*

"Away from the hull!" I yell.

Crew dive free as metal rips apart.

I'm thrown back hard, seeing stars as I connect with a bulkhead. "*Urgh!*"

When the attack is over, I stumble upright. My ears ring and my vision is fuzzy. The passageway is flooding fast with new water. Foam froths around my waist and debris tumbles past—a waterlogged book, a ration pack, one of those stupid bobblehead toys.

And in the middle of it all, a tooth-marked twig.

I gulp a breath and dive under, hands flailing 'til fingers grab a jacket. I drag a limp body to the surface, grateful when I see it's Blue.

"Blue? Blue!" I shake him, then drag him up a ladder. When I can, I put my mouth over his and give several quick puffs. *There's a song that helps this next part—what is it?*

The ship groans and creaks as it's squeezed. It's on its last legs, but I ignore it all. The screams and cries, the dying ship, the cracks and retorts? I block it all out, humming "Stayin' Alive" by the Bee Gees as I compress his chest in time to the rhythm.

I'm giving up when I feel movement beneath me. A cough and sputter. Blue rolls over.

"Thank fuck," I groan, leaning back against a railing. "Thought you were fucking—"

Metal shatters as something wet and rubbery wraps around my ankle. I'm yanked from my feet and dragged into open water.

Then I'm fifty meters above the ship and upside down. I've gained a section of railing, which came with me when I was taken, and lost my Defender and Militia buffs. I have just enough time to think *not a good trade* before I look down and my eyes widen.

Oh, we are *so* fucked.

Part colossal squid, part stolen turtle, the kraken is easily as large as the *Canberra.*

Shell covers most of it, though a mass of tentacles rise from the front. The thick, rubbery appendages twine around the *Canberra*, ripping components free. I watch as the remnant of a hatch is dropped onto an enormous sucker near the base of the turtle shell. The metal sticks, becoming new armor.

Organic matter isn't quite so lucky. Scraps of MMPU hang like wilted spinach between teeth larger than a lifeboat. The maw is ridged by smaller tentacles with spines up their lengths. I recognize them immediately.

"Those are the fuckers that punched through the… *ungh.*"

I clutch my ears, nearly braining myself with tubular railing as our big guns fire, my MMPU dampeners unable to compensate this close to the action. Shells chip and flake at the kraken's stolen armor, but the angle is wrong. Even explosive rounds can't do serious damage. The ship creaks as tentacles crush the life from it.

Crew hack madly at the spined limbs with little effect, though electric skills seemingly do some damage. I watch one appendage get shocked free, then two more take its place. Our automated point defense systems are down—out of ammo, Mana, or disabled. We're fighting a losing battle.

Dolphin teams harry the beast from the water, their lasers burning arcs through rubbery flesh. Drakes and giant birds attack from the air.

The kraken's eyes are huge, bulbous affairs on the top of its head. An obvious weak point, they're protected by the kraken's angle from our guns, but not from Ivy. She screeches as she rakes at an eyeball but is repulsed by tentacles before she can do serious damage.

The beast is just too big. We're barnacles on a whale. Fleas on a waterlogged dog. We're nuisances—nothing more—fighting above our weight and out of our depth, only alive 'cause we're too stupid to give up and the Captain is fast spending our Credits.

Gold ripples traverse the ship as section after section is repaired, then crushed, then repaired again. A third Typhoon is ripped from its mountings, brought with an inhuman screech to the giant teeth. One snap and the base disappears. Another and I see only barrel. It's like watching a goddamn emperor eat grapes and the gun is an amuse-bouche appetizer.

I look at the railing in my hand, discounting it immediately as a weapon. If the kraken can bite through steel as thick as my arm, thirty centimeters of hollow pipe will do nothing.

Swapping it to my left hand, I pull free my upgraded pistol. *Eat laser, you goddamned freak of fucking nature.*

As tiny beams soak into colossal rubber, I realize my mistake. The kraken had been ignoring me, a tasty morsel it could save for later. Now, I'm lifted lazily forward.

Shit, shit, shit! I snap my gun back to its holster, intending to draw my knife. Instead, I yell "*Fuck!*" as I watch the gun, knife, and belt tumble. The ancient leather has snapped and now… well…

Fuck you, Blue, and the broomstick you rode in on.

Okay, powers. Powers. I'm out of weapons, but not defenseless. What Skills do I have? Mentally, I cycle through them.

Brew? No luck.

Yeast Cultivation? I try halfheartedly.

Scrub? To my surprise, it works—barnacles disappear around the tentacle holding me. In desperation, I try the Skill again. Another patch is scrubbed clean, this time of detritus and metal.

An idea hits me and I target armor, hoping to remove that next. It polishes to a brilliant shine but is otherwise unharmed. Great—now the fucker can sparkle while it kills me.

My passage toward the teeth slows, as if the beast is confused about what I just did. It's not like I've done damage or even cleaned more than a square foot. But maybe conductive metal is sensitive to more than just radar?

I blast the skill again and again. I'm being pulled away from the mouth now and toward one of the beasts' eyes. High above the colossal shell, a watery orb soon fills my vision.

Could Scrub irritate it perhaps? I try, but soon admit defeat. I keep cycling through my skills, trying to find something to fight back with.

Poison Resistance? Nope.

Frat Party? No, no, no.

Unclog? I move on. Unclog only works on pipes.

… wait. Pipes.

I ram the hollow railing I still hold in my left hand against a tentacle.

Unclog

Effect: Pull organic matter through pipes one meter or under.

Cost: 15 Mana. Continuously channel Mana for increased duration.

Skin bulges, drawing tighter and tighter. And then something bursts on the kraken's surface.

Well fuck me, it worked! Didn't do a thing to stop the monster, but still… I feel brief pride at my actions, choosing to continue the Skill though the damage is pitiful.

Dolphins, drakes, the crew… hell, even the ship's cat does more destruction. But as I continue to pump Mana into Unclog, that slowly changes. The suckers around me shrivel. Innards geyser through the makeshift piping.

Only when the kraken drops me with a shriek do I consider my actions. I'm fifty meters high in the air, hanging above a monster! My own shriek is considerably tinnier. I crash onto an eyeball then bulbous rubber, rolling and bouncing 'til I hit shell.

Ungh… Lying on my back in a daze, I note a shadow above me.

Fuck! I dive to the side then keep running as truck-sized tentacles lash down. Dodging left and right, I take stock of my surroundings.

Right. So I'm running across the back of an armored kraken. I'm separated from the ship, can't swim, and—looking at the mass of tentacles, some big, some small, in the water—don't even want to. I can hurt the kraken, but then lots of people can. But I'm here right now. And they're not. So what can I do?

I look up at the eye I was just gazing into. The *Canberra* can't hit it.

But I can.

Sprinting back along the shell, stumbling and falling over giant ridges, I leap finally onto the kraken proper. The mantle is slick but spongy, allowing me footholds once I find my rhythm. The bulk of the tentacles are on the other side, grappling at the *Canberra*, but I still have the smaller, spined fuckers to contend with. They slap at me, curling and grasping, but here, my size is a bonus. Though the tentacles seeking me are the smallest of the kraken's limbs, I'm even smaller. I trigger the skill Drunken Stumble and sway easily around them.

Halfway up, I encounter the remains of the Typhoon. All that's left is a meter-long barrel. "That's not a pipe," I mutter, stowing my bit of railing. With a grunt, I heft the Typhoon barrel. "*This* is a pipe."

I scale the rest of the way, then shove the metal straight at the kraken's pupil. Eyeballs are soft, fleshy things. But the kraken is so large, even its sclera is hand-thick leather. My pipe hits its surface and stops, sinking only millimeters and causing no damage.

But that's not how my skill works. My skill *unclogs*. And right now, I've got a pipe with one blocked end and a whole lot of Mana.

The kraken screams as thick, clear gel fountains from the Typhoon's barrel. I've hurt it! Adrenaline surges through me as I push my advantage. Leaning into the pipe, I try to dig it deeper. Gore covers me, making everything slippery. But though I'm doing damage, my heart soon falters. The blasted thing's so big! Could anything one person does ever truly…

You have received a Buff!

Compounding Interest: All buffs in the next 30 seconds stack!

You have received a Buff!

Bitch slap: Handheld weapon damage enhanced by 15%

You have received a Buff!

Street fight: Improvised weapon damage enhanced by 12%

What the fuck? I look over toward the ship, still floundering. And then at the deck, where sailors are pointing in my direction.

You have received a Buff!

Drill Master: Piercing attacks cost half Mana.

You have received a Buff!

Field Surgeon: It's now easier to cut flesh.

You have received a Buff!

Head Shot: Attacks to the head enhanced by 100%

You have received a Buff!

King Hit: Attacks to the head have a chance to stun.

You have received a Buff!

Stripper: +10% damage if your opponent is wet!

You have received a Buff!

Kaiju Hunter: +20% damage if your opponent is more than 10 times your size.

…

The buffs keep coming and coming. My muscles swell. Power courses through my veins. And the viscera ejecting from my pipe suddenly fountains. Naval strength has always been about the team, and the crew's just given me a metric fuck-ton of buffs.

My pipe bursts through the outer layer of the eyeball. Another scream of pain from my opponent. I'm doing real damage now, and the beast knows it. Tentacles make a desperate grasp for me and I swing, curling around the deep sunk pipe like a gymnast.

That is, 'til the pipe wobbles. It's implanted in gooey eyeball, not something solid. I keep the tube lodged only at the cost of my body—foregoing the swing to stabilize and keep pumping.

A tentacle taps an ankle, crushing it. I scream but refuse to let go. Though my Mana is draining fast, the eyeball deflates and shrivels.

You have been hit with a spell!

Mana Swap: Your Mana has been swapped with that of the caster.

On the deck, an officer slumps as my Mana rockets upward. I continue pumping.

Finally, metal groans as my adversary releases the *Canberra.* I know what it's going to do—what I would do, were I a giant monster. As it gains distance from the ship, I get closer to the water. But I don't let go. I drag in lungfuls of air, preparing futilely for the roll that will kill me.

Eyeball goo coats me as the fountain tilts, getting in my mouth. I wash it down with a beer that I produce from my chock-full inventory. It's my own special brew—*heals even as it gives you a headache.* My vision swims, but the ankle gets better.

As the water gets closer, my only regret is that I can't swim.

No, fuck that, I think in a moment of clarity. *I'd just drown slower.*

Then from the corner of my eye, I spot twin white lines in the water. They're speeding from the *Canberra.*

I just have time to think *well fuck me* before the kraken shudders.

More lines now. Released from the beast, *Canberra* can fire its torpedoes. The kraken screams as huge chunks of flesh are blown free, each successive blast drilling deeper and deeper. A tentacle flies free into the air. Then another and another. I know we've hit something vital when its skin flashes grey then green around me.

A slurp at my back. I turn to see a whirlpool, the kraken's shell pulling free from its mantle.

Our lone Typhoon blasts the creature, spraying me with flesh, blood and chunks of viscera. I curse *Canberra*'s aim as I stumble behind the kraken's bulbous head, but don't blame my crewmates. *Survive, protect, defend.* I'm done for, but the ship sails on.

A death cry, and the beast sinks. Notifications flash across my vision. There's water around my ankles, now my knees. I climb, scaling the dying beast like a cliff face. When I reach the crown, I stand, panting, to face the ship and salute. Then thinking better of it, give Blue the finger. Hope the asshole's alive to see it.

Soon, the water's back to my ankles. I'm going down with the ship, and there's not a fucking thing I can do about it. Should I just jump, make it quick?

I shake my head as water crawls past my knees, a strange feeling overcoming me. I should be panicked. I should be crying. But instead all I feel is… satisfaction. We did it. *We fucking did it!* I laugh at the sky as pockets of air bubble around me.

Then cold water hits my waist, truly soaking my MMPUs. My laughter stops abruptly.

Should have learned to swim.

On the deck of the *Canberra*, the crew are shouting, organizing ropes. A Zodiac is being lowered into the water, but I'm sinking too fast. It will never make it.

A beer appears from my inventory—just a regular brewski, nothing special. I crack it and take an awkward swig as water hits my chest. *Wonder if Blue made it?* I think over a long draught. This one's for—

Screeeee!

I startle, then scream as claws sink into my shoulders. *What the fuck?*

My beer splashes into the ocean as I'm heaved into the air, water sluicing off me. I stare up. Azure undercarriage, and a smell I'd know anywhere… Ivy? *Ivy!*

"Atta girl, you magnificent smelly princess. Extra fish for you tomorrow."

***

I'm standing on the deck, covered in gore, as the crew cheers around me. So this is what it feels like to be a hero. I think back to my fight and my injuries. How I saved Blue's life, dangled fifty meters above a kraken, played dodgeball with its spines and in the end, plumbed the thing to death.

Congratulations! Boss defeated.

For defeating an armored kraken, your group earns 184,920 XP.

Your share is 804 XP.

Faaark. We take down a Titan and I still don't level. That's what you get when experience is divided by two hundred and thirty.

Suddenly, I notice something in the distance, out on the sea.

I rush to the ship's edge—not too close, there're still no railings—but close enough to see bubbling water where the kraken was circling.

Really? We're crippled, near dead in the water. Our escorts have scattered. We're exhausted, low on ammunition, and even lower on Credits. Yet the System sees fit to throw another monster at us?

I close my eyes. They snap open as the klaxon wails.

"Survive. Protect. Defend."

My words are echoed by the crew around me. *We're the motherfucking* Canberra.

But then the monster surfaces, and my mouth drops open. Periscope and sail hit sunlight first. Then a long, tubular body. It's a submarine. A regular, human-made, *gods-damn-it-am-I-dreaming* submarine!

Sucker marks scour its body. Its propellor is twisted and bent. It must have been hiding on the bottom from the kraken.

Congratulations!

You have found a hidden quest: Rescue the Survivors.

1 of 10 military units discovered.

Chills crisscross my body. And then the crew cheers. I can't help but smile.

Survive. Protect. Defend.

Yeah, that's the Australian Navy for you. They thought humanity would flounder. That we'd all capsize and sink.

But instead, we're learning to swim.

Courting Rituals of the Human Subspecies

Updating the venerated work *Courting, Mating, and Propagation of the Galactic Species Under the Aegis of the System and Your Best Tactics to a Successful Extension of Your Genetic Line* by Professor Gl'xxmmas, we are adding the various new races and subspecies that have joined the Galactic System since the publishing of the 298th version. As such, we are looking for a variety of stories highlighting the courting and mating ritual of the human species.

- Professor_Adjuct_Qussa_Frill_1897th_Spawn_of_the_27th_Branch

Larsbeyond_WanderingASMR – Did you intend to use the singular form? I know English translations can be tricky.

Professor_Adjuct_Qussa_Frill_1897th_Spawn_of_the_27th_Branch – Of course singular form. Don't tell me these Humans are another barbarous group with multiple accepted mating rituals.

CoyoteMutant9882 – Can I tell him? Please, can I tell him?

Professor_Adjuct_Qussa_Frill_1897th_Spawn_of_the_27th_Branch – Mana Spawn! I only have a week to finish this work.

Ugland_ChairDwarFTW – If that is the case, I recommend the vast repository store of mating rituals also known as "romance novels," along with their ancillary dataset of "romantic comedies." I believe the period between 1970-1990 is considered the peak documentation time.

Professor_Adjuct_Qussa_Frill_1897th_Spawn_of_the_27th_Branch – Thank you!

Luke_Ascension999 – You're evil.

CoyoteMutant9882 – I have a few works from earlier periods. Try looking over my data stores here. I'll expect a proper reference though. I particularly like the attached recording, purchased direct from a System download of a nearby Voyeur Prime. High quality download, I tell you. Also, not as risqué as most of his other work.

Luke_Ascension999 – Risqué you say? Do tell.

CoyoteMutant9882 – DM incoming. Mods do not look kindly on further discussion in public forums.

McGregor_mod_Hunterzone111 – No, we really don't.

Seeking and Finding

By Chelsea Luckritz

Grantham, Grahm to his friends, watched the door of the Adventurers guild, a converted bar littered with tall, round tables around which were clusters of people and aliens. The voices, as plans were made or jokes shared, never carried above a hum. To Grahm, it almost felt like the old small towns he used to visit while he drove around gathering businesses' earnings for banks.

A woman came in, and as usual, he did a quick scan of the newcomer.

Anastasia Sloan (Librarian Level 43)
HP: 430/430
MP: 430/430

She's going to be swindled, he decided as he took her in.

She was average in height, perhaps reaching up to his shoulder, with brown hair worn in a medium height ponytail and brown eyes. Only her slightly overfull lips, turned up at the corners, refused to meet the boring standard. Her clothes were beige or brown business casual, lacking in wrinkles. She left no impact as a physical specimen, except to make Grahm wonder how she had managed to remain so wholesome. It was enough that a few others in the room took note of her.

She scurried to the side and motioned another patron through the door as if she were a butler. *Too polite.* She stood on her toes and craned her neck to search for something or someone. *Too obvious.* She saw him, their eyes meeting, and she smiled. *Oh crap!*

He genuinely considered avoiding her, but it wouldn't reflect well on his reputation if he ran from women. She licked her lips as she approached him.

"Mr. Morris?" she asked with a mild smile. He nodded once. "I would like to hire you, sir, to escort me to Trenton."

He ran his eyes over her body one more time, hoping for some change in impression now that she was closer, but no. She was clean, pale, soft, and utterly civilized.

"Why me?" If this was some scam…

"I was referred specifically to you by Mr. Blaine," she said. "His exact words were, 'If you insist on this lunacy, hire Grantham Morris to guide you.' He was rude about it, truth be told." She pouted her displeasure momentarily before producing a note. "He's sponsoring me. He told me this was the fare I was to offer you. I've drawn up a contract already if that suits you."

He checked the amount and fought back shock at the outrageously high amount she was offering. "Who the hell are you?" he asked, no longer able to pretend to be completely aloof. If she had Blaine's backing and this kind of Credits available to her, she had to be special, no matter how boring she looked.

"Oh, yes! My apologies." She quickly wiped her palms on her trousers and stuck out her hand to shake. "My name is Anastasia Sloan."

He shook her hand, appreciating her firm, business-like grip. At least there was something about her that wasn't soft. Her name didn't mean anything to him.

"You can call me Tasha if you wish."

"Okay," he said, but it came out as a question. "And why are you going to Trenton?"

"Well"—she brushed back an errant strand of hair—"I heard a rumor that someone there has managed to rescue, salvage, or hide a great number of books as well as art. I would like to speak to them." Her eyes brightened with her obvious excitement, and it gave her face a warmth that Grahm much preferred.

"Why?" There was too much money on the line for her to visit an impromptu museum.

"I'm a librarian and there aren't a great deal of job opportunities for a librarian now. I've found a new calling in preserving not just library books. I've… decided to be a historian for humanity. There are children living even now who will never know the way we humans carved out a place for ourselves on this planet. They'll never know the excitement of looking up at the stars and wondering if some alien species might be doing the same…" She waved a hand. "I think it's important to preserve some of that, if I can."

It seemed like a waste of time to him. There was no going back, and children now needed strength, not excitement. But Blaine was backing her, so he pressed on.

"How are you with combat?" he asked.

"I've not had much experience in that. I was with Blaine at the beginning of the System." He frowned, and she added, "But I'm healthy and I have gear. More than anything, I need someone to help me stay on course. I'm terrible with directions."

He winced. His Class was a Treasured Conveyancer, so if Blaine had named Grahm, directions weren't what she was buying. Even if she ignored his Class, one look at him should have told her what she was dealing with. He had always been fit, but he had made himself into a weapon in the two years since the System changed everything. Between the muscle mass he carried and the scars crisscrossed across his nose and left cheek as well as down the length of his right arm, he knew he was imposing.

"Can you take orders?"

Her eyes widened in surprise, but she nodded.

"Because if you can't, when shit hits the fan, you could die out there."

"Don't attempt to frighten me," she said. "I'm quite determined. If you won't take the job, simply say so and I'll go on my own."

If she did that, Blaine would most likely kill him. The man was insane. Grahm didn't really have a choice.

He sighed. "I'll take the job."

Her face transformed as she smiled, and he had the crazy thought that she was probably a cheerleader in high school. She had that "prettiest girl in town" charm when she smiled that wide. Weird how he hadn't noticed that before, and he wished he hadn't noticed it at all. The woman was his responsibility now and he didn't need the distraction of a pretty smile.

"I'll have some preparations to make," he carried on before she could say something that would tick him off… like thank you… "We'll start tomorrow morning at seven. I'll meet you out front."

"Lovely. I'll see you then." She turned and left. She wasn't exactly skipping, but she most certainly wasn't walking either.

Grahm groaned and swiped a hand down his face. "Damnit." And then he left to get a few supplies.

***

The next morning, Grahm arrived on the street where he would meet Tasha and almost turned back around and went home because he could see her. From all the way at the other end of the street, he could spot her. He had never seen a pink like that before. Ever.

He ignored her smiled greeting and asked, "What are you wearing?"

She looked down at herself. "My gear. I had been planning to take up hiking before the System arrived."

He squeezed his eyes shut and forced patience into his mind. "That's not going to work."

"Why?"

"You're fucking kidding, right? Do you not see the difference between what you're wearing and what I'm wearing?"

She looked down again. "Mine's newer?"

He stuck his hands on his hips, looked at the ground, and swore. Profusely. Creatively. Until he ran out of breath. He grabbed her hand and hauled her up the street to a local gear store. Cheaper than buying at the Shop, it would work well enough for what she needed. Anything was better than the atrocity she wore now.

"She needs a jacket," he announced to the man behind the counter.

"I have a jacket," she protested.

Luckily, the storekeeper cut in. "Are you trying to be a target out there?"

Grahm nodded slowly.

"*Oh!*" Tasha said with a laugh. "You could have just said the color was too bright, Mr. Morris. It was an honest mistake."

Understatement of the century. He'd be willing to put money on that.

The shopkeeper obligingly saw her fitted out, blessedly inquiring after the rest of her gear while he had the opportunity.

Finally, they stepped outside and Grahm laid out the rules. "Your job is to be quiet. As quiet as you can be. And when we meet up with something, you hide while I take care of it. That's the way this goes. Got it?"

She nodded agreeably, so the journey began. Not without some trepidation on his part.

Grahm had been prepared to constantly remind the woman to be quiet so as not to attract anything, but she was obedient about being quiet. She was obedient about hiding too. Skirmishes came and went with her tucked safely out of sight and silent. For three days, he trekked and fought with her shadowing him. And nothing else. *Nothing* else. She walked silently, ate silently, breathed silently, and slept silently. It was starting to get creepy. How could any person be so ghost-like when tromping through the woods? Especially an amateur?

After setting up camp for the night, he finally buckled. "You're good at this. Some people stomp around and attract monsters."

She graced him with a huge smile. "I have a Skill. Enforced Silence. It was my first choice when the System went live."

He nodded. Silence fell over them again and it wasn't broken for another two days.

***

A twig snapped and Grahm froze, his instincts flaring to life. He activated his Detection Skill and found they weren't alone. He followed with Analysis.

Pardus Fallax (Level 39)

HP: 1440/1480

Crap. He gave Tasha the signal to hide and waited for her to slip back out of danger.

The creature, with spiked, tail-like tentacles at its waist, was as sleek and black as a panther. The thing was notoriously difficult to see, even knowing it was there. Its camouflage in the thickness of the forest was otherworldly, after all, and that didn't even account for the way it tricked the mind into believing it was in a slightly different place than it actually was. So he had to draw it out. And that meant opening up his back for attack.

He thundered forward in a run and twisted at the last second when he felt more than saw or heard the beast jump at his back. The beast got the horny end of a tentacle on his jacket and wrenched him under its body. Not the worst-case scenario, but not the best either. He would get out of it. He always did, but this one could be painful.

He scrambled, trying anything and everything to stay out of the beast's jaws. He got a hand on one of his knives and slashed at a tentacle before the beast could slam the spiked end into his chest.

"Shit. Shit. Shit," he found himself chanting.

"No!" Tasha's voice broke into his concentration.

What the hell was she doing? She was supposed to be hiding.

"I said *no*!" she said with calm authority.

To Grahm's amazement, the Pardus Fallax stopped trying to gut him. It looked over its shoulder at Tasha and rumbled a low warning in its throat.

"Go away," Tasha ordered. Grahm watched her flap her arms at the beast. "Shoo. Go on."

Ridiculous woman! Grahm took full advantage of the creature's distraction. He thrust his knife into its stomach and sliced up to its chest before pushing it over to the side, dead. Grahm lay in quiet amazement, staring at the treetops, until Tasha stepped forward and held out a hand to help him up.

"Are you all right?" she asked in a tone of motherly concern.

He couldn't take that. No, just no. He jumped to his feet in an explosive burst of angry energy. "What the hell?" Grahm shouted in Tasha's face.

She blinked rapidly. She cleared her throat and nervously said, "I'm good with animals."

"That wasn't an animal, Tasha!" he snarled. She backed away, which gave him the pleasure of stalking into her space until her back hit a tree. "That was a Pardus Fallax, spawned by the System, not a house cat."

Tasha frowned. Her hands came up to brace against his chest. They slid through the blood of the Pardus Fallax until she gripped his shirt at the shoulders. "I've got a boon that helps enforce obedience on cats. I got it when the System came active."

"Why the hell would you get that?"

She blushed and looked away. "I was kind of a young version of a cat lady."

"I don't actually give a fuck. Why the hell didn't you tell me about this earlier?"

She cleared her throat uncomfortably. "Well… because I'm not stupid." She met his eyes defiantly. "Have you told me all your abilities?"

He curled his lip. "I didn't hire you for protection."

"I didn't hire you for protection either," she shot back. "I hired you for directions."

"You thought that's what you hired me for. But if that was what you really needed, Blaine would have sent you to Andre, not to me."

She furrowed her brow. "Are you implying that Mr. Blaine misled me?"

He leaned even farther into her despite her desperate attempt to push him away. "I'm not implying anything. I'm telling you Blaine thought you needed protection." He shook his head and laughed mirthlessly. "Probably because you were hiding all these nifty little tricks. What other surprises are you hiding?"

Her eyes were wet with unshed tears, but she firmed her jaw. "I'm not telling you that. I'll use them if they become necessary."

He glared at her, wanting to wring her neck.

"Just like I did today," she tacked on nervously.

He continued to glare, trying to decide how he would make her talk. He hated surprises. And she had way too many of them.

"You're looking at me very oddly." She shrank back against the tree, pale and breathing in a jerky, uneven rhythm.

He raised an eyebrow. "Oddly?" Murderously was more like it.

"You look like you might kiss me," she said and swallowed hard. A tic had started near her left eye.

He blinked out of his glare, surprised. He hadn't for a second considered kissing her. She was a job, not a woman. He took in her trembling form, braced against him. Frightened. As she should be when he was pissed. So why would she make such a stupid conclusion?

He purposefully glared and asked, "This is how men look to you when they want to kiss you?"

She slowly nodded. "An ex told me it was the only legal thing to do. I never quite understood what he meant by that."

She relaxed a fraction when he didn't move. But she continued to observe him warily through leaking eyes. Grahm could only gape at her, agonizingly aware of her fragility. She had been so stoic that it had been easy to relegate her to the recesses of his mind as a job, a mere package to be delivered. What stood before him was much too alive for that.

"You're nuts." He brushed the tears off her face. "Look, don't cry, all right? I wasn't trying to make you cry."

He didn't like being the creator of those tears, didn't like the way it made him want to hold her until she wouldn't confuse him with a brute.

Tasha brushed aside his hands and wiped away her own tears. "Let's just go."

She tried to sidestep away from the tree he had pinned her to, but he shot out a hand to keep her where she was.

"I need you to tell me any other little secrets that might come in handy," he said, working to keep his face clear and his tone even. He needed her talking, not terrorized into silence.

"It's none of your business what I can do."

"We're alone in the wilds together and you think it's not my business what you can do? When I first saw you, I thought you looked like a helpless, unprepared, unremarkable person. Then you pull off silence better than most of my clients. Now you've disobeyed a rule meant to keep you safe in some hairbrained scheme to save me—and for the record, I don't need saving. If you refuse to give me forewarning before you do something else you shouldn't be able to as a helpless, unprepared, unremarkable person, I swear I will put you over my knee and paddle your ass. Do you understand me?"

She scowled. "Let me get this straight. Because I have not been problematic, because I have the skills to be helpful even, you are threatening to spank me? Does that actually make sense to you?"

Not when she put it like that, but watching her eyes roam down his body, that didn't matter. He preferred to have her sizing him up than weeping in terror because of him.

"Yes. So, are you talking or are you planning to risk the spanking?"

She took her time thinking, tapping a finger absentmindedly on his chest. His body tightened in response.

"I-I don't think I have anything else particularly surprising or helpful," she said, but she looked nervous about it. He didn't release her. The answer was too vague to satisfy. "The odds of it being necessary are extremely low… I think."

"You like to live dangerously, huh?" he said.

She licked her lips and he wanted to close the distance between them, to taste her. He stared, mesmerized by the idea. She tipped her head down, away from him. Clenching his jaw, he focused on the matter at hand.

He studied her long enough to decide she was telling the truth. He pushed off the tree. "I won't spank you," he said as he strode away. "Because that was honest."

He knew she was hiding something. But he would let her keep her secret because she had let him threaten her. It hadn't occurred to her to threaten him back with whatever she was hiding, so it probably wasn't dangerous.

"Ever?" she asked, trailing him.

He smirked. "No promises, Tasha. If it keeps me from kissing you…" He glanced back in time to see her jaw drop. He laughed.

He restarted their trek while he shook his head, thinking about how much trouble she must have been before the System. She was plenty of trouble now, that was for sure.

Her silence didn't freak him out as badly this time. But by the end of the next day, he was getting disturbed again. It was that smile. The smile she always wore. The one that was a little vacant, as if she were a harmless idiot. The one that looked a little bit like a creepy doll. The one that didn't fit *her* the more he learned of her.

Halfway through their dinner, he couldn't take it anymore.

"Stop it!" he snapped.

Tasha looked all around her. "What? Stop what? Who?"

He rubbed his eyes, exasperated with his own outburst. "Why do you smile like a brainless idiot?" he asked in a calmer tone.

Her brows drew together. "I don't know what you mean."

"Yes, you do." He was pretty sure he was right.

The creepy smile slipped, a blank expression as she studied him. "Is there something wrong with smiling? I know you don't, but…"

He raised an eyebrow. "I smile when it's appropriate. You smile all the damn time. And not like you're actually happy."

She gave the slightest frown.

"If I'm upsetting you, you can frown. Scowl. Sneer. Curl your lip."

She made a face something like a wince and said, "I'm tired. I think I'll turn in."

"That's not the way to handle a person like me," he told her quietly, and she blinked at him. "Lay down a challenge like that and I'll pick it up."

"What challenge?" she exclaimed.

"The brush-off."

She sighed. "Isn't it better to be around someone… pleasant?"

"Pleasant is good. Honest is better."

She raised an eyebrow, her eyes glittering with emotion. Imperious, angry. "For whom?"

"Everyone," he said.

"Wrong." She turned away.

"How?" he asked, fascinated by her genuine disdain and fury. It was so huge that he could feel it in the air all around them, but it wasn't showing on her face, in her hands, in the volume of her voice. She was enduring it, containing it.

"This world is survival of the fittest, is it not?"

He nodded.

She shook her head. "If it was, can you honestly say I would still be here?" He frowned, and she carried on. "The problem with survival of the fittest as most people see it is that 'fittest' always means 'physically strongest.' But there are other kinds of fitness and other ways to fit in. A fit mind that produces technology, for example. A fit mother to bear the next generation. Or in my case, the carefully woven persona of a person who never fits the description of a person that others wish to see hurt or dead. Pleasantness is my armor, Mr. Morris, and politeness, my weapon." She took a calming breath. "Now, if you don't mind, I'm tired and will sleep now."

"I mind," he said, mostly because he was happy to be facing an actual person at last.

She had dropped the creepy doll smile and he was enchanted by the change. There was something beautiful about her anger, even as contained as she kept it. And he could understand someone as soft as her wanting to fly under the radar.

"Sit a while more," he said with a smile.

"Why?" she asked in a drawn-out whine of sound. Perfect. Exactly how she ought to be with him. He should have aggravated her days ago.

"I'll tell you a secret." It was only a feeling that she couldn't resist knowledge, particularly illicit knowledge, but he would have bet his best gear on it.

She crossed her arms and studied him as if he were a particularly slimy creature before she sat back down. "What is it?" Suspicion was heavy in her words, but she leaned toward him eagerly.

Then he realized he hadn't had any particular secret in mind. He met her eyes steadily as he scrambled internally to come up with something. When she looked as though she might stand again, he blurted the first embarrassing thought to run through his head. "I haven't had sex since the System went live."

He felt his cheeks flame even as he watched hers do the same. He blamed her for that line of thought. Why had she leaned forward with her arms crossed? Didn't she know how it put her curves on display?

She giggled. "Ummm…"

"I panicked." This was the kind of idiocy that resulted from noticing his job was a woman.

"I see that." She admirably fought more giggles and lost. "Mr. Morris, I promise to keep your secret."

"It's not that funny," he groused, hating that he was pleased that at least she seemed inclined to stay and remain human.

"I-I just don't understand why it's a secret," she said.

"It's not. I panicked." And he was absolutely never going to tell her that he had sex on the brain because of her. She had rejected him once. That was enough.

"I haven't either!" She bit her lip.

"Oh… I'm sorry… and good." No. He wasn't going down that road. Her sex life had nothing to do with him. Even if her eyes had dilated. Even if her hands clenched on the log. Even if her breathing became shallow as she looked at his lap. "Anyway… tell me about your plans to preserve human history."

She jerked her eyes up. "Mr. Blaine and a few others are financing several of us as we go about finding books, art, music, and simply stories from elderly people who experienced the most recent past. I know, of course, that they see the financial possibilities in keeping those things and I know some things are already lost to the alien races that took souvenirs or to the monsters that spawned and destroyed. But… it's ours. Monetary value or not… it's ours." Her face had firmed as she spoke. Her determination shone through.

"This is the face you should show the world, Tasha."

She blushed. "I don't know what you mean. I really am tired. Good night."

"We'll make it to Trenton tomorrow," he said and got a small nod in response.

He almost regretted that their time together would be ending. She was interesting and funny and more beautiful with every conversation. He wouldn't mind learning more about her, which was the wrong attitude to have about a job. Perhaps it was better that they were parting ways soon.

***

Around midday, they crested a small hill and the city that they knew harbored a Safe Zone appeared as if by magic in the distance.

Tasha smiled. "Thank you, Mr. Morris. I believe I can handle things from here." She snatched up his hand, pumped it twice, and started down the hill, suddenly in a hurry.

Not at all suspicious.

Grahm fought down the urge to scoff and followed her, strangely determined not to let her out of his sight. "I'll let you know when my job is complete, Tasha," he said low and near her ear.

Her spine stiffened, and she threw a startled look at him over her shoulder.

"Blaine wanted you protected," he found himself lying. He was the one who was worried about her. The troublemaker had weaseled her way into his thoughts.

"I'm fine," she argued.

He ignored her and continued to dog her steps.

"Employment ends when the employer says," she said with a hint of temper. "I'm not going to keep paying you."

He smirked. "That's fine." He stretched. "What will a protection specialist in the middle of nowhere do with himself?" He managed not to sound sarcastic. "Oh look! A town, likely with an Adventurers Guild building or at least a bulletin board with job postings. How convenient!"

Tasha glared at him. He liked it. He liked that she wasn't hiding behind politeness anymore. It seemed that he had earned his way into her trust.

"That was unnecessary," she said primly.

He shrugged. "I told you that the brush-off was the wrong way to handle me."

She was quiet for a step. "Yes, I suppose you did. Honest mistake."

She stopped trying to get rid of him after that, even after the notification that they had crossed into the Safe Zone flashed. She didn't acknowledge him in any way either, but that was all right. He was fascinated by watching her. She had planned ahead. She asked the first person she saw, in the most frighteningly polite way possible, for directions to the Eagle Ridge Bar and determinedly followed them.

At the bar, she tiptoed and craned her neck, just as she had when he had first seen her, to find her target, who turned out to be a serving girl. Tasha wove through the crowd to the girl, introduced herself, and explained who she wanted to meet. The girl flicked her eyes around the room, then handed Tasha a slip of paper.

They had to stop at two more places like that, and Grahm was beginning to get grumpy from wandering all over without dinner.

It was well after dinner time when Tasha knocked on the door of a bland home. The door opened and hands shot out to pull both of them into the building, where a beam projector was placed firmly against each of their foreheads.

Grahm sighed. "Seriously?"

There were six men, all Classed variations of "Security" with varying strength between them and the man Grahm assumed owned this house.

John Smith (Technician Level 49)
HP: 700/700
MP: 810/810

Grahm didn't trust anything about that notification. False name, most likely. Possibly a hidden Class as well. A technician wouldn't need this kind of security. He didn't like this one bit.

Tasha continued her politeness, in spite of the fear that thrummed visibly through her body. She introduced them to "Mr. Smith" and explained why she was there. She produced all the identification and references the paranoid collector wanted. Only then did he agree to show her his treasures… if she left Grahm behind.

"Not happening," Grahm said.

"Thank you," Tasha said, shooting Grahm a glare for his attempt at protection.

Grahm ignored her, grabbing her wrist so she couldn't leave without him. He glared at "John Smith."

"You don't have the references I require," the man said.

Tasha addressed their host. "It's all right. Let me talk to him." The second the man had put some distance between them, trailed closely by his guards, she hissed, "What is wrong with you?"

"You're not going anywhere alone with that man," he said. "He's too jumpy."

She rolled her eyes. "Given what he's got hidden, I'm not surprised. I'll be fine. I promise."

Grahm groaned.

"Please. This is important and not just for me."

He didn't like her begging. It wasn't right for her to beg. She kept looking at him with those brown eyes, the ones he had thought boring, and he forced himself to let her go.

"If you scream, I'll come. Don't try something stupid like you did against the Pardus Fallax."

She grinned, nodded, and followed the technician away.

Grahm paced the house's entrance hallway and tried to decide how long was too long for her to have been gone. *Too long.* The thought crossed his mind. He walked with purpose toward the door that had closed after her and stared at it, willing it to open. *She's strong. One more minute.* Then the pacing resumed. Again and again, he convinced himself to wait.

When she finally came back, Grahm felt relief like he hadn't known before. But then he realized that the man was propelling her forward, hands on her shoulders.

A strained smile was on her face. "But, sir, I have no reason to lie. They're all forgeries."

"*Get out!*" Smith thundered.

Tasha jumped at his volume and surreptitiously slipped something into Grahm's jacket as she came up next to him. That was when Grahm knew things would only get worse.

"Fuck it," Grahm said, snatching her up against his chest. He activated his Skill En Passant.

En Passant *(Level 1)*

Effect: Instantaneous teleport for the user and a target in physical contact to a safe location within 25 meters. Safe Destination must be within line-of-sight or a previously traveled location.

Cost: 250 mana

He activated it five times in quick succession, running in between to get them farther from the irate stranger. It left him sweating, but they were close to the edge of town and the edge of the Safe Zone by the time he was done. He grabbed Tasha's wrist and dragged her toward the woods.

"Where are you going?" she asked, looking around.

"What's in my jacket?" he countered.

She cleared her throat. "Now, Mr. Morris, it was an honest mistake—"

"I doubt it. So we're putting some distance between us and that… man."

She jogged to walk beside him and look up at his face. "He can't report me even if he wants to—everything else was a forgery and I'm pretty sure the paint was still wet on some of it."

He was so mad he almost couldn't speak. "Tasha… shut up before I spank you."

"You said you wouldn't!"

He gritted his teeth. "You left me behind. Then you stole from a man so twitchy he greets people at his door with a squad of security guards and a gun to the head—while he's in the room. And you put it in my jacket… whatever it is. So now I'm walking around with your stolen goods and the knowledge that you have some incredible skill in theft you didn't warn me about."

She licked her lips. "It's… not a Skill. Not in the System anyway."

They had made it to the woods. He pressed in far enough that he couldn't see the town behind them, then he pinned her to a tree. She didn't react with terror as she had before. Her lips parted and her cheeks flushed.

"Talk."

She shrugged. "I, uh… I like magic. You know—card tricks and coins behind the ear. That kind of thing. I've found that it works for getting around the System." She pursed her lips.

He closed his eyes and breathed out a string of curses. "And what is in my jacket?"

"*Persistence of Memory*" by Salvador Dali. I couldn't leave it with him. He wasn't treating it right." She was babbling in a hurried rush.

"Tasha!"

She snapped her mouth shut, her pulse visible in her throat.

"You're insane," he said calmly. "And I'm furious with you."

"You don't look like it."

"Don't *ever* leave me behind like that again. Understand?"

She frowned. "No. Are you mad that I left you behind or that I stole a master work of art?"

"I'm not mad. I'm furious."

"You really don't look like it."

She was right; he didn't. A small smile had formed on his face from the moment she started babbling about the theft as if she had rescued an abused puppy. The smile had only grown larger since then. He was furious and had been since the moment she begged him to let her walk into danger without him, but he was realizing it was because he liked the crazy woman. Watching her turn her back on his help had made him angry. His inability to stand by her crazy little butt had turned it into rage. And God only knew what fool errand she would want to go on next. But he wanted to go on it with her.

He wanted her quiet strength beside him. He wanted to make sure she never lost that. He was in so much trouble.

"My name is Grahm. Use it."

"I'm very confused. Are you angry or not?" she asked.

"I'm angry. Very angry. Livid that you left me behind," he said, leaning back to catch her eyes. "Don't do that again. I'm serious, Tasha. I will paddle your butt. I will not let that pass again. Do you understand?"

"Wait. Let me get this straight. Because I know how to take care of myself, you're angry. And furthermore, you will cause me pain if I don't pretend that I can't take care of myself. Does that actually make sense to you?"

He was loving this. "You're asking me to use logic right now?"

"You keep threatening to spank me. I'm defending myself."

"You just stole a masterpiece right in front of the crazy owner…by using a parlor trick. If I didn't threaten to spank you, I would be a bad person. The fact that I *haven't* spanked you is the sign that I like you."

Her face flamed crimson. "I beg your pardon?"

"I like you. How do you feel about me?" His heart was suddenly in his throat, but she was still soft, meeting his eyes with desire tinting her own.

"Mr. Morris, I—"

"Grahm."

"I do like you, but we barely know each other," she said.

"That's easy to fix. We're alone in the woods together. What do you say? Yes or no?"

"Yes," she said. "Grahm."

He pulled her into his chest and kissed her until they were both breathless. "Guess you've avoided a spanking again, but you sure do like to live on the wild side."

"I do not!" she protested as he released her and led her deeper into the woods. "Wait, aren't you going to kiss me again?"

He would do more than that as soon as he found a place where he could be sure they wouldn't be interrupted. "Patience, Tasha."

Exclusive: Redeemer of the Dead and the Forbidden Zone (Paid Content)

One of the enduring mysteries, what happened to the Redeemer of the Dead during his time in the Forbidden Zone? Well, drawing from myriad sources including a System tap, Mana vibrations and a Master Class Psychic, we have the answer!

- Celebrity_PreviewsAlpha_188XV77AS

Kanundraspies981 – Mod, I thought we banned these guys?

McGregor_mod_Hunterzone111 – Out of my hands. They keep the server running with their contributions.

J-EdgeHunter_Gates11 – I paid for it. It's well-written fiction, but this work should be under fan fiction. We all know you can't get System recordings from the Forbidden Zone.

Celebrity_PreviewsAlpha_188XV77AS – This is not a work of fiction nor conjecture. Every piece released by Celebrity Previews is well-researched, sourced from multiple reliable sources, and verified by an independent body.

J-EdgeHunter_Gates11 – That you pay off. We know your tricks. It's garbage.

CorruptQuestor42 – I don't know about that. My sources say that this particular work is ninety percent accurate.

DeBruyn_Collapse211not – Certainly reads like that vengeful maniac and threat to Galactic stability.

AintGonnaLetYouDown001A – Only one way to know. Got to click the link.

DeBruyn_Collapse211not – And now I'm not going to.

When Our Hero Kills a Ten-Story Behemoth

by Tao Wong

A Behemoth walked in the distance, its figure shifting as it undulated through the ruins. Ten stories tall, its body built of stone and corded, steel muscle. An elongated neck, almost drakeish in appearance, jutted from its grey torso, multiple folds of skin flopping about with each movement. Eyes, so many eyes taking in its surroundings. Beneath its multiple legs, monsters screeched their defiance, a wandering herd of flame and aggression seeking to guard their hunting grounds.

They screamed till they were stepped upon, squashed the same way a human would an ant. Ignored, unconcerned. The Behemoth occasionally dipped its head down to snatch up an unlucky monster, killing with a quick snap and swallow as it continued its never-ending trek through the pale-yellow and grey sands.

"And I'm supposed to kill that?" John Lee, Erethran Honor Guard, Paladin-wannabe, and lost-human, said. The Honor Guard sat on a distant cliff, staring at the creature with a conflicted look on his face, double-lidded eyes tight with concern.

"Just about, boy-o," Ali said, the orange-jumpsuit-clad, bearded, and olive-skinned Spirit idly revolving around the human. "If you ever want to complete the Quest, you will."

John groaned, running fingers through dark-brown hair. In his other hand, he conjured the simple bastard sword that was his Soulbound weapon from the ether before making it disappear, again and again. It was a reflexive action and training, as he pulled against the Mana that permeated the Forbidden World, working it such that it became second nature.

"Well, cutting it isn't going to work." Even with his Skills, System-infused formulas, and magical spells that allowed him to be a living wrecking ball, John doubted he'd be able to do more than irritate the Behemoth. For one thing, the Fire Elemental it had just stepped upon would have been a real fight for him.

And worse, there was no way to Level. No System-enabled way to gain strength, not in this Forbidden World. No, whatever solution he came up with, it would have to be…

Different.

"Welp, I've seen enough for now," John said. He stood up, the worn, self-repairing tactical jumpsuit pulling tight against his body. Multiple Levels, a genewash, and years of constant combat had seen his once half-starved, pale form grow muscular and lean, his skin tanning under the harsh alien light.

Ali snorted, floating down to take his usual place beside John. A flick of his hands brought up additional System screens, few enough in this place. Their connection to the System was broken, muted, and distorted, but at the least they had some local control. Enough that he could watch for additional threats.

"There's a herd of Epilsaurs down to the left if you want to try some training," Ali said. "Or we could head back to base and get some shuteye."

"Tempting. But I want to test something out first," John said, bounding down the hill in the direction of the Behemoth. "Rest won't get us anywhere."

"You're insane! You can't just rush in and kill a Level 150 plus monster!" Ali shouted after John as he floated alongside.

"I won't know till I try, will I?" John said, grinning savagely. A small monster popped out of its burrow, a barbed tentacle shooting towards John in a surprise attack that was thwarted by a simple sword conjuration and cut. The next second, a gleaming arc of energy flew from the Soulbound sword, tearing apart ground and cover to lay low the creature.

"Gods, I hate you so much, boy-o," Ali grumbled. By this point, the Spirit knew better than to try to dissuade his linked partner. All he could do was scan and plan for the eventual retreat.

***

Dealing with the monster herds was going to be the first major obstacle to killing the Behemoth. There were, of course, ways to do that. John had a few area-effect Skills, a few environmental control spells that would alter the shape of the terrain to give him time and space to attack the Behemoth. Unfortunately, that probably would not be enough—not with the Level disparity between himself and the monsters. As an Advanced Class that skipped the first tier entirely, he was seriously under-Leveled for this region.

That left John with one of two options: Lure the beasts away or avoid them altogether. After scouting the upcoming terrain, he had chosen the second. A simple enough canyon ridge allowed him to take position—after killing a couple of other monsters who had the same designs—before he hunkered down.

Stealth skills and a propensity to hide in the ground itself allowed John to wait till the Behemoth was within range. After that, all he had to do was pop out, cast a Skill or two, and deal enough damage to get the information he needed before running like a ten-story Behemoth was after him. Which it would be.

It'd help to target a weak spot, but considering the entire creature was built of stone and corded muscle, there didn't seem to be any clear critical sections beyond its head and neck. And years of fighting monsters had informed John that such weak spots could just as often be covered with ridges of bone, corded muscle, and, in some cases, extradimensional shielding.

Timing was important, since his most powerful Skill, his opener here, took time to set up. He couldn't just pop up, pull a trigger, and be done. Instead, John waited till the monster had begun its rhythmic swing and search on the other side of its body before he rose, already triggering the Skill in his mind.

Around the rising human figure, swords began to appear in a halo of pointy objects. Replicas of the one he held in his hand, a dozen weapons formed around his body. Bracing his legs against the rocky ground, even as the Behemoth sensed his appearance and had begun its turn, John swung his hand down. And with it, he pulled the formed Mana into being.

System Mana, drawn from the environment, formed into brilliant arcs of light and force, an explosion of power that followed the initial attack that started Army of One. It struck the creature at the edge of its jaw as it shifted towards the tiny figure, energy released like the solar flare rising from the heart of a sun. The attack burnt bright blue and yellow, grinding away at the stone and bone of the Behemoth.

A grunt, a roar of anger, and John was jumping backwards, eyeing the rising smoke as the attack finished. A pockmarked jaw, a minor dip in the flesh, and burnt-away muscle, only for the creature's unnatural regeneration to kick in, the wounds disappearing at a visible rate.

His gaze narrowed, John skipped back as the multi-eyed creature returned the favour, releasing a volley of magical beam attacks from its eyes. Before it reached him, John triggered Blink Step, disappearing into the distance. Once, twice, thrice, as fast as he could reappear and reorient himself, he fled.

Multiple kilometers away, John took a second to breathe, to allow his Mana to regenerate. A second was all that was needed for a single beam, homing in, to blast him in the back and throw him forwards. Faceplanted, he tore through earth, shattering bones and misshapen alien vegetation to come to a stop.

"Owwww," John said, rolling back onto his feet, staring at his Health. The attack had cut right through his Soul Shield and torn away half of it. A single attack. "Well, that could have gone better."

"You think?" Ali's sardonic voice returned as the invisible Spirit caught up with him. "Now best get running. It's still coming."

Groaning, John took off in a sprint, cycing his slowly regenerating Mana. He would blip away again when he could. Till then, it was time to pound earth.

***

"I'm not sure if I should be insulted or thankful that it gave up so easy," John muttered as he slowly stretched. He glanced at his life and Mana, both having returned to full after the ten minutes of running and teleporting, and sighed. "So, how'd we do?"

"Full numbers or percentages?" Ali said, floating down beside John as he stared around the five-foot-shrub-filled forest they stood within. Small monsters moved through the woods, preying on one another but staying away from the large predator within. Occasionally, the vegetation—all part of a single plant—would sway, rise up, and capture one of the running monsters before pulling it back down into the earth to be consumed.

"Percentage is good," John said, eyeballing the tiny creatures that hopped around. There were quite a variety of monsters about, but the one he was studying looked like a cross between a grasshopper and a rabbit, with the least cute parts of both. Still, it was more edible looking than the others.

Living on an alien planet for months on end had expanded his culinary preferences. Thank the gods the System had made most monster meat edible.

"Four point three, after all damage adjustments," Ali said. "If you hit a noncritical part, you could see it decrease to just over three percent or as high as five or so percent."

"That low, eh?" A flick of John's hand had his blade form and cut into the monster before he grabbed its corpse, dumping it back into his inventory. Simple enough to store the body that way, and he could pull it out later to eat. "What was his regeneration rate?"

"Interestingly enough, seven percent per minute, or just shy of that."

"Only seven?" John said, his head rising. The usual number was 10 percent per minute, putting a normal monster or individual back at full Health in ten minutes.

"Yup. I can't say why, just yet, but it's going to be an innate Skill or resistance."

"Nice," John said. Still, he had insufficient Mana to kill the monster, not and dodge all the attacks he knew would be coming if he stuck around. His best shot took just under half of his Mana pool after all. "So trying to fight it head-on is a losing proposition."

"I could have told you that."

"Yeah, but we had to try," John said. "Any good scientist needs a baseline number to work from."

"What, you going to make assassinating a Behemoth a scientific experiment?" Ali's voice went higher, incredulous.

John grinned. "Tell me about his resistances, or what we could pick up."

"Fine. From the damage we did and what was coming from the various herd members…" Ali began reciting while John kept his head turning.

With barely any setup and little more than a twitch of his legs, he bounded across the forest, recalling the sword he'd left behind halfway through the jump to land and skewer his next target. Food first, information in conjunction, and plans later.

After all, even if he was lacking in chocolate, he could still eat properly.

***

Roast rabbithopper-monster drifted in the wind, mixing with the smell of rendered fat and charred meat. The merry crackling of firewood rose in the air, filling the broken-down ruin and reflecting off the leaning walls, leaving twisting shadows to dance in accompaniment to the meal. A pair of stuffed fur makeshift beds lay in opposite corners of the room, one nearly twelve feet long and the other a more human seven.

"You've gotten better at cooking." Suhargur Aungur, last Paladin of Erethra, sat with a full roasted monster in hand, sharp teeth flashing in a smile before she tore into the corpse. Just a shade over eight feet tall, broad-shouldered and muscled like a bodybuilding contender, the pale-blue-skinned, coral-eared Erethran lounged with easy confidence. Still, her eyes never stopped roaming the perimeter, checking for potential problems visually and via their truncated System.

"I've had a lot of practice," John said, eyeing the discarded remnants of seven other rabbithoppers, with another four more on the fire at the moment. "System-enhanced bodies require a heck of a lot of energy. Still, thank you. The salt you lent made a big difference."

Suhargur chuckled, her voice melodic but slow, each word carefully picked out. "And your first attempt at the Behemoth?"

"Went about as well as you'd expect," John said, turning over one of the roast rabbithoppers and basting it from the pan of drippings he held in one hand, ungloved. No reason to worry about damage; his resistances were more than sufficient to handle a simple cooking fire.

"Then?" She raised a single, plucked eyebrow.

"I'll try something else, in a few days."

"Good."

Silence fell between the pair. John knew better than to expect further advice or aid from the Paladin. This was his Master Class Quest, one she had given to him as a max-Level Erethran Honor Guard. It was his to complete. And if it seemed impossible, well, that was his problem.

That was the test.

***

What do you do before a test?

Study, of course. Crouched low, peering through mangled binoculars, one lens cracked and showing a fractured world, John studied for his great examination. At least, the greatest till his next challenge. A Behemoth of over Level 150, a creature so far out of his range that it should have been laughable to beat it. And yet he was tasked to end not only one but four of these titans.

Impossible. If not for the simple fact that others had done it before. Few enough, in truth. But it had been done, it had been accomplished. And knowing that was half the battle when it came to the seemingly impossible.

The other half was being willing to sacrifice whatever it took to get there.

In this case, John watched, trying to understand the monster in the distance. Trying to grasp its behavior, the rhythm of its life and existence. When it slept, what it ate, what it desired. What hated it—everything that breathed—and what it feared—only other over-Leveled monsters. And then, from there, devise a plan to win.

He watched the herds of monsters attack it, throwing themselves at the Behemoth in futile contests of strength. Watched parasites climb upon twisted flesh, burrowing into stone armour and corded skin, draining it of blood and life while other prey stalked the parasites themselves. An entire ecosystem lived on its body, growing stronger. Only to die when the members disturbed the Behemoth too greatly and the monster sought relief by brushing itself against nearby cliffs or turned about to snap and tear and blast the monsters off its own back.

John watched it all, watched as it damaged itself, just for a few moments of peace. To rest, recuperate, and then move on. Days passed in a slow, torturous grind for the human, for the Behemoth never slept, never stopped moving, only avoiding the domain of other monsters like itself.

He spied, charting damage types as herds of lower-Leveled creatures threw themselves at the monster. He judged the attacks that pierced the Behemoth's defences. Watched as it reacted to aerial assaults by lashing out with eye beams, stomped upon creatures that burrowed under the ground, and tore away at its footing. He studied the elemental strikes, the flame and ice, lightning and sound that assaulted the creature and that it returned.

Through it all, the Behemoth stalked the desolate plains of the Forbidden World. Barely paying attention to the vast majority of attacks, confident in its strength, in its defences. Engaging its lessers only to eat or to wipe away a cluster of annoyances.

John observed it all, his Spirit floating by his side, taking notes. Thinking and planning, before he began his experiments.

***

"Poison?" Ali wrinkled his nose, staring at the boiling cauldron of stone, the dark-green bubbling mixture's vapour making his Mana-formed figure melt upon contact as he hovered over the cauldron.

"Yup," John said, reaching into the gap in space where he stored the bodies and alchemical ingredients the System had generated for him. He tore open another sac of poison, feeling the caustic and necrotic ingredients eat away at the skin of his hand. "If we can make something that can hamper his regeneration, it'd be a start."

"Not sure you can classify it as a him," Ali said.

"Her?"

"Not exactly. It's sort of sexless at the present moment. And will alter its sex when it encounters another of its kind, with the pair competing to be the female," Ali said. "Also, you do realise just tossing various poisons into a stone cauldron and boiling it together isn't really concocting or alchemical brewing, right?"

"Yeah, of course. Still, I remember some talks I've overheard, and this should work well enough. With enough poisons," John said, wincing as he pulled his hands back after dropping the latest batch within. He stared at the bubbling flesh, System-enhanced healing warring with the damage. He drew a deep breath, forcing the pain aside, the sensation of skin reknitting, and the way the System influenced his body. "Just got to let them do their own thing, mixing together. Some might counteract one another; others will combine and be stronger. And some will just coexist. All of it should do damage."

"Yeah, sure," Ali drawled. "How do you intend to actually deposit it in the damn Behemoth? You do remember its stone skin, right?"

John grinned. "I have an idea."

"I really hate it when you say that."

***

"This is your idea?" Ali said, eyeing the near-score of corpses that had been extracted, dipped in the vat, and then stored away again. In another time, in another place, they could have Inspected the bodies and have the System levy its judgment on its efficacy. Here, they could but stare at the simple information displayed.

Poisoned Corpses x 17

"Yup. Ugly's hungry, mostly." John frowned. He'd had to range ahead of the Behemoth for days to locate and end them, storing their bodies in his Altered Space to prepare for this fight. "Especially for these guys."

"These guys?"

John nodded, waving at the brown-furred creatures. "The Behemoth constantly eats. I think it's why it never stops moving. Sort of like a cow—constantly eating, constantly needing to fuel its body. Even under the Mana overload in a Forbidden World, it can't contain its size without that. So, food."

"Obviously. You going to try teach a Goblin to mate, too?" Ali said.

"At first, it didn't seem to care what it ate. Except…these guys. It always ate these guys." John waved again at the bodies before him. "I'm guessing they're the monster equivalent of good chocolate."

"So, you poisoned its chocolate?"

"After hunting every trace of them down for the last few days." John nodded. "I figure, if it's anything like me, it'll snap up the corpses the moment it sees them. Thus, poison."

"Great, you've figured out how to feed it now. But what happens next?" Ali said, crossing his arms. "I doubt even you would eat poisoned chocolate twice."

John gave a sheepish grin as he recalled other times, other places. Then he looked into the distance where the fast-approaching Behemoth was arriving. He noted the hordes of monsters moving around it, flowing ahead, and sighed. A surge of will as he backed away put Sanctum in place. His single-use, unmoveable protective shield Skill. It would keep the poisoned food safe, at least until the Behemoth arrived. If he had timed it properly, that is.

John sighed and Blink Stepped away to a prepared position. Crouching low, he pulled a monster-hide cloak from storage and threw it around himself as he scrunched down. He didn't have to wait long, for the monsters and the Behemoth moved fast, crossing ground in the way that only a ten-story creature could do on open plains. Almost exactly on time, the Sanctum shield failed, leaving the food exposed to the world.

Monsters that had moved around the glowing yellow dome headed for the newly revealed pile. A few, sensing danger, skittered away, but many others chose to ignore their instincts to feed on the corpses. Noticing the change in the herds below, the Behemoth looked over. The next moment, it released a roar of triumph that shook the earth itself, scaring away even more of the scavengers.

As the Behemoth gorged on the monster meat without stopping, the Honor Guard breathed a sigh of relief. A lesser, unspoken worry had been the matter of taste. It was not as if he was going to sample the meat for any changes, so he could only try his luck. Yet if there was a change, the Behemoth seemed not to care as it tore into the corpses with gusto. Only when it was done did John take action, triggering the next part of his plan.

A simple Blink Step took him a few hundred feet away, high in the sky. A channelled spell kept him floating while his Skill formed around him, glistening swords in a deadly halo. He did not wait, even as the creatures screeched in surprise and anger at his appearance as he unleashed the attack. This time, he struck the Behemoth on the body, just below and behind the slope of its left shoulder. A location where, theoretically, heart and lungs should be. At least, on most quadrupedal Earth creatures with the vaguely same shape and size.

Guesses. All of it guesses. But it was better than nothing. Another brief moment as John triggered his Blink Step after his attack had dug into the monster, fleeing once again while Ali, invisible to all, watched and studied the damage.

The Honor Guard's escape was too slow to avoid the various retributive beam attacks by the Behemoth, or its ire. Yet John knew that game. Run, run, and take the blows till the homing beams were done. Then run again. Beaten, blasted, and injured, but alive.

Hours later, the Spirit returned, stroking his thin beard.

"Well?" John demanded.

"Regeneration rate of two point one percent. Lasts for just over six minutes at that level and then steps down, over the period of two hours," Ali replied.

"Two percent is good," John said. Between his own regeneration, which was just over nine minutes long, he could do the equivalent of 5 percent damage every three minutes or so. Which meant he could—in theory—kill it. If he managed to keep hammering away.

And keep the loss of regeneration rates at the original amount. Which, as stated, was not about to happen. Still.

"It's a start."

***

To assassinate a target, you needed to know only a few things in the System. It was something his friend, his teammate, had once told him. A long, meandering conversation late at night over a cup of coffee, homemade bannock, and monster meat stew.

You needed to know how much damage you could do.

You needed to know how much damage it could regenerate, normally and via Skills.

And then, you needed a way to deliver that damage.

If you wanted to survive afterwards, you also had to know how to get away.

Simple, really. Getting to targets was often easy with monsters and hard with sapient creatures. Figuring out how to deal with abnormal regeneration and Skills was the obstacle with monsters. After all, those were often much higher, including a higher Health point base.

The Behemoth had Health points in the hundreds of thousands. A normal attack would barely be a scratch. Even if John had been lucky enough to miss retaliation, he could have stood in front of the monster and hacked at its body and done nothing, not against its base regeneration. Not without using his own Skills. He had to deliver the damage in a way that could override the regeneration rates.

So.

Special methods.

***

The ground beneath their feet was broken, shattered. Made of a top of hardened earth and a bottom layer of softer, more porous rock. Rain and overflowing water had taken away portions of weaker stone, leaving the beginning of hoodoos—plateaus of land that jutted from harder stone far below, slowly ground away till they would stand, alone.

"What are we doing here, exactly?" Ali said, floating beside the crouching human. "The Behemoth's never coming this way, you know that."

John nodded. The creature was not dumb. Not sapient, but not foolish enough to travel all the way here. It was too big, too heavy to walk on the rocky columns. Its very presence would shatter the land beneath its feet.

"Think I could draw it here?" John said curiously as he let the soil dribble through his hand.

"Not a chance, boy-o," Ali said. "Higher-Level monsters are smart. It's not like the Salamander you fought early on. This one would figure out your intentions pretty fast. Never mind spotting the danger a long way away."

"Figured as much," John said, sighing as he dusted his hands. His next words were interrupted as he spun aside, barely dodging the leaping six-footed lizard, claws brushing against his cheek and drawing blood. The monster landed a short distance away before it reared up on its back four legs, front claws gleaming as it readied itself to charge the Honor Guard. Distracting the human, or at least trying to.

As if the first failed attack had been a signal, other such creatures crawled from the cracks in the earth, shedding their camouflage.

"Well, look who's here," John said, conjuring the first of his swords. Another push of will and three additional copies of his weapons appeared within arm's reach. The swords floated beside his body, following the trajectory of the original as he shifted his stance, creating a gleaming and edged defence.

His back mostly turned, the first of the creatures leapt at John. Instinct had him sidestepping, sword drawing a long line against its torso as he passed. Duplicate weapons mimicked the motion, the angle of the attack, as they tore into the body of the first assailant, the remaining floating blades fending off the other creatures as they attempted to close.

Never stopping, John kept moving. His Soulbound weapon, the original sword, disappeared as John discarded it into the ether. He ducked low, dodging another leaping monster before conjuring his weapon back into his left hand. A deep lunge took a third monster in the chest. Duplicates shifted direction, following the path of the new weapon, twisting around John's body and altering angles. His first assailant fell, the second and third blade plunging into its hindquarters as it attempted to tear into John's side.

A twist of his hand, then the blade disappeared only to be conjured into his grasp again to deflect another attack. A shift of his body, a disengage and cut, the floating weapons around him mimicking his motions. A portion of his mind kept track of where each blade was moving, another where the monsters were, and the last integrated the two and his own motions so that their trajectories would meet lizards. Turning the very air around him into a floating, macabre charnel house of ghostly butchers wielding glowing metal swords.

Until the battle was over, the last few monsters twitching on the ground. The beasts almost never ran, driven by an insane fury to rend and tear, to Level.

Breathing hard, his nose filled with the acrid stink of emptied bowels, torn muscles, and the iron tang of blood, John's dance finally came to a halt. Around him, the floating metal swords dispersed to create a crimson rain that stained the dark earth.

John tilted his head from side to side, staring at the bodies, staring at his sword. A thought forming.

Only to be jolted to the present by Ali. "Looks like this was a waste of a trip then."

"Not exactly." John shook his head. "You see—"

"Don't say it."

"—I've got an idea."

***

"This was your idea?" Ali screamed as he floated alongside the fast-moving Adventurer. Beside the man, behind him, were the floating swords. Every few seconds or so, John would Blink Step forwards and upwards. The weapons did not teleport with him, but as John moved directly at the Behemoth, they followed their original trajectory.

"Yes!" John shouted back, a grin on his face. "Try to cheat the damn System to make the swords cut through it."

A giant head, moving unexpectedly fast, lunged. John twisted in midair and then Blink Stepped out of the way. Not far, just twenty feet, but enough to avoid the attack. He landed on the monster and cut downwards with his sword as he ran, pushing the weapon deeper into it. Then, as beams fired from those numerous eyes, he tucked himself in a ball and rolled off the long body before Blink Stepping away onto the other side.

Behind him, the swords plunged, following the motion, spinning through the air and cutting as they were programmed to do so. Following the unerring path carved by John as he ran, to strike at the Behemoth.

Only to glance off stone skin.

Cursing, John twisted around as he fell, angling his body to crash into a leg. His hand extended as he attempted to dig his way through the skin, to tear a hole in the stone armour with sheer strength. Only to fail, again. Even using his momentum, the full force of his System-granted power, the creature was too strong.

"Damn it!" John cursed, allowing himself a moment of frustration.

A momentary lapse of concentration, a shift in movement. A Skill burst forth from the monster as it called down fire upon itself. Burning the very air around the human, forcing him to flee by Blink Stepping away as his body was wreathed in flames and energy, his defences wrecked.

He ran, chased by tracking eye beams and the scent of his failure.

Neither of which he could easily escape.

***

When once you fail, you dig a bigger hole. Head down, hands wielding an oversized shovel that he used to shift the dirt before depositing the load in his Altered Storage, the Honor Guard worked underground, tearing into soft loamy earth and widening small monster burrows. Hanging beside his eyes was a 3-D map of the trap he was building, the many-layered tunnels he was creating. Occasionally, when his Altered Storage was filled, he would step outside to dump its contents before returning.

The work itself was simple, even if he had managed to bury himself a number of times before he learnt his lessons in underground tunnelling.

System-enhanced physiology and the ability to reorient himself via Ali's sight made sure that cave-ins were a nuisance instead of a life-ending event. Even so, even wielding a Mack-truck-sized shovel made from monster body parts and bones, digging was a chore. Which meant that Ali's company was an annoying but necessary distraction.

"So, you decided to become a rabbit?" Ali said, a pair of notification windows hovering beside him. One was the a replication of the same 3-D map John was using that showed the surroundings. The other ran an unending loop of Buster Keaton films. "One failure, and you stick your head into the ground and get to digging?"

"No. I'm just prepping," John said. "And thinking. We've got a poison that should take its regeneration down to dealable levels. But to kill it, I need to dish out enough damage to both overcome regeneration and reduce its Health.

"Using my swords don't seem to work, not directly. And even if they did, I still want—no, need—to keep adding to that damage beyond Army of One. Since I can't Level up or buy more Skills, I'm trying to figure out my other options while working on, well, the plan."

"More debuffs?" Ali offered. "You started with poison, but there're others. Cold? Fire? Lightning? We could work on your affinity."

"That's more your thing," John said. "You throw lightning while I keep the coefficient of friction down. It'll help contain the Behemoth."

"Oh, my job is to throw lightning, is it?" Ali shook his head. "You know I have trouble conjuring much by myself."

"Right. That's an issue…" John heaved, lifting earth off the ground. Now held aloft in his hands, he shifted the entire shovel and its contents into his storage before extracting it again. Another motion and he stuck the monster-spade into the earth once more before he tugged on Mana.

A Portal—a slit in the space–time continuum—formed in front of his hands, allowing John to step through it. He walked a short distance away, holding his other hand out to release the earth and rocks contained in his Altered Space, watching this cascade down the hill. Still holding on to the Portal, John stretched his back out after staying hunched over in the tunnels for so long. High above, covered in clouds, the alien sky looked down upon him, a sight filled with a midnight sun and half a dozen visible moons.

"I might have an idea," John said after a moment.

"Oh hell," Ali said as he floated through the portal and followed the Honor Guard's gaze to the sky. "This should be…fun."

***

"Wahoo!" The Spirit let out a whoop as he spun through the air, swooping on errant gusts of wind, feeling the thrum of energy all around him. The pair floated in the clouds, hair standing on end for John and the materialised Ali as they manipulated the electromagnetic force holding electrons to their atoms. Forming a world of potential that sparked and lit up the very atmosphere itself, lighting the pair in stark relief with released energy.

Beneath, a herd of loping carnivorous monster deer chased down a lone respacat. Caught by surprise, the respacat attempted to escape the closing jaws of the deer, their wild cackle oh-so-reminiscent of African hyenas reaching the rarefied atmosphere of the duo above.

"Now, this is fun!" Ali said, giggling to himself as he flung his hands wide. Lightning crackled at his command, the already charged air responding to his whims and releasing its stored energy in minor displays of power.

"Focus!" John snapped. He flexed his fingers, wincing in memory of past burns, of electrons tearing through his form. Hours setting this up, of bringing down rain clouds and adjusting the very fabric of reality. Hours creating an environment ripe for exploitation.

"You really are no fun," Ali said, floating back to the angry man. "I could do what you're asking in my sleep."

"At full strength, sure. But you're hampered just like I am. So, focus!" John said. "And when you're ready, show me how much damage you can do."

"Calculate this, Ali. Look that way, Ali! Throw lightning, Ali!" Muttering to himself, the Spirit began to wave his hands around, the Honor Guard feeling immediately the shift in potential as his companion took action. "Sit quietly and let me read about my stupid damn Quest, Ali!"

Lightning birthed itself, racing down the lines of power. Some arced away, shifting along natural areas of least resistance. The majority of the charge followed Ali's guidance. More lightning fired, the clouds above unleashing their stored rage. In their wake, thunder rumbled and roared, deafening in proximity.

Below, the herd were struck, corpses fried and crisped. Again and again, lightning touched down, racing through bodies, grounding and cooking monstrous flesh. Those close to the unfortunate targets were thrown aside, limbs and tails convulsing as stray strands of energy dug into them as well.

Cackling like a demented tiny demon, his form aglow with energy, Ali unleashed the stored potential of the atmosphere they'd gathered in a few brief seconds. Eventually the clouds themselves quietened, unleashed potential spent. It would build up again naturally, but for now, it was quiescent.

"Owww…" John groaned, rubbing at bleeding eyes to clear them. Already, his body was fixing the damage, sorting out frayed nerves and burnt-out corneas. His eyes glistened with tears that he wiped away, his sight returning. "So?"

"I could do this…" Ali said. "But it isn't that much damage, you know." He waved below, where even some of the creatures struck directly by the lightning were staggering to their feet. Monsters were hardy, and without the aid of the System, even natural attacks could be resisted.

"Every little bit helps, as my father used to say." John paused, lips twisting as he remembered his parent, complicated feelings of anger and loss rising up. Once more, he shoved them down, pushing the emotions aside. Compartmentalising. "Pretty sure he was talking about saving money, though, not throwing lightning. But what can I say? You gotta make do with what you've got."

Ali rolled his eyes even as he tugged a stray gust of electrons towards him, building up a small ball of electricity between his hands.

"Sure…" Ali muttered.

***

More earth, more digging. Each motion was simple, repetitive. A moving meditation, like John's fights before, but much less violent. There was a certain degree of peace in doing the same thing over and over again—digging the earth, shoring up sides with wooden beams and packed stone columns. Portalling above to dump earth before returning underground once again. Repeating the action.

Days on end, as he tested other options to injure the Behemoth, to kill it.

Spell created fire, enhanced by his own elemental affinity, helping it burn longer and hotter. Thrown at the Behemoth's body to wrap around wrinkled flesh. Only for the fire to gutter and die within seconds as stone skin refused to catch.

Cold, in this case requiring a two-week trek northwards till he made it to the spot where a weird Mana mutation had created a pool of liquid nitrogen, had been more effective. Stone skin had cracked and shattered upon striking, leaving a gaping wound in the Behemoth. But considering John could only keep the liquid nitrogen in his Altered Storage, the volume of skin affected was minuscule on the ten-ton Behemoth. Insufficient for his purposes.

Esoteric elements like gravity were out of his hands. No spell, no Skill. He had tried dropping a large metal spike from the sky, but between the difficulty in ensuring accuracy and the resulting issues with consistency, that plan had been abandoned.

Acid had been his next attempt. Unfortunately, unlike poison, the Behemoth seemed to have an unnaturally high resistance to the corrosive substance. No matter what kind the Honor Guard dropped on the creature—all of it gleaned from the acid sacs of hunted monsters—the Behemoth had ignored it. Even on open wounds, the connection failed to take hold.

Outside of damaging the monster, John had attempted to take the creature on directly. Timing himself to learn the beast's attacks, the way it dealt with specific provocations. Again and again, John threw himself into direct conflict with the Behemoth, tearing into its body with his swords, cutting at its stone skin, destroying eyes with Army of One. Blink Stepping around its form, conjuring Sanctum when he needed to buy himself the ten minutes to heal and return to the battle.

Or, in so many cases, to run away.

By this point, the monster had grown used to the constant harassment. It still ate its food, it still wandered the steppes and open lands, but it ignored him otherwise. It refused to be led, refused to alter from its meandering circuit through its territory. Swamps were ignored. Hills and steppes were traveled through as necessary, but never between gullies and canyons that rose further than waist-high. Never in such a fashion that John could use the environment to impede or slow its motion.

Changing directions, John targeted the monsters the Behemoth preyed upon. Herds were attacked or driven off, their alphas and their mates murdered from a distance. The lower-Level monsters were easier to manage, easier to taunt. They could be driven towards traps, murdered throughout the night in hit-and-run tactics. Predators could be drawn to them long before the target arrived, and the corpses consumed. All with the goal to starve it.

Starved and angry or not, still the Behemoth roamed. Uncaring—or ignorant—of John's tactics. As much as the Honor Guard did, he was but one man and the monsters were an unending wave. All his actions built but a dam of bone and carnage, only to see repeated rushes of fang and fur washing it away. Leaving John mentally exhausted and Mana short and his true opponent only mildly hungry. The debuff from not consuming sufficient food was a small decrease in Health and Mana regeneration.

Attempt after attempt, test after test. And in between, John dug deeper and deeper, spreading the burrow across a wide stretch of land. Leaving the ground beneath cratered, but deep enough that those above knew not what happened below.

Far away from the Behemoth, till one day, time ran out.

Research.

Preparation.

Practice.

And now, the true attempt.

***

Ten minutes to draw the Behemoth to him. That was the time limit created by using Sanctum to keep the poisoned bodies untouched. Any longer than that and other monsters, scavengers and the like, would have access. And while some could die, others might have sufficient resistance against poison to consume his hard-created bait.

Never mind the fact that a bunch of newly poisoned corpses might be a bit of a giveaway.

To further encourage consumption of the poisoned meat and to provide a debuff, John proceeded to attack monster hordes days before. Bouncing between the herds, killing the alphas, murdering the powerful and the young, and leading the others on a merry chase. Until they met another monster horde, where amidst the clash of angry forms, the Honor Guard continued to prey on the injured combatants on the sidelines.

A running, murderous battle, only viable due to his Blink Step Skills and increased attributes. A constant cyclone of blood and death that saw him nearly slain himself multiple times before he escaped for a few short, painful minutes. And then, he returned, for violence and pain were the hallmarks of the Forbidden World and he had a quest to finish.

Days of running battles, thinning the herds. Killing, storing, and dumping bodies to starve the creature for that minor debuff, to keep it hungry and searching. And then, finally, he was ready.

Blink Step took him a short distance from where the Behemoth was moving and in the direction it was currently heading. John squatted, breathing hard, recovering Stamina and Mana, the low visibility of the early-morning fog making him grimace. For a moment, he considered pulling out his other weapons, the limited stock of high-tech tools he had left from his time on Earth. But there was no resupply, no way to get more. Not here.

Better to wait. He could acquire the materials he wasted on this attempt again amongst the monsters he fought. Still, that meant he had to gain the Behemoth's attention in some other way. A rifle shot from a few kilometers would work—even he could hit a ten-story building at those distances. Magic, however, was harder, more difficult.

A challenge, then.

Grinning savagely, he drew in one last breath, tasting the iron of shed blood, the slight cinnamon smell of the monsters, and the hint of sulphur in the air, and dismissed it all. He focused deep within himself to the spell constructs that were embedded in his mind by the System. Teased them apart like his once-mentor had shown him, tasted the flow of formula and spells.

Once he ascertained and confirmed the portions that needed adjusting, he took hold of them with his mind, triggering the spell. His Mana churned, flowing into esoteric runes and glyphs that he had formed, following the System's pre-built structures till they hit the portion he controlled. The spell shuddered, jerked, and almost failed as John attempted to restructure the runes within. Caught between a lack of knowledge and the impetus of the System, the spell tore at the bindings he placed upon it and released.

He watched the flames from the Fire Storm spell engulf the sky miles ahead, high in the air where it caught naught but the shaded grey of the morning mist. He winced, squinting at the bright light, and wiped at his nose, his hand coming back red as he tasted the warm feedback of liquid failure.

And tried again.

Six times more, he weaved the spell, attempting to adjust cadence and distance. Six times, he failed, the spell burning the environment before him as monsters were engulfed by the explosion or caught nothing but packed earth or open air.

Six times, he paid for his failure in pain and blood, in a pounding headache and nerves set alight as the spell feedback tore through his body. Still, he continued, for pain was an old friend. And though physical agony was crippling, ego destroying, it was nothing compared with what he held within, for the loss of his family, his friends, his world. The grief over billions of lives lost, a society destroyed by an uncaring universe. Compared with that, physical pain was but fuel for the rage that lay within.

And if he never did succeed in laying the fire upon the Behemoth—though he got closer with each attempt—John did attract its attention. Gouts of expanding fire, the scream of monsters, and the crackle of flames drew the Behemoth to him. Till finally he could cast the spell within its System-defined range and could begin the plan properly.

***

Tracking beams of light, dodged at the last minute, melted sand to create dark furrows of gleaming glass. Feet bent, absorbing the impact as John finished jumping, a twist of his hand and a surge of will bringing his sword into his grip to skewer an opportunistic, spiky predator. Galvanised high-tech rubber soles dug into the ground, pushing against loose soil to launch the Honor Guard into the air once more. He twisted in place, swinging his sword to block another blast of energy as he released his own attack in return. Slowing the beam by a micro-fraction of a second.

More than enough time for a surge of energy to pull himself through space as he Blink Stepped away to safety. Mana flowed and hummed, his body reappearing kilometers away in the line of sight of a fast-moving Spirit who zipped in another direction, always moving.

John rolled as his weight impacted the ground, before he launched himself to his feet, pushing past the grasping vines that erupted from the earth as it attempted to trap him. Behind, the Behemoth roared in thwarted anger, reorienting itself as the pesky mortal reappeared. Like the moving building that it resembled, the great beast stomped forward with unrelenting pressure, booting aside unlucky monsters as it chased after the human.

A hand raised, pulling a potion from inventory. The dark-blue potion tasted like bubblegum and electrodes as it slid down a parched throat. A flood of Mana surged through the Honor Guard's body, even as booted feet pushed him forwards ever further.

"Three. Two. One…"

Counting under his breath with each step, eyes darting from one corner to another, John turned and spun, hand and sword rising. Duplicate weapons appeared once more as the Skill moved in unison, discharging their attacks with his movements. Concentrated beams of energy, forming a single massive strike, burrowed into the monster, landing just off from a fast-closing wound.

The Behemoth roared, a portion of its shoulder blistered and cracked as it wept dark fluid. Even as John ran from the newly re-enraged monster, he noted how the creature's regeneration had already begun fixing the damage. In return, another stream of attacks were released, the first to arrive shattering his Soul Shield and leaving him vulnerable.

Another Blink Step and he was away, even as Ali shifted direction again. Each second, each motion brought them ever closer to the small blinking dot in the corner of his mini map.

Poisoned food, an underground trap, and more. Weaving around approaching agitated monsters, many driven insane by the overflow of Mana, the smell of shed blood, and the anguished roars of the Behemoth, John fled, the edges of his plan coming together.

Finally.

***

A glistening dome of yellow, a sphere of protection that was impenetrable to any attack. It should have been waiting for him, but instead it was gone. In its place, a pile of poisoned food, three-quarters the size that it should have been.

"What the hell happened to my bait?" John snarled. A simple Blink Step via Ali's point of view had taken him away from the Behemoth into a hidden cavern. From it, he squinted down at the pile of corpses and the still-furious monster. A glance to the side indicated he had mostly restored his Health, his body sacrificed rather than using his dwindling Mana stores. His Mana levels were even worse, at the edges of complete emptiness even through his abuse of potions.

"Sanctum went down early," Ali, floating beside the Honor Guard and invisible, replied.

"Why?"

"We're in a Forbidden Zone. That means regeneration and spells work better, do more damage. More Mana—more damage, right? Well, sometimes, when we're talking about ongoing Skills or spells, it works the other way because System Mana gets corrupted. Deeper you go into the Forbidden Zone, the worse it gets."

"It hasn't happened before," John said. Worse than the reduced size of his lure were the corpses around the meat, the victims of the poisons. While the mixed concoction was insufficient to deal with the Behemoth itself, the damage it could do to the scavengers was profound. John could even spot some monsters rotting from the inside, necrotic tissue eating away at Mana-empowered muscle and skin.

"Oh, it has. You just haven't noticed it," Ali said. "Blade Strike ranges too short. Mana Imbues decreased. Even your Soul Shield has been weakened. It's just never been to this degree, I'll admit."

Fist clenched in helpless rage, John leaned forwards. Hidden as he was, he could only wait to see if the Behemoth would return to its basic, unthinking behaviour. Of all the Quest targets, the Behemoth, with its mindless need to eat, kill, and wander, had been chosen for its very nature. It might be strong, but it was also easy to predict.

Theoretically.

But even the dumbest natural predator would not eat obviously poisoned meals. It would grow wary at seeing those corpses. It would hesitate. It would consider. And it would move on.

"If this fails…" John would have to try again. Hunt more suitable creatures. Mix their bodies and poison glands. Pray that the new mixture was stronger for the combination and not weaker. Spend more time digging up the ground. Waste weeks, if not months, as he tried to find a new solution.

A large, swaying head turned. Multiple eyes shifted, some focusing on the surroundings, some on the thinned herds below its grey feet, others on the food presented to it. Alien gaze burnt with anger as hunger warred with instincts. It stopped, searching the surroundings for a threat.

"Thousand hells," John swore, seeing its hesitation.

Movement in his peripheral vision caught his attention. A smaller monster, dusty-brown skin almost invisible against the same-coloured earth, crept forward. It ignored the Behemoth that loomed over it, driven by greed and hunger as it crept towards the bait. It was smaller than its brethren, a runt of the herd that clustered around the Behemoth. As John focused, he realised the creeper was gaunt and shrunken, starved of sustenance. Before it—a veritable feast.

If it noticed the corpses around, it cared not. Life in the Forbidden Zone was violent and short. Only a small few managed to claw their way to the top, to survive longer than a bare handful of weeks or months. The pyramid of consumption was tilted, a warped ecology reinforced by Levels and the uncaring nature of the System.

The runt approached the bait, body low to the ground. The other members of the herd, knowing better, stayed away from the poisoned food, but the creeper ignored the danger. It stuck its head into the stinking pile of corpses, partaking of its first—and possibly last—meal in a long while. It bit, it chewed, congealed blood dripping anew.

The Behemoth, enraged by the creature's temerity in stealing from it, attacked. Large maw enclosed the scavenger and a portion of the pile of poisoned corpses in one fell swoop. It bit, once, and swallowed. And then repeated the action, tearing into the bait. It ate, disinclined to share even this poisoned meal with the others. For the Behemoth was the master of all it surveyed and would not have another be its equal, in any shape or form.

The master of all it surveyed. It feared nothing. Not even the obvious trap.

"Yes!" Far away, hiding like the bug that he was, John grinned and briefly pounded the earth in glee. Now he just had to wait for the opportune time to begin the next step of his plan.

***

Bite. Chew. Swallow.

Twice more, the Behemoth moved to consume the pile of food before turning its attention to the corpses that surrounded the bait. Having dealt with the easily claimed meals, it returned its attention to the monster swarm that tore at its flesh. The insect that had injured it, taunted it, fed it, was forgotten. The Behemoth had better things to do—other locations to visit, to defecate upon, and from which to swallow all inhabitants.

Then the earth rumbled and began to buckle. It twisted beneath the Behemoth's many feet, cracking and shattering as muffled explosions emerged from the ground. Mines, high-explosive and gravitic, triggered deep underground began their assault upon the integrity of the land above. Layers upon layers of passages carefully constructed gave way as the prepared explosives—too much in parts, too little in others—unleashed their fury. Starting from the lowest level first, the damage rippled upwards, and tunnels built like a demented ant nest crumbled.

The Behemoth reacted by trundling forwards, attempting to escape. Legs pushed against falling earth only to find that the range of the collapse was greater than its ability to flee. Not to be outdone, the Behemoth reacted. A suffused red light cloaked its body and its legs found purchase where there was little to offer, as it moved ever faster with each step and left the trapped zone.

"Goblin shit!" John cursed.

A pulse of power and the Honor Guard reappeared via Blink Step on the plains. Reaching deep within himself, he tapped into the frayed ends of the System, towards the attributes that made his altered body what it was. He had hundreds of points in Strength and Agility as the System registered it, but all too often he could not exert either properly on the world around. The concept of Strength or Agility was a shorthand for a thousand, tens of thousands of different physical equations that helped balance the world and his impact upon it. It dictated how well the ground held together, how wind resistance and friction between surfaces managed faster than human speeds, how heat and noise replicated when individuals breached the sound barrier. A thousand visible and a million invisible concepts held together in one single word.

John stripped control from the System, taking hold of his attributes directly. He removed the balancing aspects to dictate higher levels of physical strength and speed, to push himself forwards. Thunder rumbled as he breached the sound barrier, heat bleeding off his body as air friction increased, the earth shattering as each step was taken.

All as he charged the monster.

Beside the Honor Guard, Ali blipped into existence, hands held out. The Spirit shifted and adjusted the coefficient of friction beneath the creature's feet, made it harder for the Behemoth to get a grip on the earth. The beast slowed, but forward momentum and its vast bulk carried it onwards as it exited the forming pit.

"You shall not pass!" John snarled, just before he struck the ten-story monstrosity.

Flames washed away from the impact, a spreading circle of energy and sound. On the Behemoth's chest, stone armour crumpled and shattered. Momentum arrested and then reversed, it was thrown back and over the edge into the newly created hole.

Its fall shook the ground, additional caverns and tunnels giving way beneath its weight. The Behemoth rolled and roared, struggling to its ungainly feet. Shaken and poisoned, it was still only annoyed by the bug that dared to attack it, its Health barely changed.

A short distance away, at the edge of the pit, the aforementioned bug was attempting to stand. One shoulder was dislocated, collarbone jutting from skin, arm bones pulverised. Ribs cracked or broken, vertebrae in the neck dislocated, an ankle twisted. Only the rebound had kept him out of the pit itself.

"Come on, boy-o. No lying down on the job, still got a monster to kill," Ali said, floating over to the human.

"Just…a second," John groaned out loud.

"Nope. He's already eating the ground."

"Whaat!" Staggering to his feet in surprise as adrenaline coursed through his body, the Honor Guard managed to peer down at the Behemoth. Pain sloughed away as the System and adrenaline took it to the edges of his consciousness. On its feet, the monster was using its mouth and eye beams to gouge a way out of the trap.

"I knew I should have made it deeper," John said.

As much as he had worked, no matter how far he had dug down, the monster was still ten stories tall and the pit only reached the tops of its hips. Too high to step out of, but not too much for the Behemoth to look over. Or dig its way out.

"Right. Fire in the hole." John's hand, the only one he could raise, pointed at the monster. Focusing, he unleashed a Fire Storm, the spell a cloud of flame that wrapped itself around its body. The spell burnt the air, held in place by Mana and will, and crisped the stone skin of the creature.

By his side, Ali clapped his hands together, agitating the atmosphere. He lowered the electromagnetic force, allowed energy to transfer easier. Not to the monster that was protected by its own innate mastery of Mana, but into the surroundings. The ground heated, smoking before the spell finished its duration.

"Again," Ali said.

Not needing encouragement, John had begun another casting. He limped along the edges of the pit, adjusting the angle of his attack as he sought to stay out of sight of the Behemoth.

Flames lit, swirling around the pit. Again and again, the pair wielded Mana and affinity. Ground, once firm, heated and then melted, grass and roots no more than ash as it liquefied entirely.

"Enough?" John asked.

"Close. Hit it with the big one!" Ali said.

A leap, straight into the sky, as the Honor Guard eyed the side of the pit that the Behemoth stood within. It had torn down a portion of the wall, giving itself the start of a staircase, but even that had begun to liquefy. Still, given time, the monster would escape.

Swords, energy, a swing. They coalesced into Army of One as it tore into the creature from behind. The attack was targeted for the back of a hind leg, burrowing through armour and defences. His greatest Skill struck his opponent unopposed, energy breaking free to deflect into and contribute to the burning environment.

Blood gushed from the wound, skin falling to melted earth. In retaliation, the Behemoth spun its head around, finding John. Energy erupted from its eyes, aimed at the Honor Guard who was already fleeing, his leg repaired, bones half stitched together from healing potion and regeneration. Even as he ran, John cast another Fire Storm.

Energy beams rent the earth around him, kicking up dirt and searing his skin in proximity. Spinning and jumping, John dodged as best he could, never stopping, taking the occasional homing attack on his Soul Shield before picking himself up again and running. And all this time, the Honor Guard threw his own attacks back into the pit, lashing out with Skills and spells as the Behemoth grew ever more frenzied. Frenzied as the lake of lava beneath it grew ever deeper and it sank.

For John, every step, every moment, a whisper away from calamity as his Health and Mana dropped precipitously.

***

Hours later. A charred body broiled as a humanoid figure staggered away from the cloying smoke of an infernal pit. Poisonous gas, released by the Behemoth as it fought, had been trapped within the chasm. Mixed with its own noxious blood, it had formed a dastardly mixture that boiled upon contact and stripped the very cells from the Honor Guard's lungs. In the pit itself, the shattered and bloody body of the Behemoth lay, twitching in the lake of lava and poisoned by its own attacks. Its skin cooked, its muscle rotted, open wounds littered its body, but it still lived. Occasionally, broken legs twitched as muscles and tendons regrew ever so slowly.

"Time?" John croaked to the frayed form of the Spirit. Ali had contributed in his own way, enforcing his control of his elemental affinity to hinder the monster and expanding his own energy in doing so, leaving him ragged and broken as well.

"Look yourself."

Grimacing, John stared at the countdown clock Ali had conjured for his sight that estimated when the poison flowing within the monster would end its effectiveness. He pulled up the record of their battle, the estimate for damage done and its regeneration. There was only one conclusion.

"Not enough."

The plan was simple in execution. To kill a Behemoth, you reduced its regeneration, made sure it could not run away, layered on as many types of ongoing damage types as possible, and then attacked it till it died. Restricting its ability to flee had been the focus of the pit. The addition of fire damage from the magma they created was just a flaming cherry on top of the trapped cake.

For all that, the monster still had too much Health. John had been forced to duck into the hole a few times, using his weapons and abilities to cripple its legs rather than focus purely on layering high-damage Skills and spells. Even then, the Behemoth refused to die. Poisoned, burnt, blasted, it struggled to survive.

"Run away?" Ali said.

Teeth clenched, brown eyes darkening. The Honor Guard was exhausted, his body racked with pain. Monsters kept trying to kill him while he fought, even as the Behemoth unleashed its area attack whenever it could. A momentary slip of attention and he'd be caught out, forced to take the brunt of the damage. Forced to retreat to heal. And always, always, he felt time running out.

"No. We finish this," John said as he conjured his sword. A bunching of muscles as he threw himself through the air, sword held out before him. Air whistled pass as he held his breath, knowing he would be plunging into the poisonous mixture below.

John sensed, more than saw, the creature snake its head out as he neared it. Rather than dodge the attack, he conjured his other blades, using the floating weapons to adjust his movements midair. Just enough to pull himself aside from the attack. He bumped into the creature's lips, even as the rest of his duplicates plunged into the Behemoth's mouth, following his falling trajectory.

Tumbling through the air, John Blink Stepped just before he impacted the ground. He reappeared high above the pit, falling again, his velocity ever increasing. His swords, caught in the motion, continued to plunge through flesh, bumping against stone skin and rigid bones as the creature's insides refused to flex.

Blade braced before him, John focused on his ultimate Skill, ghostly weapons from Army of One creating a halo around him. He unleashed the attack and groaned, his Mana bottoming out once more. The attack burrowed into broken flesh, revealing cracked bones and beating organs within.

Before the Behemoth could squirm aside, it found itself sinking ever deeper into the lapping magma. Ali adjusted the flow of energy once more, decreasing the melted rock's viscosity. Lava lapped at its body, bubbling around its skin and exposed wounds.

Finally, the human landed, weapon leading the way as he plunged into exposed organs, blade piercing beating heart. Sword and body burrowed into the monster to be surrounded by caustic flesh and blood. Eyes closed as skin and muscle were eaten away, John gripped his weapon tight and spun. Ghostly blades tearing through neck and throat were dismissed and conjured beside him.

Wading through flesh, he burrowed ever deeper with each step, having nothing left to give but his Health and will, his stubbornness and refusal to stop. Blood flowed, organs throbbed, his very body cracked and healed over and over again but he refused to stop.

Till a blue box floated before him.

Level 152 Behemoth Titan Killed!

+&!&#@~!error XP Awarded

Blink Step.

Freedom.

Back to the cavern, he stumbled and fell, clothing but a memory, nerves exposed to open air, eyes but gaping sockets. Even so, a smile was on his ruined lips as the previous notification floated in his mind's eye.

A notification and one other.

Paladin of Erethra Master Quest Partial Completion!

Slay 4 Monsters of Level 150+ Alone.

Results: 1/4 Completed

The Honor Guard just lay there, soaking in his minor victory.

He would rest. Sleep. Eat. And then do it again.

Because that's what you did on a Forbidden Planet.

Criminals?

What it says. I'm not a hard mollusk to please. Looking for varied stories about criminals. I'll take anything you have, but I'm a little tired of biker gangs, mafia overlords, heart-of-gold triad enforcers, and corrupt businessmen, so if you've got other forms, I'll be accessing those first.

As always, dirty water to all of you.

-----FromtheDeeptheyComeandweworshipthemAll544

*%22^^KilltheBuzz – Criminals should be consumed by the purifying flame of the System!

McGregor_mod_Hunterzone111 – *%22^^KilltheBuzz, you've been warned about preaching.

*%22^^KilltheBuzz – I am not preaching! I am stating the requirements of my religion.

***%22^^KilltheBuzz has been banned for 48 hours**

McGregor_mod_Hunterzone111 – I said, test me today.

FromtheDeeptheyComeandweworshipthemAll544 – I'd ask people to stop messaging links.

YellowSub_xxs118.471 – I have a series of treasure hunters who have been raiding mermen dungeons, if that's of interest?

8*8-DinnimanandDonuts – Slavers of any interest? There's a bunch of stories of Hollywood agents taking on a series of galactic clients that were great reading.

XanBRedMage-Crystal44 – I got one about some criminally underlooked types of villains, the downtrodden, the repressed. Check it out.

The Tower of Doom

By David R. Packer

The plan is simple. Simple, because we know it'll fail. Plans always do, and that's fine. This plan is to walk into the tower, grab the box, and leave.

Jackal and I have learned that our best strength is improvisation. In the heat of the moment, we can think faster, and react faster, than anybody else. We've got the stats to back it up, but mostly it comes from our pasts. I had my personal apocalypse before the shared one.

We're both used to having our worlds turned upside down, so we don't get freaked out when it happens. That gives us a few precious milliseconds lead on our opponents. So our best results tend to happen when we get good and close to someone and cause as much confusion as possible. Back home, they refer to me as a pint-sized chaos grenade.

I like it.

Feels like me.

Of course, you can't just plan on charging in and making random shit happen. That's suicide, and I'm crazy but not that kind of crazy. So I like to plan.

Jackal is quick on his feet, but he hates planning and refuses to learn anything complex. That's how our partnership works. I make deep and elaborate strategic plans, and Jackal stares at me blankly until I can reduce it to small words and simple steps. He's not dumb—far from it—but he knows what works best for him.

Forcing me to break down my elaborate plans into concrete steps has given me some amazing levels in planning. Hell, if the System ever goes away, I'll be able to make a killing as a project manager now. Or not.

Entirely possible that without the System, I'd fade back into my old self. I'd rather not go back to being homeless, with a less-than-concrete handle on reality. Have to admit, despite the hardship it's been for everyone else, this new world seems to suit me just fine.

This will be a risky job. We've been hired by a wizard, can you believe that? An actual wizard. The nutjob's grown the full beard and has the pointy hat and all. Craziness did not universally go away with the advent of the System, if you ask me.

Anyway, Gand-elf (yes, that's what he calls himself) has a bit of a rivalry with the wizard who owns the tower. And tower-wizard has something that Gand-elf desperately wants but refuses to pay for.

Enter Jackal and me.

Thieving isn't something Jackal nor I like to do, to be honest. But we're good at it. Our skills complement each other's in ways that make this not a bad career. Jackal is surprisingly light-footed and nimble for a giant tanky warrior, and me? Well, let's just say my former mental issues gave me some skookum skills for going places people don't want me. And our home, Tanelorn, needs the funds right now, so we're out earning some extra credits for the old homestead.

The tower is well-defended. The owner isn't an idiot, and he's hired a good security firm to protect the place. Strong System tech everywhere, grey-uniformed guards with that ex-military look. And all fairly high-level, to boot. Only an idiot would try to break in.

Fortunately, I'm the biggest idiot in the world. That's why they call me the Fool.

***

The tower has three levels up and a number of subterranean levels. We learned that by eavesdropping on conversations between off-duty security guards. As best we can tell, our goal is on the top floor. We've also learned we want to avoid the lower levels at all costs, because ye olde tower wizard does some dark, dark experiments down there.

Avoid like the plague. Do not go down to the dark. Nothing good there.

Bottom floor is where the guards are and where most of the day-shift Artisans work. The wizard makes most of his money by offering magical items for sale. That's why the top floor has a big opening. It's a hangar for some sort of flying craft the wizard owns. He's out adventuring and Leveling up pretty often. Probably hunting for parts for his personal Artisans to craft into goods with his help.

Of note, said wizard is supposed to be on the verge of Master Class. So we're aiming to enter when the wizard isn't home. No tangling with Levels that high. No profit there.

So top floor is a hangar and living quarters for the wizard. Second floor is storage, an apparently extensive library, and a kitchen. Mr. Wizard is apparently a gourmand who likes to have in-house meals whenever he can. He's also the highest Level around, other than our employer, so he has every chef in town on a rotating weekly schedule so he can have his favorites predictably.

And that's the key to our plan, in a nutshell.

Wait until he's out of town, but due back the following day, and bluff our way in as delivery folk for the next chef rotation.

We've already bribed the chef. Actually, we bribed every chef in town. I mean, we scammed every chef in town, but they think we bribed them.

As far as they know, we're the sole Earth providers of an intergalactic semi-hallucinogenic wine that is very human compatible. Tastes like bubblegum, which… I don't know. Some people's tastes, I guess. Jackal thinks I should have just said it was a rare bottle of French wine, instead of making something up, but he doesn't know gourmands the way I do. We need a truly exotic offering, and what's more exotic than something I made up?

We've offered each of them an exclusive supply of their own in exchange for letting us slip in a bottle to the wizard along with a surprise gift—a direct portal to a well-known resort planet, with an all-inclusive week included. All the wizard has to do is accept our invitation to a sales meeting regarding some of our rarer vintages, only sold to a select handful of folks, once a year.

We'll have to set the portal up ahead of time, so to provide the smoothest experience for the wizard, we'd like to sneak in and do the prep work first. It's a little fishy, but greed blinds people.

Of course, it's all a bluff. The wine samples they tried were just grape juice, but that's my Skill at work. Trickster has a lot of useful Skills.

The actual plan is to get in, disable anyone we need to disable—or preferably, sneak up to the third floor—secure the object, and exit via the roof hangar with a single-use flying carpet we were provided.

Easy, right?

If we get stopped by the guards on the way in, Jackal will take them out fast. Ugly, but fast. He's good at that. Brute force the door, then put my skills to work and add some solid chaos to the first floor. Then walk casually through the resulting mess. Or otherwise hide us. Risky, because we don't know what protections they have in place. I'd rather skip using my Skills.

By the second floor, we should be okay. From what we've overheard, it's mostly unoccupied. We won't be alone though. The rest of the chef's crew will be there. But they're all Artisans and not up to dealing with anything Jackal and I can dish out. We should be able to ditch them without being noticed. We don't anticipate any issues there.

Third floor will be deserted, from what we've been told. When the wizard is out, he takes his companions with him. The door is secured, but I haven't met a lock yet that can stand up to my Skills.

Overall, pretty slack security. But that makes sense. Who's going to mess with a wizard? Anyone high enough Level to bother him probably has other things to do than break into someone's personal property.

And in this System world, theft isn't as common. It's not a common Class on Earth. Most thieves don't make it long on a dungeon world without a solid party. Eventually, that might even out, but for now, there's a gap.

Fortunately, neither Jackal nor I are thieves. We tend to be good at thieving, but that's a side effect.

***

"This is a dumb idea." Jackal tells me. Under his breath of course, because we're almost up to the tower.

I don't disagree with him, because at first glance, we look suspicious as hell. Jackal is a bit of a classic and goes for the full medieval look. White linen puffy shirt, jerkin, tight leather breeches, and thigh-high folding top boots. Nice big sword on one hip, buckler on the other. Apparently, he used to be a big Ren Faire guy, in the before times.

Me, I'm in my version of adventurer-chic. Gold-tone jumpsuit, with about a million pockets.

Neither of us look like sous chefs of any kind. But my Geas skill is in area effect mode, placing anyone who looks at me under a temporary obligation to see me as exactly that. It's a steady tick down on my Mana, but I've got the juice to manage it for a few days… as long as we're acting the part.

It's a mutual obligation. As long as I fill my end of the bargain, the System keeps everyone else obligated. The second I do something to break that obligation, the Mana cost shoots up dramatically. I've learned the hard way to cancel the Skill before I break character on one of these charades, or I'll be fighting Mana-free almost instantly. Only had to learn that lesson once.

I'm not entirely sure what counts as breaking the obligation, but even thinking about what Jackal said is causing a noticeable strain. Gotta stay in character. I just have to imagine that he's talking about our cover story, our Geas within a Geas. It works, and the Mana load drops immediately. I can't even scold him without risking more drain.

And he knows it. I see the glimmer of humor in his eyes. I'm going to make him pay for that when this is over. Not thinking about that now.

I focus on the security guards. It's okay for me to be nervous about them, because that's in character. The Geas can work with that. They're a professional lot, for sure. Mostly human, with a few recent alien hires. Solid grey uniforms with black piping. Some sort of automatic rifle slung just right for quick action. Familiar looking rifles actually. Then I laugh as the nerd in me recognizes them for what they are.

"M41A Pulse Rifles! No way! How did you get those?" I say before I even realize I'm speaking. Yeah, I was a fanboy as a kid.

One guard looks at me in confusion, but the other is smiling.

"Specially made for us. The company founder was a big fan. That's where we get our name from," he says.

I can see that now. I hadn't noticed before, but the company name on all their patches is "Colonials" with a stylized xenomorph head on a spike. Nice.

"That's amazing!" I say, and I'm not kidding. Those rifles look completely cool, and suddenly I want one. Mental bookmark. Get one later.

"Are they available in the Shop? I'm not gonna ask if I can hold it, but that is so cool! Do they handle like the ones in the movies?"

"Absolutely! Same ammo even. I mean, I'm glad we haven't had to try them against any actual xenomorphs, but they work like a charm on every dungeon run we've taken them on. I fucking love these things." He's grinning ear to ear.

Bastard. I hate it when I'm jealous. But now's not the time. I've got a job to do.

"Not as good as a phased plasma rifle in the 40-watt range," Jackal says in an absolutely perfect Terminator voice. He's scary for a second, because he's got the same build, only about a foot taller. One of his Class Skills has him grow an inch or so with each level. He's one of the tallest and widest humans I've seen yet.

Thankfully, the Geas has modified this, but for the briefest moment, the effect fades and the guard jerks back… but then he smiles again as the Skill pours back into effect. I'm grateful no one has a high Mental Resistance among this group.

"I wish!" the guard says. "I might look for one of those with my next bonus check. Never even thought to look for one."

And that's that conversation done, and the guard waves us through with a smile. Just a couple more chefs for the big meal tomorrow. Perfect. It costs a few extra points of Mana, but I can't help but let out a sigh of relief.

Just like that, we're through the first of our obstacles. Behind the door is an office. It feels like a bit of a jarring contrast, but the tower started out as a three-story office building. The medieval tower look on the outside, according to the locals, is the result of the wizard making changes. Inside are more guards and an actual reception desk.

The receptionist doesn't even look up, nor do any of the inside guards. We're more invisible than even my Geas skill can make us because nothing is more invisible in any world than hired help. As long as you don't make a mistake, no one wants to know you exist.

Even with the System, people want to hire people they can ignore to do the things they don't want to do. It's the best way for us to gather intel and do our other tasks.

The lead chef walks right up to the stairs, and I try not to look around. Try not to be suspicious, try not to wonder how they can't suspect someone as large and dangerous-looking as Jackal. But they aren't.

I love it.

This is really my world now. So much better than the old one.

Two short flights of stairs, and we're on the second floor. It's an open floor plan, with the last flight opening right up onto the floor. The kitchen occupies one entire wall, and there are all sorts of other workstations around the rest of the floor. It looks like it would be a lovely place to work. Wizarding apparently pays extremely well.

The chefs all peel off to their workstations as soon as they exit the stairs, and we aren't even halfway across the floor before the noise level shoots up as they start meal prepping. It's still going nice and easy, and Jackal and I keep up the casual saunter, as if we're heading for our assigned place. As if we've done this a million times before. No one is even looking at us when we start up the stairs at the far side. We're completely forgotten by all of them.

I drop the Geas as soon as we cross the threshold, because now we are far out of expected behavior and the Mana cost is about to shoot up. I definitely want a full tank for the next bit, in case anything goes wrong.

Jackal takes the lead, and I'm okay with that. Magic and Skills are wonderful, but for my money, you can't beat a giant wall of muscle for dealing with surprises.

I'm ready behind him. I don't know exactly where we need to go, but we've done this sort of thing before. I'll take the left and Jackal the right. Quick and efficient, we'll give each room a quiet toss while we look for the prize.

In this case, we've been told to look for a wooden chest with gold clasps and heavy glowing runes carved into it. We're told it's unmistakable, that we'll know it when we see it. We're also told it's the centerpiece of the main room and that we can just walk straight forward to get it.

But we know better than that. We've been burned before, and people move things around all the time. So we'll stick to our plan and move from room to room.

And honestly, we're gonna grab anything else that might have some value.

Things go wrong as soon as we step off the last step and onto the third floor. Not in a bad way.

There's a black cat staring at us.

Cute little thing, just a little bigger than a kitten. Big golden eyes. I don't know about you, but my rule is you always pet the cat. Doesn't matter what kind of job you're doing, doesn't matter what the circumstances are, the kitty always gets a pet. Jackal sighs as soon as he sees the cat, because he knows my rule.

He doesn't pet the cat, but he waits for me to do so. Nothing wrong with small superstitions in this new System world. You never know when something is more than it seems. I think of it as my own Geas with the

System. I pet the cats, and the kindness of cats is always on my side. I'm sure it's a valuable gift, regardless.

It's a good kitty, and a soft kitty, and it bumps my hand and purrs as soon as I pet it. I boop its little nose, and it flops on its back and looks up at me. I grab one of its little paws and give it a shake. This is the nicest cat I've seen in a long time. I'm trying to remember the last time I saw an actual house cat that wasn't some sort of demonic beast, when it rolls over and leaps up on my shoulder.

Well. That's cool. I look at Jackal, and he's shaking his head. But he splits off to check out his rooms.

I turned to head toward mine, trying to carefully juggle the weight of the cat on my shoulder. Turns out to not be a problem, as the kitty seems to know exactly the best way to ride on a shoulder, and it hugs down on me in a way that doesn't seem to affect my stride at all. A very good kitty.

I'm not seeing too much in the first two rooms. No doors, and clearly set up as different kinds of lounges. Next is a bathroom—literally a giant bath, not quite a pool but some kind of giant over-sized hot tub thing. Decadent. Definitely see one of those in my future.

The next room is sparse, just a bed, a desk, and a chair. Must be a guest room of some sort. Past that is an open space leading to some big view windows, and when I turn to the right, it's a big hallway that runs the length of the tower, cutting right through the middle of it. On the far side, I see Jackal. In the middle, exactly as we were told, is the box.

And next to the box, looking at me with absolute fury, is the next thing to go wrong.

One really pissed off wizard, who is somehow not out adventuring.

Fuck.

The cat rockets off my shoulder first, and for some reason, the wizard is tracking the cat, not me. What the hell?

I feel the Mana pull as the wizard powers up something nasty. That's one of my other Skills, and one of the central fun bits of being a Trickster. But we'll get to that in a moment.

Right on cue, Jackal does his thing. Scream and leap. Or bellow and smack his sword into his buckler. Either way, it's a hell of a lot of noise and very distracting. Some kind of attention-grabbing Skill too. The wizard falls for it, spinning to face the charging warrior.

Turns out the wizard is some kind of summoner, because Jackal doesn't make it even two more steps before some kind of actual demon rakes a claw at his face. It's a vicious and fast swipe, but he's more than up to the challenge.

Even the wizard stops for a second to watch the battle. It's a pretty damned high-level demon, but Jackal is made from the mold of the heroes of old. And some excellent Skill selections and careful point allotments. This is his jam, and he's enjoying himself. The two of them are putting on one hell of a show.

Which leaves me a split second to deal with the wizard.

No fooling, he'll end me if he gets the chance. But I'm a Trickster, and my Class is all about making sure no one ever gets a fair chance at anything.

In this case, I'm relying on my No Fair skill, which can neutralize any one part of anyone's character sheet, but only for the briefest flash of time and with unpredictable results.

It's an almost useless Skill, unless you back it up with a ton of perception and intelligence and a good smattering of luck. I've got another Skill related to that called Talent Scout, which lets me get a deep sense of what and how somehow is using their Skills. That's how I can tell when the wizard is pulling in Mana. And when he's about to focus it and release it.

Which is right about now, when he's noticed me. And with a massive surge, he's about to fry me where I stand. In less than a second, I'll be nothing but super-heated vapor.

So I trash his Mana. His hand extends toward me, and there's a bright flash. A little glowing bubble of plasma floats off the tip of one of his fingers. It pops in front of his face with a tiny *blup*.

I book it.

Wizards specialize in high intelligence and other fun, so I've got no doubt that he's already figured out what I've done and has a plan to work around it, so I'm not counting on the same trick working more than once.

I hear the clash of steel and demon skin, so I know Jackal is still hanging in there. Best thing I can do for both of us is run as fast as I can and hope something comes up in the next second or two.

I mean, this is what we do best. I have faith. Always faith. Something always comes up, until the day that it doesn't, but I won't care after that, so I'm not going to care now.

I'm out of time. I feel the Mana pull again. In a second, that wizard is going to come around the corner and flay me alive. But right in front of me is a spear with a bright silver head. It's the most beautiful thing I've ever seen, and even though I'm not one for using weapons, I grab it as though it's the salvation of my life. I'm not holding out any thoughts that it'll do anything against a near-Master Class wizard, but at least I can die fighting.

Who am I kidding? I have no intention of dying. I burn up my Mana and summon Coyote.

Or Raven.

Or Loki.

Whatever you want to call them. My patron saint. The god of Tricksters. The Mana-festation of every trickster god there ever was. Or maybe just one. He's not telling, and I've given up asking.

I don't actually summon them as much as become them for a moment. For the merest moment, I'm so much bigger than the room. I'm touching something vast. And something amused.

I hate this. I really do.

The Trickster is fickle, and no matter whether they help me or hinder me, I'm in debt to them. My life is in their hands until the debt is paid, and they'll use me anyway they like until I pay that debt. It's an apex tier Class Skill, and I've only ever used it once. I'm still not ready to talk about what that next year was like.

But no choice. It's that or death, so I let my god into my soul for a moment.

And they laugh.

Because the moment the wizard comes storming around the corner, he trips on the cat. Falls forward right onto the tip of the spear I'm holding.

And that spear… it's something special. Something… evil.

The wizard screams, and for a tormented second, I know what's happening. The damned spear is a *stormbringer*. It's eating the wizard's soul, or trapping it in some other dimension, or something I really don't want to know about.

I let go of it as fast as possible, because I know how cursed weapons work and I want to be farther away from that thing than I wanted to be from the wizard a moment ago when he was still alive.

I'm not even taking a second to catch my breath. The laughter of my god is still echoing inside me, but they've already moved on. I sprint around the wizard without even pausing to search the corpse, because god knows what else is in this cursed place. As I round the corner, I see Jackal looking at me with a confused face, the demon turning to smoke in front of him.

We both look at the box.

A moment later, we're at the hangar. I've got the magic carpet rolled out, and we're off. Time to deliver this box and get our reward.

***

Gand-elf is ecstatic and doesn't even wait to open the box. "Yes! It's all mine! Take that, you stingy fuck! You didn't deserve this!"

Weird dude, but as long as his money is good…

"Thank you both. You've completed your quest most satisfactorily. Enjoy!"

I revel in that sweet notification. It's a nice payday. We're more than set for the next few months, even living it up a little.

But I'm still a little curious. We never asked what was in the box, and Gand-elf never volunteered. Now that it's over, I take a chance to be curious and ask. He's happy to share.

"It's the most remarkable thing. It's the rarest wine, no one else on the planet has it yet. It's supposed to taste like bubblegum, if you can believe that…"

Gand-elf is happily babbling away, and Jackal gives me his best perplexed look. I just shrug. I guess next time I make something up, I'll check first to see if it's real.

***

I'm not even surprised when we walk out the door and see the black cat waiting in the street for us. The Trickster always demands a price, and somehow, I know this is it. Not surprised at all.

I am surprised when the cat leaps up on my shoulder, turns toward me, and says "So, what's next, boys?"

Athletic Competitors

So, "Olympians" and "gym rats" should be a higher percentage of the survivors, right? Just like angry loners, but it seems like, you know, not much variance. I got a friend, a Statistician, who says it ain't the truth and I don't get it, you know, for why wouldn't they? They're the alphas of their people, the lead wolves, the prowling tigers and lions of humanity.

- MusclesaretheWay881

Hmmaas_Baldree8x7 – You're assuming that human levels of athleticism matter. A newly weaned Yerrick without System aid is twice as strong as your average human. They're a weak species.

Serial-Tanner99 – And don't forget that we know, initial survival statistics, especially in high density areas, are positively correlated with high degree of existing community levels, rather than prior preparation for apocalypse scenarios. The only higher correlation has been military levels, access to firearms, and firearms training in the population.

MusclesaretheWay881 – But strength and training and mindset of an athlete should carry through! Why, you need to only watch the latest competitions put on, since the stabilization of the environment.

ZDan9kmma9NN – Saw. Race Clipper. Lousy athletes.

MusclesaretheWay881 – Sailing isn't a real sport. You'd call humanity's "pool" a sport next too. But let me take a look…

Clipper Race

By Corwyn Callahan

Year 4 of the System Apocalypse

I looked at my hand and flexed it hard and fast. The System made so much of the world harder and easier. The Clipper Race was another one of those things. Technically the distance had not changed. The only differences were Skills, stats, and the monster zones now that Earth was a Dungeon World.

Manila wasn't a big scary zone compared to others. It was more of a starter zone. The Philippines in general was not a bad place to have been when the world went crazy. The big concern was all the water surrounding it.

The ocean had always been a cruel mistress, and now she was a banshee with three different baby daddies and a chip on her shoulder if you looked at her funny. But everyone who was registered for the Clipper Race had to launch from Manila. From there, you traveled the world by boat. There was a four-hundred-page rule guide to clarify everything on what was and was not allowed. It was now to be a straight run with no motors or mana engines, and very few Skills were allowed.

It was kind of crazy. But the prize was the hook. The seventy thousand Credit entry fee was steep, plus you; had to factor in the transportation to get to Manila and the fees to enter the city at all. But it was the twenty million Credits for the winner that I was after. Twenty million Credits would buy six serfs and transport them back to Earth, hopefully.

The sheer number of Credits was appealing to every alien and human on the planet. Circumventing the globe in a small wooden boat would give most people chills, even pre-apocalypse. Still, the Clipper Race had drawn over a thousand different people and aliens. Everyone was nervous and on edge.

The ocean was a danger to one and all. While the islands were peaceful and for the most part pacified, once one was feet from the shore, the Level requirements required to survive fluctuated so wildly that the beaches were never in use.

I waited in line for what felt like forever; it was almost as bad as waiting on a Disneyland ride before. Then it was finally my turn to be inspected and have my craft deemed acceptable or forfeit my entry fee. Already, humans and aliens had been disqualified.

"Name?" the bored Movana attendant asked without even looking up.

"Brent Winslow," I said as clearly as I could. It was difficult, even years later, to deal with what I still thought of as Elves. It didn't help that most seemed to have high charisma or something that made speaking difficult.

"Craft?" The Movana was still doing whatever he needed to do without bothering to look up.

"A handcrafted yacht." I coughed but got the words out clearly.

The Movana sighed and looked up. "Show me."

Pulling out a small template made by the System, I placed it down to be inspected. I was certain there were ways to cheat, but that stupid template had cost thirty thousand Credits by itself. I would hate to think of what a cheater's version would have cost.

As it was, I did not need to hide anything. The Yacht was basic. The design was purely me and something I had been playing with for years. Nothing on it was illegal though. I picked up on some of the glances the Movana sent my way. The ship was unique but legal.

"Interesting. It passes. But I recommend selling the ship and recouping your losses. This race will not be won by a human. It would be cheaper and much healthier for you if you sold that ship to someone else." Staring at me for a moment he continued. "An Advanced Class should be smarter. You have a long life ahead of you. Do not squander it."

I took back the template without saying a word. There really wasn't much to say. I was an Advanced Class, but I knew the ocean would be lethal if anything from the deep came after me. Let alone whatever Alien decided that I should be removed from the race. The past few years had hammered that point in very well.

Whatever was circling in the deep dark abyss of the oceans made all the committee members worried. They wanted a race, not a slaughter. Anything that might undermine that look would be crushed. The Committee was wanting to build up the Race to make it a Galaxy Attraction.

But killing the ocean life made you forfeit, so for the committee, the race was a quick payday. If none of us survived. Or we survived but forfeited the prize by killing something for us to live. It was crazy. But the betting pool on everything about the race was lively.

Muttering about idiots and fools, the Movana waved me away and called the next person. Which was nice. It gave me time to settle down. Not much, but some. The jitters I felt were not going to go away completely.

The race was important. A return to some sort of normalcy. And hopefully a return for some people who were no longer on Earth. I had been shocked to find out that slavery was possible even in the System. But this race would help bring a few people out of bondage. In my case, some particular people.

Assuming, of course, I was able to survive and win.

I took deep breaths and moved to the docks. The race had a starting point in the bay but buying a slip to have my ship ready to go was too expensive. So, I was using the launch pad to pull my ship from my inventory and put it in the water. Doing so would force me to reveal one of my trump cards. It was nice, but it was not that unique in the grand scheme of things. Though having a ship that could minimize to fit in your inventory was somewhat impressive.

The launch pad for ships was bare. It was set aside and available, but according to everyone, it was a waste for the most part, since Skills that allowed for Ships to go into Inventories was expensive unless it was part of your class. It was meant only there for the rich and affluent who could afford purchasing that expensive of a Skill. Idiots like myself who wasted Skill Points or buying Skill Points were too rare on Earth for such a niche Skill. Maybe one day that would change. But for now, it was an easy way for the aliens to tout their superiority. Humans really had not managed to accumulate those kinds of resources yet. Because of my species, I was forced to show more identification than normal to use the launch pad, which meant I had attracted a small crowd of humans.

Pulling out the *Windless Beauty* brought even more whispers and conversations. Aliens and humans talked while I looked everything over. I pulled out the sails and checked them for tears visually and with Weaver's Sight.

It was one of those Skills that sounded dumb and pointless, until you dumped four or more points into it, then it became much more impressive. With five points in the Skill, I could augment and repair the sails visually. Properly stowing them away afterward even gave them extra durability.

I checked coils of rope and rechecked the tension and suppleness of the lines and weight. Putting my hand on the small yacht, I used my Wood Affinity to check for anything that might be dangerous or out of sorts with the wood. I needed a clean hull and everything watertight.

Barnacles had become more dangerous since the System arrived, and they had a nasty habit of telling other ocean life that a ship was nearby. And there were creatures that could worm through any crack in the hull to hunt their prey.

Communing with wood was a thrill and something I had picked up with my small Perk when the System arrived. I had found that the more I used it, the stronger I could make my affinity grow. It had started from Low, and I had practiced for four years and managed to get it barely to Average.

The biggest problem was that increasing an affinity took a lot longer than raising a Level. So, I stagnated on levels while increasing my affinity. While in theory I was only an Advanced Class, I had learned that I could punch harder with my affinities than my Level would suggest.

I wasn't a genius, but practicing with various woods had been extremely helpful, as well as the level of Mana the wood had been forced to deal with since the world had been inducted. Even trees that were the same species at the start had evolved differently depending on the Mana saturation levels.

In my mind it felt like hours, but the reality was mere minutes. I was comfortable with the yacht, so I used my Water Affinity to move my yacht to the start. It was the second Perk I had taken with the System. It was helpful and downright a necessity when I had found myself in the Mojave Desert when the System arrived.

Between my Wood and Water Affinities, I had managed to eventually make my way to civilization. I had hated my Basic Class while in the desert, but now, a Sailor Class was much more helpful. And my Advanced Class allowed me to sail using methods other than water.

Using my affinity was much easier now. With so much water, moving and propelling anything took little Mana. The natural movement of the tides and currents gave me wings. The wind was wrong for going to the starting line even though the current and tide were good. My position was poor and without the use of my Water Affinity, I'd have been tacking and maneuvering for most of the time before the race began. I would have no doubt been exhausted when the race officially started and been in the worst spot and shape to move forward.

Keeping stationery in the bay was hard. A thousand ships of various makes and models dotted the view. Every one of them was fast and nimble.

The goal was to end up back here without using any Skills to affect the weather or draw attention to your ship or the others. There were roughly eight check-in stations around the globe. Pre-System, the race would have taken a few months. With the System, the judges were assuming it would take a month. Assuming the ocean did not eat everyone beforehand.

The check-in stations would start and stop your time. You had limited shore leave to fix and repair your craft, but the deadline for completion was thirty days total with five days of shore leave. Making for the necessity of having a crew of three or four to make on-the-road repairs. Less than that put you in danger of everything above and below the ocean.

I was aiming to complete the journey solo so I could buy six serfs who the Twilight Steel Sect had carted off to a different world. They had taken more, but the six were people I knew or friends of friends. The Sect wanted three million per person to even think about ripping up their contracts and bringing them back. They also had an assortment of fees that would be another million or two. The Sect Head on Earth had been kind in informing me that those fees accumulated the moment the deal had been negotiated and settled upon.

That made having a crew difficult. No one could work for free. Anyone I knew had their own problems to deal with and could not afford to take off leveling or earning money for a month or longer. And those who were willing were not built for this kind of race. Too many had perished or been taken.

I didn't have the build to be a heavy-hitter, or so I thought. I did have the ability to support and, hopefully, keep the weaker people of Earth safe. There was already talk about various Legendary figures, who were strong and capable, growing among humanity.

A Skill, or gadget was in use and gave a countdown. I tried to take in everything, watching how everyone was moving and preparing.

10

9

8

7

6

5

4

3

2

1

With a quick flick of my Wood Affinity, I dropped my sails and moved the water with my Water Affinity to help *Windless Beauty* soar. Cheers and roars could be heard from the shore as we launched forward. Already, ships were barreling through small gaps or, in some cases, crashing into one another. The benefit of my crappy starting position became evident by the fifth or sixth crash.

Unfortunately, that also started the small crews on those ships using Skills and abilities.

The rules were clear that you couldn't directly attack anyone. Didn't matter to many. Apparently, the damage to their ships would put them beyond the five-day limit for repairs. So, they decided to attack others. Or they decided to vent their frustration on the people they'd crashed into or who had crashed into them.

Either way, I was dodging and weaving and keeping myself to the outside of the pack. The wind was better where the action was, but I didn't want to have to contend with fireballs, lightning strikes, arrows or bullets. It took an hour for most of the people to make it out of what I was considering the starter disaster.

Once we got to the open ocean, everyone spread out a bit more. The notifications of new zones and dangers were pinging, and the ocean was deep and treacherous. Even close to Manila, the zone from the island to the Pacific was a big jump going from level 40 to level 80 in the blink of an eye.

Safety on the ocean was more about being distant from your neighbors. Monsters were more likely to attack large shipping convoys since they churned the water and disturbed more than one alpha or nesting site. Easier for small groups or single ships. Masking one's position was a necessity.

The merpeople only occasionally informed coastal cities they might be in danger because an idiot merman or mermaid had pissed off some creature and they had decided to rampage about over the offense. Of course, it didn't help that the fishing fleets did the same thing as well.

I slipped into meditation and channeled my Affinities and Mana into the ship. I could not do it long term, but it was my biggest ace. Channeling for two hours with two affinities was like doing one for six hours. Working them both allowed my small yacht to make some headway on the trail.

Two hours channeling, four hours off. Back and forth. I worked on my carving as much as I did watch and sleeping. Carving was the best way to help with my Wood Affinity right now.

Enhancing and changing the wood at the atomic level to create my pieces was mind-numbing and painful. More than once, I earned a face full of wood shrapnel when the piece I was carving blew up. Even low-grade wood packed a serious punch when I screwed something up.

By the second day I had managed to pull ahead of everyone. I did not leave them in a cloud of dust, but the closest craft behind me was a few leagues back. Some ships had managed to attract attention. Some people had tried to attract attention to other ships. It became a curious game and race. Sleeping was hard and stressful. Even hour-long naps held the danger of someone trying to encourage something from the water to notice you while ignoring them.

By the third day, it was a smaller group still racing and chasing each other. My extra leagues had widened, increasing every time I channeled. Even without that, *Windless Beauty* kept pace with some of the faster vessels, the less skilled aliens. I was sure I was winning more because we were just a little backward Dungeon World, hardly worth their best.

When they'd said that off-handedly, I had been torn with indignation and fury. Now, I was more than happy that less of them were around.

By day four, I had picked up a dangerous tail. It was a flying fish, one of the more unique migration fishes around now. It did not technically fly, still constrained to gliding. But the fish was no longer limited to the Caribbean, and its fins now had the ability to slice through anything it ran into with ease.

The little bugger was zipping back and forth around my ship, occasionally slicing the rigging and the sails.

Seeing me run around fixing things seemed to bring him joy. He made certain I was finished and settled back down before attempting it again. The intelligence in the fish's eyes clued me into his knowledge that he was aware what he was doing, and he was just having fun.

The closer I got to Honolulu, the more destruction the flying fish seemed to want to cause. Once I limped into the safe harbor of Honolulu, I was thankful for whatever Gods, Guilds, Sect, or Settlement Owner killed that fish for me. I also cursed whatever committee member had demanded that the racers not kill any of the wildlife. Surely, such a pest was not necessary in the ocean.

Docking, I was met by a few different representatives for the race. Each of them looked angry. I ran through what they could possibly be angry about, but I came up with nada. Having obeyed the rules and having people who looked angry to meet me was not a good sign.

"We need to inspect your ship," an overgrown shrub said in a thick Russian accent.

I stared for a bit. Shrubbery was not supposed to talk. I was getting used to weird aliens, but this one took me by surprise. I needed to collect myself.

"What for?" I hadn't broken any rules and the officials had said they were able to monitor the race and our actions, legal or otherwise.

"We have had complaints of cheating," said a humanoidish panther with what I thought was an Indian accent.

"I haven't cheated." That was ridiculous. They'd inspected my vessel and had a way to monitor the entire race. How could I cheat?

"Step aside, *human*," the shrub growled and pushed me out of his way.

Only the panther stayed next to me. The rest trooped down to the dock and did whatever they wanted. Any time I tried to move down; the Panther put a paw on my shoulder. Nothing more. But I couldn't exactly shake the paw off. So, I waited and waited until eventually everyone came back up.

"Okay. Now your inventory, boy," the stupid shrub said menacingly.

Before I could say anything, Panther and some weird alien that looked like a dog with tentacles for a beard held me. A beautiful Movana with a smile ripped open my Inventory. It was not physical, but it felt like it. She pulled things out, looked at them, and so did everyone else before they put them back.

I wanted to scream, yell, swear, but my voice didn't work. My Skills were all locked out. When they were done, they discussed things as if I was not there. I could not do anything, so they really were not too far off.

"You can continue or use some of your shore leave. Either way, you can continue," Shrub said. Like the personal violations did not matter and neither did anything else.

I glared at them. I wanted to kill them. I wanted to do lots of things. I even wondered if eating the stupid shrub counted as murder or veganism. I debated internally and fantasized, all while they walked off my yacht with nothing more than a look.

I thought about leaving. But that was stupid. I needed sleep. I needed to calm down. I needed to focus on the prize. And right now, the prize was all that mattered.

I debated staying on the *Beauty*, to save money. But I was willing to splurge a bit just to have a different view and different smells. Finding a room for the night was simple. Finding a cheap room for the night was difficult. After two hours, I finally settled on a room that cost me double what I thought it should. I sacked out and enjoyed the non-creaking bed and uninterrupted sleep.

It had been a long four days and an extra-long four-hour interruption. I needed sleep before the next stop. I was curious if the four-hour delay would be counted against me. I really did not want to ask.

That wound, like so many old wounds, bled in my mind as I slept.

Six hours later, I was awake. An hour after that, I felt somewhat human.

I used the launch pad reserved for the racers. Pulling out *Windless Beauty,* I did my commune with it. Grabbing logs from my inventory, I let them merge and flow into the ship, repairing the nicks, dings, scratches, and gouges.

I scraped off the barnacles and let the wood meld and strengthen again. It took fifteen minutes but after that, the *Windless Beauty* was as good as the first day of the journey. The sails I just swapped out. I could have mended them, but time was everything.

I took the time to meditate and clear my head. I needed to focus. The next stop wouldn't be until what used to be Panama City. It was owned by some Sect and had been renamed, but the important part was that it was the next stop in the journey. It was a longer stretch, but there wasn't much between what used to be Hawaii and the Americas.

Nothing we wanted to talk about anyway.

Heading off, I did not bother to look long at those coming in. They looked exhausted, but they were still here. I doubted that any of them would stay long in Honolulu. The race was still in its infancy and the prize money would make us all cut corners. There was not much to do or see on Hawaii unless you wanted to hunt. So, making my way, I channeled and rested. And prayed I would be left alone at my next stop.

***

Four days of running and hiding on the ocean was stressful. More than one mutated sea creature aimed for me. Thanks to my Water Affinity and Wood Affinity, I had survived at the cost of some blood and a lot of tears. On the fifth day my luck ran out. As far as I could figure, I was off the coast of Mexico. Off coast like it was a speck of sand on the horizon.

When I saw the ship, I did not pay it too much mind. They weren't in the race. It was only when they veered, approaching me, that the pit in my stomach dropped.

The ship was small and fast. Built along the pirate lines before the System arrived. It wasn't designed to take a hit, only to run fast and snatch whatever they were after. Once they were closer and I could see them, my anger flared hot.

It was the annoying shrub people. I thought about attacking them, but the rules of the race flashed in my mind. I had no clue if attacking someone outside of the race would get me kicked out, but I also had no clue that it wouldn't.

So I channeled and weaved and tacked, knowing deep down it was a losing battle. Their ship had a motor. Mine had sails. Eventually I would lose. I just had no clue when.

Sea battles are a lot of maneuvering and very little damage given or taken. Before the System, we probably could have launched attacks and only worried about someone seeing us. But now… well now, the sea creatures could and did notice us. Wandering into their territory was as good as any reason for them to attack us.

My Water Affinity gave me a leg up. It allowed me to minimize the disturbance I created. So did some of my other Skills—Skills I was allowed to use, to run on a passive level.

Unfortunately, the shrubbery didn't have that. Whatever they kicked up eventually noticed me too. The Beast was not a typical Earth creature from before the System. Having an eye, the same size as me, with tentacles and fins made it eye popping. The churning water gave me a good estimate on size. But nothing to identify the beast that decided it was going to play with both ships. The shrubs might have magical-technological shields, but I didn't. Though I wondered if the shields would be able to take a hit if the monster got serious.

My maneuvers and Affinities gave me a slight advantage but not much. Enough to minimize damage, not negate it. For hours, we played the game until one of the shrubs threw a fireball and hit my main sail. Even dousing it with water wasn't wonderful. I was losing speed.

The three forwards shrubs kept throwing fireballs. I doused what I could and dodged what was possible, but between the sea life and the shrubs, I was losing too badly. Soaked canvas wasn't resistant to System fireballs.

My only saving grace was the stupid sea creature was busy attacking us both. The shrubs' ship shuddered from the creature's latest attack. The shrubs looked at each other, but I could tell they knew they were doomed.

Even now, whatever it was, I couldn't see as it moved deep beneath us. Just shadows and impressions of darkness beneath me.

The sea creature didn't stop though. One dying ship apparently wasn't enough for it. It took the beast only three more hits before I heard my keel crack. Not a minor one. More like it snapped and broke the ship.

Looking down at my beautiful baby, I wanted to cry. I couldn't.

So much was riding on this. So much I wanted to do.

Gritting my teeth, I decided to try the one thing I thought might work.

I headed down to my cabin and opened the one empty closet door. Grimacing, I stepped into it, a little tube made to shoot down into the water. It was the one stupid idea I'd had. Well, probably not the only one. But the one I had for saving myself while sailing.

In my coffin-sized escape tube, I shut the door and locked it. I pressed the release button, and it gently depressed and sank. It dropped gradually, which I hoped would make everyone think it was debris and not my escape.

I didn't bother trying to guide myself using water. Not because it wouldn't have worked, but I didn't know if it would alert anyone or anything in the area. I had found more than one creature that was sensitive to Wood or Water Affinities. But most ocean wildlife tended to only care about water.

I only used my Wood Affinity to keep the wood sealed tight. Pushing the carbon dioxide out of my little coffin and pulling the oxygen into it. It wasn't simple or easy, but it did give me time and more importantly, it occupied my thoughts. I only had about an hour of air in a tank in my inventory, and I needed the area to settle before I made for shore. Swimming was a lot more dangerous now.

It took an agonizing three minutes to hit the bottom of the ocean. I only knew that because the thud of hitting the ground was jarring. Then I began my countdown of when I could attempt to leave. It wasn't something I attempted to think about. It was constantly in my surface thoughts. Thinking about Vicki or Jeb didn't help. Nor about Thomas or Annabelle. Everything kept coming back to me being at the bottom of the ocean.

After ten agonizing minutes I decided to try opening the door. It wouldn't open.

I wanted to yell, but limited oxygen stopped me. I was going to scream when I got up to the surface, I decided. Putting my hands against the door, I opened myself to both Affinities to feel around me.

Normally my Water Affinity would not be trying to drown out my Wood Affinity. But now my Water Affinity was yelling about what was all around me. While my Wood Affinity was barely even a whisper in comparison. Water almost made me feel like I was drowning in information, buzzing loudly and constantly. Sorting through them was a mess, but eventually I pieced together my situation. I was next to a shipwreck. I couldn't open the door since I was pressed against the hull of the ship.

The other sides that I could possibly open to make a new door felt like it would open with limited spacing or none. Wood could tell me if I was pressed against other objects, but I hadn't ever tried to tell the difference between metal or earth. Water could tell me how much space it filled but not the objects that determined its final shape. It felt like rocks were spread around close by and various creatures were moving in the water. But I didn't exactly have an idea of what everything was. My Water Affinity could tell me the area the creatures displaced with water, but not the Level of anything. I needed to see the creature to identify it.

Reaching out with my Wood Affinity, I navigated through the hull of the ship and my door. Keeping my hands pressed against the door, I started the melding and merging. The shipwreck's wood was old and water-logged. Severely so. But I ignored that, connecting the wood to make a chamber. And prayed to every God I could think of that none of them had an Affinity to Water, or at least not a better Affinity than mine.

Using my Water Affinity, I siphoned the water out of the chamber, taking the sea creatures out with it.

Ten minutes later, I was able to open my door and walk into a decrepit ship. The air was tangy with salt and metal. But what made me stare was the Spanish gold and silver. The bags had rotted away to nothing, and the iron-banded chests had corroded away, spilling their contents. That was fine. The gold and silver remaining was the good part. The Silver fusing in parts wasn't great. But hopefully that enhanced the value to someone.

Gold and silver had had plenty of value pre-System. Now, not so much. At least, not the raw stuff. But I was fairly certain some of this gold and silver would be bought by collectors. This wasn't just any gold after all, but old lost Spanish gold. And if there was one thing collectors liked, it was things with a history.

Opening my inventory, I took out everything. Ripping apart clothes and dumping out bags, I started filling bags and crafting more. I wouldn't be winning any awards in my makeshift bags.

All this treasure would maybe be enough to buy the serfs their freedom and bring them home. Maybe. If not, I decided then and there to change my damn occupation. No more sailing in idiotic races. Treasure hunting paid well, or so I hoped. Humans had paid, like, ten times more for old Spanish gold, so hopefully aliens would pay a lot more too.

It was the best I could do for a friend. His wife and children would come home.

I just hoped they would forgive him for dying and not being there to welcome them home.

Crafting stories for inclusion in work focusing on prejudiced Artisan-based minorities

Looking for an Artisan- or crafter-based story to include in a publication focusing on prejudiced minorities following the Artisan path. It has been decided by the minority inclusion committee that the latest addition to Galactic races—the humans—should have an introductory story added. As such, we're looking for a story that is both uplifting but also showcases the powerful boosts a crafter can provide to the more common Combat Classers.

- OverworkedInternZeta107121

Daiyu_Frass-singer0991 – Seriously, what's with the flood of requests we're getting today?

Bla's8kkm – Galactic Council funding cut-off. They need to get their publications sorted in the next six standard days.

Professor_Adjuct_Qussa_Frill_1897th_Spawn_of_the_27th_Branch – We take offense at that! We're conducting our research because humans have been an area of great focus for the Professor.

Bla's8kkm – In a forum meant for enthusiasts. Sure. Pull my other tentacle.

OverworkedInternZeta107121 – Bla's8kkm is right. I got thrown onto this project last minute. So, really. Any help. Please.

SharkEater_Gss-9811 – How about some fishermen? Got a bunch of stories featuring them. Follow the link.

AintGonnaLetYouDown001A – Follow my link too.

Kanundraspies981 – Don't!

OverworkedInternZeta107121 – Too late. What is this? It is quite catchy. Also, thank you for the link at the end.

AintGonnaLetYouDown001A – You're welcome.

IntheWebNoOneCanHearYouScream_02 – Are you telling me he's actually helpful?

McGregor_mod_Hunterzone111 – Why do you think he's not banned? Now, why don't you try that?

IntheWebNoOneCanHearYouScream_02 – Fine. How about this one? I was spending time researching a group known as "hicks" and came across this file.

The Audacity of Soap

By E. C. Godhand

We leave the trading post empty-handed. Again.

Point Bank used to be where we kept our money back before the apocalypse hit. Ever since then, it's been a trading post. So theoretically, I guess they still keep most of our money.

Outside feels colder than a banker's heart on foreclosure day at the orphans' home. I pull my sweater tight around me. My uncle Frank, his friend Bob, my brother Harlan, and I won't get materials for our crafting businesses at this rate, let alone a turkey for Thanksgiving or a cake for Memaw's birthday on Saturday. Holidays and celebrations are important to her, and she won't speak to us for a month if we forget again. The last year hasn't gone well for us, and she blames our bad luck on not following tradition and remembering how things were before. "These small things keep us connected and human," she says. Even so, despite our best efforts, we've been all over the small village of War Trace since the sun came up and had doors slammed in our faces when we didn't have enough Credits.

"It's that flannel," Frank says to Harlan. "You should've washed it last week. Besides, it makes you look like a redneck."

"This is my favorite shirt. It's lucky," Harlan replies. "At least it doesn't make me look like an extra out of a spaghetti western." He eyes a spot of sauce on Frank's leather jacket. "Emphasis on the spaghetti…"

Bob lights a cigarette and shakes his head.

I heave a sigh and look between my uncle and my brother. Since I'm a soap maker, they leave the laundry to me, but they never actually put it in the basket. I'm not about to go into grown-ass men's rooms and pick it up off the floor.

Tired of their bickering, I step off the curb into a puddle of icy slush and feel a tug at the back of my sweater as Harlan pulls me out of the road. A

Jeep packed with folks holding higher level guns and weapons barrel past us, hollering and laughing.

"How many points do you think she'd be worth?" a man calls as he rests a long sword against his shoulder.

As they drive off, a young woman in torn low-rise sweatpants and fishnets smacks him across the cheek with the butt of her shotgun. I chuckle. Revah hasn't changed since high school.

"There was a dang stop sign there!" Harlan cries after them.

"Damn combat Classes still think they're better than us crafters, huh?" I mutter.

Frank and Bob lift their weapons, a skinning knife and simple bow respectively, but put them away as soon as the danger passes.

Frank leans against his red truck and checks the remainder of our Credits on his HUD. "You better settle, boy. That Hunter's still got you in range."

"They almost hit Bailey Ann!" Harlan says in my defense.

"They got a Preacher too," Frank adds, frowning at his screen and dismissing it with a wave.

The threat of a man of God being against him got Harlan's attention. He huffs and crosses his arms. If Mama were here to see him roll his eyes like he did, she'd knock them out of his skull. We haven't seen her since this all started. Grabbed Ol' Tick-Licker off Papaw's mantel over the fireplace and said she was "goin' huntin'." Wandered right out into the woods with the Winchester and we ain't seen her since.

"How long we going to let them push us around?" my brother moans. "They won't sell us materials because we ain't got no Credits, so we got nothing new to craft with. And then we got nothing to sell to get the Credits. The Warden here won't even let us hunt more turkeys, so there's nothing for the holidays. Memaw's gonna cry again and my heart can't take that." Harlan kicks a tire on the truck and Bob frowns. "We can't keep scavenging after them like vultures. We'd be better off working together."

I agree with him. We could only make the same low-Level items over and over before we stopped seeing any significant experience gain, and low-Level items aren't in high demand anymore now that everyone else had Leveled up. We need money to make money. Same as it always was. At least no one is collecting on my student loans now.

Frank shrugs. "They slowed down, didn't they?"

My brother lifts his giant hammer as if it's nothing more than a sack of potatoes. "If I started beating them with this hammer, and they asked me to stop, and I just slowed down, you think they'd agree those words are the same thing?"

Frank motions for us to get in the truck. Bob grunts and hops in the passenger seat. He's not a man of many words, which I'm grateful for. Last time he spoke it was to rant about how the System was a lie cooked up by the Russians. When I pointed out the literal giant message on a blue screen that had appeared so the aliens could explain what was happening and why, he quietly loaded his rifle and said, "That's just what the government wants you to think."

Yeah, no shit, Bob, they do want you to think that. Because it's true.

I shrug off the memory and hop into the bed of the truck. "Where to next?"

Frank slams his door and starts the engine. "I was thinking if the creek don't rise, we head on down to the 'Allmart and try our luck tomorrow."

I groan. "Whole world ends and we're still shopping at the 'Allmart."

"If by shopping you mean fighting our way through the dungeon mobs and taking what's left, sure," says Harlan, joining me in the back.

I grunt. "Ain't much changed."

Three years ago when the System apocalypse happened, Memaw and Papaw refused to leave the homestead. Said they had to keep the lights on for Mama. I'm glad they still have hope, because the majority of the town's residents disappeared during the integration into whatever the hell a "Dungeon World" is.

After Mama left, Harlan and I took refuge with Uncle Frank at his ranch out in the sticks. His friend Bob hunts and takes care of the farm animals while Frank does the skinning and leatherwork. Papaw is a Miner just like he was before, while Memaw makes do as a Homesteader who grows her own food and medicine.

As a family of Crafters, we aren't fighters like the combat Classes. At best, I'm good at dodging monsters and bites because I used to be a veterinary technician before it all went wrong, and my Class has the advantage of being extra slippery.

So now? I'm a Soper. I make artisanal soap. And I still don't make money.

Basic Class: Soper

A crafter who specializes in manipulating chemistry to make cleaning products.

Class Abilities: +1 Intelligence per level. +1 Agility per level. +1 Perception per Level. Additional 3 Free Attributes per Level.

Most of my basic Skills focus on the different production methods to make body products—Cold Process, Hot Process, Distillation, Emulsification, etc. Some are more analytical, like Litmus Test, or focus on making the most of what I have, like Lye Discount or Rebatch. Mass Production was expensive to buy but helped a lot in the beginning because I could make a lot of soap rather quickly from fewer materials.

Others are meant to help me survive my own craft, like how Lye-er protects me against caustic damage, or some are meant to increase the quality of my products, like Aromatherapy. Ever since I hit Level 31, I've been itching to try a new set of skills that had previously been locked. I'm not sure what each of them does yet, and too much depends on me choosing the right one to save my business to pick one at random.

You'd think people would still need soap in the apocalypse, right? Apparently, a total system collapse of invading aliens turning the world into a dungeon like out of a video game didn't do much to encourage humanity to wash their damn ass every once in a while.

At the start, they did. But when adventurers discovered a spell in the Shop called Cleanse that removed all the sweat, gore, dirt, and blood they tended to accumulate, I was out of business.

A hick town in the Heartland isn't big enough to catch the attention of any of the Artisan Guilds, and a small business doesn't do so well when there's the Shop or the trading post or the Allmart turned mid-level dungeon just down the road.

Worse so when the town is full of adrenaline-fueled combat junkies looking for their next rush and the Allmart went from the one-stop shop for a variety of goods at low prices to a dungeon filled with monsters run by a mad taxidermist who allegedly "hires" weaker adventurers by force.

Even after the W fell off the sign when the lights went out three years ago, the big box store always had been and always will be. Rumor at the swimming hole is that every Allmart dungeon is the same and has a secret portal to Bentonville in the general manager's office.

I'm not so sure about that, but they had been right about how Karen Whittaker morphed from the head of the PTA into a monster with a particular affinity for terrorizing stores.

After we pull into the long driveway of the ranch, Frank shuts off the engine. "Bailey Ann, next time you drive."

I open my eyes. "Why's that?"

"What if a Hawk Moth or Hellbender attacks us like last week?" says Frank as we hop out of the truck. "What are you going to do, throw soap at them?"

"I might try that. Maybe they'll slip."

Frank slams the door and spins on his heels. He waits until Harlan and Bob carry what meager supplies we scavenged into the house, then he leans against the truck and eats an apple off his blade. I stand still and wait patiently for the lecture I know is coming.

"Now listen," Frank finally says, "I ain't charged you or your brother rent because you're kin, but you need to either stop being too poor to paint or too proud to whitewash, you hear?"

I glance down with a pout.

Frank frowns and tosses the core out into the woods. "Use the sense your Mama gave you and figure something out with that lil' soap-making thing you do *tonight,* or you stay in the truck tomorrow. Your mama will tan my hide if anything happens to you."

"Yes, sir."

Frank scratches the back of his neck and sighs at the crud under his nails. "Man, I reek bad enough to gag a maggot. I don't reckon you got something for that, do ya?"

That got a smile out of me. And an idea. I used to feel that if I had any idea how to save the business, it'd die of loneliness, but this one just might work.

***

Before it gets too dark, I gather all the lye water from the buckets by the rain barrels off the porch. Everyone who lives in the country knows you aren't outside after the sun goes down, and if you hear voices in the woods, *no you don't.* That's even more true now with the roaming monsters.

Later, I'll have Harlan help me gather ashes from the fireplace and campfire to make more potassium hydroxide, commonly known as lye. Hardwoods like ash and beech do best, as the potassium doesn't burn away in the fire. I use Litmus Test to check the pH of the water I have now. Good, I don't need to adjust anything. As it stands, I have a long night ahead of me. After my talk with Frank, I realized I needed to expand my client base and appeal to market demands.

New customers don't want soap with names like "Mountain Rose" that smells nice and cleans well—that's for homesteading wives who still want to smell like rosemary and lavender after they finish in the garden. *That was for the world before, and the world coming after, if I live that long.*

My customers are hunters, like Mama. They have specific monsters in mind they want to attract—or avoid. The deer are in heat around this time of year, so maybe Bob and Frank can help me collect doe urine to make soap for hunters. But that's kind of a pain. I need something different.

Memaw had gifted me some anise oil with a wink over a week ago when I asked her for advice. I thought it was for the berry bug infection I got after I harvested some blackberries, and it worked for that. But it could also work as a replacement for the deer urine and attract horned monsters without the stench… or letting higher Level monsters know you're prey.

Harlan looks at me as though I'm crazy as I carry buckets of lye to the kitchen and order him to grab every pot in the house. He instinctively puts more wood on the fire in the cast iron stove and grabs my soap molds as well. I appreciate his help. He's always looked after me since Mama left.

One of the benefits of being a crafter is discovering new recipes. Higher level recipes have a higher chance of failing, but failure is how one learns. At its heart, soap making is just chemistry. Oils are liquid at room temperature and contain more carbon-to-carbon double bonds than fats, which are solid at room temperature. The goal is to use a caustic base, like lye, to condense the long fatty acid chains to pack tightly together and have a higher melting point, also known as saponification.

I pull on my protective gloves and goggles. Safety first.

Harlan heaves a giant pot on the cast iron stove for me. I pull out my recipe book—one of the first things I did was record everything I did and its success rate. Then I took the Skill of the same name. When I first make a new recipe, I gain extra XP, and if I make it again, I have a higher chance of success. I've sold a few recipes to the System, but most had been discovered already. I need something *new*. Something *useful*.

The first thing I'm making I name Improved Hunter's Soap.

I first add water, then potassium hydroxide instead of the standard sodium hydroxide. The order is important. One never adds water to lye, only lye to water. Doing otherwise will create an exothermic reaction and blow us all to kingdom come. Even doing it properly, I have to be careful as the alkalinity burns skin and can even destroy materials.

I cover my mouth with a wet cloth and so does Harlan as he opens the windows to vent the fumes. Frank knows my process well enough to go outside and enjoy the fresh air. I see him out on the porch with Bob, smiling in the shadows with a cigarette between his teeth.

Lye Discount allows me to put less lye into the recipe so it'll harden faster without affecting the quality. In the past, I've experimented with using milk, tea, and even beer instead of water with varying degrees of success. I didn't particularly like my whole family smelling like a brewhouse last Christmas.

Harlan puts another pot on the stove, and I review my oil ingredient options.

I already have a stock of rendered fat from Bob and Frank's hunts. I add deer tallow, bacon lard, and apricot kernel oil. I add in a little beeswax too, for hardness. The tallow will harden on its own, but I don't have enough to counteract the bacon fat's softness. I don't have the fancy butters made of things like mango or coconut or shea. Those don't grow in Appalachia. We have to make do with animals we hunt or the seeds we don't intend to replant, and Memaw reserves the goose, duck, and chicken fat for her cooking.

I melt down the oil mixture, making sure to keep the temperature at 100°F. Harlan gets me a third pot and I mix together the heated lye and oils. Then I stir. And stir. And stir some more until what's called the trace appears, making the soap look like cake batter.

Normally I'd be finished, but I need these soaps by the morning, not a month from now after they've properly cured. I heat the soaps up a second time to speed up the curing process.

The last question written in my recipe book stares me in the face. I haven't done anything new, not yet.

Would you like to use Aromatherapy to infuse any additives to your mixture?
Warning: some additives may have additional effects. Some effects may be unwanted.

Memaw had insisted I use distillation to create a collection of essential oils. I had listened to her, but I've never really used them. Lavender, while it smells nice and is calming, just doesn't take the edge off the whole world going to hell in a handbasket.

Out of curiosity, I pick up peppermint oil at random and inspect it.

Known Effects:

Mint oils can repel insect-type creatures.

I know that already. Memaw grows mint around her house for that reason. I need to try something different.

I bite the bullet and sink my unused Class Skill point into Cleanses the Soul.

Cleanses the Soul

Effect 1: Grants the Soper the ability to use additives in their work to create a practical effect on the item.

Effect 2: The Soper's additives also imbue it with magic to apply status-altering effects like buffs and debuffs.

Cost: 10 Mana

A giant grin spreads across my face. I select another additive. Their effects all match the old country knowledge Memaw taught me.

Cayenne repels monsters with sensitive noses, like Wampus Cats. Pepper and cayenne in high doses scare off Dire Bears and other large animals. Humans too. Citronella disorients flying insect types like the Hawk Wasps and Cazador Skeeters that live near the creek. Activated charcoal cleanses poisons.

It's only when Harlan brings more pots that I realize I was announcing my thoughts to the house. He says nothing, supportive brother he is, and knows better than to interrupt my crafting frenzy.

For my first batch, I select a high concentration of anise oil and a small bit of vanilla extract. For the next nine batches, I experiment with all of my various combinations of essential oils and ingredients. At some point, Bob donates an old bottle of deer urine, and Frank brings me a plate of asparagus with some berries as a snack.

I'm too focused to think about eating. Into the pot they go.

When I'm done, I pour the soap into the rectangular molds and slam them on the floor to get the bubbles out. Normally it'd take weeks for them to cure, but with my abilities, they'll be usable by the morning. Or at least solid. The scent will intensify over time, and as they cure over the next six weeks, they'll increase in quality.

Everyone who wants Christmas presents for the hunters in their family will buy them. And with these new effects, they'll pay well for the soap too. For once, Memaw and the rest of my kin could have gifts that aren't more soap because I'll finally have Credits.

After I finish the first few batches, all the extra recipes I've created give me an XP boost.

Level Up!

You have reached Level 32 as a Soper. Stat Points automatically distributed. You have 3 Free Attributes and 1 Class Skill Attribute to distribute.

Hell yeah.

Normally I'd put one point into Intelligence to help with my Mana, one into Perception to help me measure accurately, and one into Agility, because that just always seems useful with how quickly I have to work. Instead, I break with tradition and put one point into Constitution to give myself a little more health and two into Charisma.

Because God bless it, I want someone besides my family to like me for once, and I don't want Frank to worry himself more.

I put my Class Skill attribute into Burst Your Bubble and laughed until tears roll down my cheeks into my kerchief mask. It takes all my willpower to not wipe them away while I still have lye on my hands.

Burst Your Bubble (Level 1)

Effect: The Soper applies, through a method of their choosing, a product they crafted to their target. This can include but is not limited to weapons, armor, and living creatures. Application methods may include directly rubbing or a diluted spray. Effects may be reduced on targets of higher Level than the product or with dilution. Duration of effects will vary depending on applied substance and other environmental factors.

Cost: 5 Mana per application.

I experiment late into the night. Soaps have a longer time of effect but take six weeks to cure. Lotions are quicker to make, since they just need the oils emulsified or whipped into a cream. Their effects don't last as long, but that's a blessing in disguise. Some of the abilities will work better as a cream if the hunters only want to bypass monsters on their way to a den, then change their scent to attract a different one.

A few more Levels and I could take Perfumery…

***

The sun hits my eyes and I hop out of bed to check the soap molds that have taken over the living room and kitchen. One by one, I pop them out into my hand and slice them into bars. A few burn my skin with a tingling sensation, and I drop them into my Inventory after reading the familiar screen.

Caustic Soap

A failed experiment. Dangerous if ingested…

Base Damage: 20

Effect: 500% damage if applied internally.

Effect #2: Chance to proc a Volcano debuff that applies 1000% damage. Interesting to watch, but a terrible mess to clean up…

There's always a risk of failure. They're experiments, after all. I'll have to use my Rebatch Skill later to repurpose them and salvage some of the materials. Maybe there'll be another use for them.

With a small lick, I test the others that didn't hurt to touch. Nothing. Perfect! I read over the flurry of screens that pop up as I empty the rest of the successes into my inventory.

Camouflage Lotion

This handmade "soap" smells of urine, asparagus, and elderberries. Just like your father.

Effect: Disguises the user's natural scent for 2 hours and decreases the chance of monsters attacking the user. Caution, hostile action toward a creature will negate this effect.

Uncured Improved Hunter's Soap

You like big bucks and you cannot lie. Smells like anise and vanilla. Let this cure a bit before you use it or you'll regret it.

Effect: Disguises the user's natural scent for 10 hours and increases the chance of ruminant-type creatures being attracted to you. This includes deer, boar, bison, goats…

Bob snatches one of the soap bars out of my hand before I can pocket it.

"Hey!" I protest.

Bob grunts and turns away. Frank laughs and sets the table for breakfast. "He says he's going to get a shower before we head on down to the Allmart."

"What's he getting gussied up for? Who takes a bath just to go to Allmart?" Then I think about it and pull out the Camouflage Lotion. "No, that sounds like a good idea."

The Warden will find out soon how bad an idea it was to use uncured soap.

I'm thinking of all the ways I can use my new Skill and soaps as I scarf down breakfast. If we can find some balloons, I could fill them with suds of the Photosensitizer Soap to make enemies take more damage while they were in the sun. If we run into Hawk Wasps, water balloons of Citronella Mint Soap Suds will buy us time to flee, or at least disorient them long enough to throw a Molotov. Papaw probably has some moonshine at his place for that. If I plan it right, I could make lures too…

Frank and I clean up the kitchen, which is a right mess after making soap ironically, while Harlan gets the truck running. We chuckle when we hear a distant scream and manly cursing. Soon after, Bob joins us smelling like licorice cookies and awkwardly scratching at his pants.

Frank tosses me the keys. "All right, Bailey Ann, you're up."

***

You have Entered a Safe Zone (The Village of War Trace)

Mana flows in this area are stabilized. No monster spawning will happen.

This Safe Space Includes:

Village of War Trace City Center

The Shop

Point Bank Trading Post

I keep driving while Frank lights another cigarette. Bob and Harlan are in the back to keep watch. We don't spend long in town. Three blocks later, we're out of the Safe Zone and on the highway again.

The Allmart sign looms ominously in the distance. Already, the parking lot of the big box store is filling up with "customers." Near the back of the lot, I put the truck in park.

Frank flicks his cigarette out the window and pounds on the glass to get the boys' attention. "All right, listen up. Y'all remember how to do quests—put your hand down, Bailey Ann—that aren't crafting related?"

Harlan lifts his hammer. "Kill anyone who stops you from completing the task."

I wince. "That's one way of looking at it. You could trade for the item, gather it…"

"Bailey Ann, if you don't settle down, I swear—" Frank sighs and pinches the bridge of his nose. "Sure. And if they try to stop you?"

"I'd hope they gave their heart to Jesus, because their ass is mine," I say.

"Atta girl. All right," says Frank. "And what do we do about the Resurrectionist?"

"Is that what we're calling Mr. Bradford now?" I ask.

Harlan chuckles from his seat in the bed of the truck. "I've been calling him the Red Necromancer."

I feigned a "ha ha" face at him. I knew Mr. Bradford as the general manager who was a bit of a weirdo who dabbled in taxidermy. Now, he runs the dungeon the Allmart has become. His "employees" are fallen Adventurers who didn't make it out in time. Whatever freak Skills he has, he's sewn slain monster corpses with the Adventurers' and brought them back as summoned creatures he controls. Dying in the Allmart only means you have a new job as his Frankensteined thrall.

"It's what his Class is. Now, what do we do about him?" Frank asks.

"Never work for Allmart," my brother and I say in monotone unison as we were taught.

Bob grunts.

"And what do we do if we run into a Karen?" Frank asks.

"Run like a bat outta hell," Harlan and I reply.

I remember my last encounter with a Karen. The woman was hunched over and limped with one heel broken, her blond hair a wild bird's nest, her eyes wide and empty. She'd take one look at you, decide you were the problem, then tilt her head back and screech to high heaven. Better to never confront her.

"Bitch is crazy…" I mutter.

Harlan throws himself over Bob onto the bed of the truck and I instinctively pull Frank down with me into the seat of the cab. A shotgun blast echoes through the parking lot.

When I peek my head up, my heart pounding, I spot Revah standing over a dead Wolpertinger next to the truck. I frown. The rabbit with bird wings and tiny antlers was kind of cute and no threat when they were small like that.

"Who y'all talking about?" she asks, grinning like a possum and hoisting the shotgun over the back of her shoulder.

"Well God bless it, Revah, act like you've been to town before!" I call, tossing Frank the keys and slamming the door.

My old high school friend gives me a hug. I oblige, then hold her at arm's length to look her over. Mama would have never approved of how she's dressed—low rise sweatpants with fishnets and a shirt that hangs off one shoulder—but I think she looks pretty as a peach.

"Hey, Bailey Ann, how's your mama n'them?" Revah asks.

I don't answer and look away.

"Revah," says Harlan with a respectful nod.

"Harlan," Revah says back, her voice as sweet as molasses as she bats her eyes and lets me go.

"You uh…" Harlan clears his throat. "You headin' in to the Allmart too?"

"How'd you know?" Revah says with a coy turn of her shoulders.

I glance between them and roll my eyes. "You comin' in with *us*?"

"You going to do arts and crafts again or do I get to kill shit?" Revah asks.

"The uh… that second one there."

Revah looks at her original group at the other side of the parking lot. The Hunter hails her, waving her back, but Revah shrugs. "Hmm. Why not? Y'all look like you could use the firepower and I still need to meet the quota on dungeon runs for my guild."

My group exits the truck. Bob looks at the dead Wolpertinger, then at Revah and frowns. For once, I agree with Bob.

"Oh, I'm sorry, Warden," Revah says sarcastically. "Do I need a tag or a permit for this? It was lookin' at your wires all hungry-like, but you know, I don't want to take more than my fair share…"

Bob grunts and walks away.

"He says it's fine," Revah whispers to me as we catch up. "Besides, only thing you really have to watch out for here are the Lot Lizards."

I laugh.

***

"I ain't seen y'all in church lately," says Revah as the Allmart's automatic doors inexplicably open for us. "You know, the church has an excellent guild…"

I stop listening as the inside is lit up with buzzing fluorescent lights. Electronics all went out years ago due to the surge of Mana, but—

"What's your Class level now, Revah?" I interrupt.

She checks the shells in her shotgun. "Level 45 Street Sweeper. What's yours?"

"Only level 45 she says," I grumble under my breath. "Hey, speaking of changing the subject—"

My words are cut off as the group of combat Classes bump into our shoulders as they enter the store. I spot the Hunter, a tall thin man with a hat pulled low over his face. He tips it to me with a side glance and glares at Revah, who out juts her hip with one hand on it. Following him are a short, freckled boy, a Duelist, carrying a banjo on his back; the Preacher in all black except for his white collar; and a muscular Brawler with a trucker's cap and the sleeves torn off his flannel.

I've never bothered to pick up their names. I just call them what Frank does. I shudder when I remember how they almost ran me over yesterday.

I'm sure they also want a turkey for their Thanksgiving feast. Why does holiday shopping have to be such an ordeal?

Harlan steps between them and Revah and me. Bob and Frank crack their knuckles and roll their necks and square up on either side of us.

"Eh, they're harmless," says Revah with a wave. "Now, what's on our list for today?"

I check the scratch paper. "For Memaw, we need a turkey, boxed cake, frostin—"

"No dressing?" Harlan asks.

My jaw dropped. "When have you *ever* seen Memaw make boxed dressing for Thanksgiving?"

"You're getting a boxed cake!" he counters.

"Because I ain't know how to bake a damn cake, Harlan."

"Well it's not like it's rocket surgery," he says. "And you know all them… soapy chemicals and shit. It can't be that different."

"I'm gonna put lye in your birthday cake," I mutter as I check the rest of the list. "Frank's getting her flowers, Bob's getting her an… oil infuser necklace? Is that right, Bob?"

Bob grunts his affirmation and turns red.

"That's right sweet of you, Bob," I say. "She'll like that."

The rest of the list I break down by who wants what. Frank needs supplies to repair the fence around the ranch before winter breaks it again. Bob keeps his list to himself. I need more soap supplies to last me until we can slaughter more livestock or hunt, and the animals will grow leaner until spring.

"Papaw just listed 'Red Herrings,'" I say in confusion. "Harlan, what'chu want?"

Harlan beats his hammer against his palm and won't look at me. "I uh… was going to get some more building supplies. Make you your own workshop out back."

"I… thank—"

A screen pops up, solidifying our desires in the dungeon, before I can answer him properly.

Quest Granted: ***Head on Down to the Allmart…***

Acquire the following items:

- *Boxed Cake Mix*
- *Buttercream Frosting*
- *Turkey*
- *Soap Base Products*

Rewards: 1,000XP, Memaw won't cry on her birthday, and you won't ruin Thanksgiving… again.

I wave away the screen. We all have our own versions. Somehow the GM who runs the dungeon can grant quests and pay out Credits and rewards.

It isn't altruistic. He doesn't want us to succeed.

The intercom crackles overhead, and an unhinged voice fills the store loudly enough to make us flinch.

"ATTENTION ALLMART SHOPPERS: ALL ASSOCIATES MUST REPORT FOR DUTY."

"Ah, hell, I thought we'd at least get to the Sports and Outdoors Section. Damn combat Classers." Frank draws his two skinning knives out of their sheaths on his belt.

***

"ALLMART IS ALWAYS HIRING. BECOME AN ASSOCIATE TODAY!"

I ignore the intercom as we make our way down the aisles. Harlan had grabbed a shopping cart for me. The boys each have their own job in a dungeon. Frank detects and inactivates traps, Bob tracks monsters and knows their weak points, and if we can't avoid a fight? Harlan is up with his mighty squishing hammer.

I push the cart.

The addition of Revah and her shotgun makes the boys bolder though. Usually, a trip to Allmart takes hours, slowly sneaking through the aisles hoping to scavenge loot the real fighters leave behind while avoiding the Associates. They look mostly human, except for their featureless faces and monstrous amendments, and carry price guns that shoot lasers, but their uniforms are crop tops that expose a giant mouth in their belly.

Most adventurers who die in the Allmart are turned into the Associates by the GM. If they're strong enough—or worthy enough, as some people put it—the GM turns them into Department Leads. Allegedly. I haven't ever seen any, but then again, our goal is never to fight the dungeon, but to scavenge.

What's for sure true though is that no one, and I mean *no one*, wants to die in an Allmart. We'd come up with another story at the wake, and it's an unspoken fear in town that one day we'll see someone working here that we recognize. Frank once said he saw the sheriff here, with arms like a bear and the body of a pig. Harlan had assured me Frank was joking; Officer Tennant had always looked like that.

Lou hasn't come around in a while though. He usually checks on us.

Sometime during the conversion, the store became more like a giant maze and many of the products on the shelves are a false front to maintain the aesthetic. The store also seems to restock itself somehow. We find actual items we can buy, but each item could also be a mimic. Bob still has a nasty scar on his hand from being bitten by the self-checkout machine.

We travel as a group, keeping quiet except for the eerie squeak of the shopping cart's wheels. The rancid smells of a dusty building that hasn't seen daylight in three years permeates the air. I try not to make it obvious that we're following Revah's old group of fighters, scavenging off the shelves and whatever loot they abandon, but we absolutely are.

I found some boxed cake mix and frosting in the baking section along with some canola and olive oil I can use as a base for soap. I picked up a jug of water too, out of habit. As we near the toy section, I make sure to avoid hitting the netted tower holding plastic balls. Last time, when we were running away with armfuls of canned goods, one of those can got loose and knocked the ball pit. What bounced out weren't children's toys but various monstrous slimes that swarmed after us.

We barely made it out.

I motion for the group to stop, then take a bit of soap out of my fanny pack and grease the wheels. Bob gives me an approving nod. I pull my hands toward my chest, curling the tips of the fingers, to gesture "I want," then I pretend to blow up a balloon.

Revah understands before the older man does. She taps my shoulder and points down the toy aisle, then to the left. I nod and hold up a finger for them to wait.

Harlan shifts uneasily and taps his hammer against his foot. I hear the Associates approaching too. I don't want to run away this time though. I quickly write out a list of items in the dust on the floor: party balloons, water guns, paint sprayers, bucket.

They nod, each crossing out the item with a toe. I exhale sharply. Thank goodness they understood. If this works…

The intercom crackles. "IF YOU CONTINUE TO RESIST GAINFUL EMPLOYMENT, YOU WILL BE ASSIGNED TO THE NIGHT SHIFT."

"Man, he's more irritating than a Bible salesman at a church lock-in," Revah says. She realizes her mistake as soon as the words leave her mouth and pumps an empty shell out of her shotgun. "Ah, hell."

"You a one-pump chump now, Revah?" I ask, our cover blown.

"You didn't do that before?" yells Frank.

Bob nocks an arrow and Harlan blocks the aisle behind us.

"Oh, hush up." The shotgunner takes point in front of us. "You still want your splashy stuff? Go get it. I'll cover you."

"You sure this'll work?" Harlan asks with his hammer at the ready.

Frank and Bob don't question it. Especially not when five Associates in their midriff polos and practical vests swarm in from various aisles with their belly mouths open and hungry. They run with their arms flailing and their featureless faces tilted toward the fluorescent lights.

Revah blesses herself and stares down the barrel. One blast takes an arm but does little to slow the monster.

Balloons. Water guns. Bucket. Paint sprayer.

The first two items are in the toy section. The last two items are in the do-it-yourself section. The auto care and sporting goods sections separate us from DIY, but fortunately, the main aisle will take us straight to it. We just have to get there, and back, fast.

Harlan moves too slowly with his hammer to come with me. I normally don't attract much attention from the Associates, and I run the fastest. Bob steps beside me as quiet confirmation he'll go. I put on some of the Camouflage Lotion and hand him the lotion as well. What better way to test it?

I rummage around my fanny pack for a bar of Caustic Soap. "Revah, can you clear me a path?"

Revah blasts the other arm off an Associate. "I mean, I can try!"

The monster sprints toward us, stomach mouth gaping with two rows of teeth and a long tongue ready to pull us in if it gets too close. I dart in front of Revah and duck low.

"The hell are you—" Revah asks.

I throw the bar of Caustic Soap into the creature's open mouth. It stops in its tracks. Gags a little. Hiccups and lets a few bubbles escape. Then foam pours out of its mouth as the creature dissolves from the inside.

"Well I'll be damned," says Revah. "Your arts and crafts finally paid off!"

"Finish it off!" I cry. It isn't dead yet.

Revah takes the opportunity to get close and fire the shotgun directly into its damaged mouth. I don't know what Skills or abilities she has, but fireworks are involved, and the thing's spine snaps.

"How many bars you got?" Frank asks, taking my elbow and lifting me to my feet.

"Not enough to do that every time."

Four Associates are left. The three people staying behind in my group can at least play cat and mouse with them long enough until we get back, I hope.

I run.

***

My soap works. It works!

Revah's gunfire echoes behind us. Historically, something would try to attack anyone who splits from the group, but not a damn thing bothers us as Bob and I hunt the shelves for the balloons.

My Skill is useful for something other than cleaning away the grime and blood of the day! I'm going to make a fortune when the soap finally cures and reaches its full effect. Hell, maybe we could even shop at the Allmart again without worry. We wouldn't even have to pay anymore; everything is free when you steal it, after all.

We just need to survive first.

I hope Memaw appreciates what we're going through to make sure the holidays are nice.

To my relief, Harlan, Frank, and Revah are still holding out near the dolls. Bob and I sneak around back by the playing cards, and I set to work pouring the jug of water into my new bucket. The Caustic Soap, being lye-heavy, crumbles like wet sand under my hands as I mix it into solution. It stings a little, like bath water that's too hot, and my hands turn red, but the Lye-er trait protects me from the worst of the damage.

Caustic Water

You really, really don't want to bathe in this… or drink it.

Base Damage: 10

Effect: 200% damage if applied internally.

I first fill the water guns and hand them out. My boys take them readily, but Revah gives me a skeptical look.

"I'll keep the real thing, thanks," she says.

I shrug as if to say "suit yourself" and keep it for my own use. The boys protect me with their new equipment as I fill the paint sprayer, then use it to fill the water balloons.

The Associate closest to Harlan takes a stream of the chemical water straight to the gut—or well, mouth. It smacks its lips and tries to clean itself with its long prehensile tongue, only to find its mouth burning as blood dribbles between its teeth.

I toss a Caustic Water Balloon to Frank, who chucks it at the damaged creature's feet. It slips on the suds and Harlan goes to town wailing on its head with his hammer.

With our new supplies, we're able to slow them down, stun them, and pick them off one by one. My bucket's getting low though and we need to save our new weapons for later, just in case. I circle my finger above my head and motion for us to head to the frozen section.

We aren't leaving without that turkey.

Revah covers our escape. I stay with her, filling the paint sprayer one last time, then I chuck the rest of the soapy water in the bucket onto the floor of the aisle. The two remaining Associates slip as she and I make a break for it.

***

"ATTENTION ALLMART SHOPPERS: DUE TO HIGH DEMAND, 'BLACK FRIDAY' HOURS ARE NOW IN EFFECT. PLEASE SEE YOUR NEAREST ASSOCIATE FOR ASSISTANCE. GIVEN THE RECENT STAFFING SHORTAGE, ALL VACATION APPROVAL

HAS BEEN REVOKED. OPEN INTERVIEWS ARE BEING CONDUCTED FOR NEW HIRES; APPLY TODAY!"

The group of fighters stares us down across the icy open freezer. Only one turkey is left, and Harlan and the Duelist both have their hands on it. All of those with weapons have them drawn on each other.

"Give me the bird," said the banjo player.

"I mean, I'd be happy to any other day," says Harlan. "But not in front of the women or the Preacher."

"Act like y'all got some sense," I moan. "Why is it always Black Friday and never Christmas around here? Where's your charity, Preacher?"

The Preacher crosses his arms. "The Lord helps those who help themselves, and we are helping ourselves to that turkey."

"The monsters are coming and you're here arguing over a hunk of meat," says Frank.

"Take your own advice and leave," says the Hunter, "and you might still have time to get home to make decorative little soaps that look like seashells or whatever it is y'all do. Leave the fighting to us."

A distant roar of collective workers called to action echoes in the store. Revah's shotgun trembles in her hands. I keep my water gun on the group and gently touch her elbow with the water balloon in my hand.

"You okay?" I whisper.

"I-I-I can't do this again," she says. "Have you seen the crowds during the holidays? It's all hands on deck. We gotta leave."

The Hunter grins. "Revah here used to work at the Allmart in the before times."

"We should go," she repeats in a cold whisper.

I take a hesitant step back. Worst case, we slaughter a chicken for the Thanksgiving feast. But Memaw would know. It didn't work last year.

"All of us," adds Revah, looking around. "Don't you hear that?"

We listen. Rapid footsteps. Jingling of too many swag pins on vests. But also… the clicking of heels on the linoleum. The fighters look around, then roll their eyes as a group.

"Nice try, Revah," says the Hunter. He snatches the turkey and lifts it like a basketball. "But this one is—"

"*Mine*!" screeches a feminine voice in the distance.

"Fall back!" Frank calls to us and we retreat to the dairy section.

Out of seemingly nowhere, Karen pounces the Hunter like a cougar. He falls to the floor, stunned, as her long, manicured nails slash him up like claws. The frozen turkey rolls to the Duelist's feet.

"Help me!" the Hunter cries to his friends with an arm outstretched.

The Duelist looks at him, then the turkey. He grabs the bird and sprints toward the front of the store like a linebacker with the turkey under his arm.

Bob comes to the Hunter's aid. Several arrows at once land in the monstrous woman's side. She pauses and looks at the Warden as if he said her hair was outdated.

"Ma'am, the manager's office is that-a-way. He's ready to see you now," Bob says. He fires an arrow far over several aisles—a misdirection Skill he rarely uses as it costs him a lot of Mana.

Karen tilts her head back and howls. The ear-piercing sound makes us drop to our knees and the store shakes. I swear I take psychic damage. She wanders off to the back where the offices are kept, following the scented arrow.

Revah and I run over to the bloodied Hunter. I take a knee and inspect him.

"The gashes on your chest I can patch up with some duct tape," I say, "but I don't like the look of that leg."

"I'm fine. Get out of my way." The Hunter pushes me away and tries to stand, only to sink back on his haunches.

I tsk. "Nope, don't like the look of that leg at all."

Revah grabs the back of her friend's jacket and lifts him to his feet so Bob can throw the man's arm around his shoulder.

"Pretty sure if the leg's broke, we gotta put him down," she says. "Ain't that right, Rancher?"

"It's not broke!" protests the Hunter.

Frank sighs. "Let's retreat to the do-it-yourself section and patch the boy up."

***

We sneak past the mob of Associates and settle down by the buckets. The Hunter's leg is infected already, likely from the dirt under Karen's acrylics. I pull out every bit of soap I have to see if there's anything useful. Harlan set about gathering buckets on the long handle of his hammer. Bob applies more of my Camouflage Lotion and grunts.

"Good idea, Bob," Frank says. "I'll come with you to get the water."

Revah patches up her buddy as I run my hands over each bar of soap, inspecting it to check the properties until I find one that works.

"What are you going to do, give me a bath?" the Hunter asks.

"Maybe I should. You've been acting real ugly."

There it is.

Uncured Wound Cleansing Soap

The combined effects of honey and silver are highly effective at inhibiting microbial growth. This may sting a bit…

Effect: Removes infection from wounds and promotes faster natural healing.

"What do y'all need a turkey for anyway?" says the Hunter. "Don't you have a Game Warden?"

"Whole point of the Warden is to make sure we don't over hunt," Harlan scoffs. "He's better at hunting people."

I put away the rest of my soaps. "Memaw insists it's tradition and we'll have bad luck if we don't put a turkey on the table. Probably explains why business has been so bad this last year."

Revah tears off the last strip of duct tape and slaps it on his chest none too gently. "You ever met Mrs. Thompson, Dale?"

Frank and Bob return with the water and I set about washing his wounds.

Dale's eyes dart back and forth until something must click in his brain. "My old grade schoolteacher?"

"Then you know she's not a woman you want to disappoint," says Revah.

Dale chuckles. "Oh, I remember." Something else pops into his mind. "Wait, you mean to tell me these are the Thompson kids?"

"Oh, bless your heart…" Revah kicks his side and points at each of us in turn. "Frank Thompson, Harlan Thompson, Bailey Ann Thompson, and you know the Warden."

Bob tips his hat.

"Your mama's name's not Rebecca, is it?" Dale asks me.

"Sure is."

"So, you're telling me you're the son and daughter of *the* Rebecca Thompson, top-ranking officer of the Guild?"

Harlan and I exchange looks as if to say 'she's alive?'. I try to hide the excitement building in my chest.

"Well, I don't know about all that… we ain't seen her in some time," I say.

Revah gives me a look. "Wait, you didn't—"

"And we almost ran you over yesterday?" interrupts Dale.

Revah scoffs. "Boy, look at her. Ain't she the splitting image of her mama up one side and down the other?"

Dale fiddles with his jacket to avoid Revah's gaze. "I never met Rebecca, but I heard stories—" He looks up. "Wait, how did you get around in this place without weapons?"

I hold up the bottle of Camouflage Lotion. "Arts and crafts." He reaches for it, but I pull away. "Ah! Check your Status too."

He does and laughs. "Well, I'll be. You crafters aren't so bad after all."

"Harlan here does building repair and construction. I bet he could make you some tree stands and fences," I say, tossing my head. "Frank's good with leather and traps. He might even repair your jacket and armor if you ask real nice."

Dale stands and shakes my hand. He turns to Frank. "Mr. Thompson, would you kindly—"

Frank crosses his arms. "Sir, you almost run over my kin, steal my mama's turkey out of our hands, and my niece, out of the goodness of her heart, puts you back together, and you ain't got anything else to say to her before you ask me for a favor?"

Dale sighs. "Bailey Ann, thank you for the assistance. May I please have some of your lotion so we can get out of here?"

"You're welcome," I say. "And I'd be happy to sell you the lotion now under the promise that you get us that turkey back."

"Agreed."

"Would you like to hear about what other products I offer?"

***

We make our way back to the registers with our shopping cart full and everyone packing a loaded bucket of Caustic Water, a couple of Splash Damage Balloons, and a water gun.

When we get there, Dale's team is overrun by Associates keeping them from leaving the building. Tongues protrude from bellies and lash at them or wrap around their ankles to pull them back into the store.

I throw a couple of my Repellant Balloons at each of them. The Associates let go and pull back their tongues. Harlan chucks an overfilled giant rubber party balloon I made for him, and Bob shoots it as it arcs over a group of the Associates.

What might as well be acid rain pours over the monsters. They stand in place and howl, trying to brush the caustic substance off their skin and smearing it, causing more damage. It's not enough to kill them, though the distraction buys us some time.

The fighters empty their weapons into the monsters while I empty my sweater pockets of any remaining soap or materials that might be useful. I don't have anything stronger that isn't undiluted—

That's it. I needed something undiluted. I search my Inventory and find a pouch of powdered lye. The first safety tip of making soap? "Add water to lye and you may die!"

I have the lye. My kin have the water.

"Bailey Ann, no!" cries Harlan as I approach the Associates.

Dale holds up his hands to signal to his team to cease fire. They do so long enough to let me empty the pouch around the monsters. The puddle of caustic water on the floor burns my soles through my boots as if I were barefoot on the asphalt in summer, but I grit my teeth through the damage.

Bob and Frank have watched me make soap for the past three years and know my rules. They pick up on my plan. As soon as I put a ring of lye around the monsters, they soak the powder in water, and I make a run back to the group.

Harlan catches me in his arms. I glance back and watch as the temperature of the water changes from corporately acceptable seventy-two degrees to boiling within seconds. Some of the monsters split at the spine to scream as it melts their feet, sealing them to the checkered linoleum. Fumes choke out the other Associates.

The group of fighters see their opportunity and so do mine.

"Toss me some soap, Baily Ann!" Frank calls.

I do. He cuts the two bars into halves and hands them out to the rest of us. Revah steadies her shotgun, and my team takes aim for the open mouths. A volley of soap, shotgun shells, arrows, and rifle rounds land in the weak spots of the monsters' mouths to the tune of lively banjo music from the Duelist.

Melted fat, gristle, and sizzling swag pins on drenched vests are all that remain of the Associates.

Revah sprints for the nearest phone on the wall and dials in a number that gives her access to the intercom. She drops her accent and says in the sweetest, most upbeat voice she has, "CUSTOMER SERVICE TO GENERAL MANAGER, CODE 4, I REPEAT, CODE 4."

I have no idea what that means, but I'm grateful for Revah's previous employment at the Allmart, because all goes quiet. Probably some "all clear" code that resets the Associates to their default departments. We push our shopping carts out the front doors.

"What the hell just happened? What did you use?" asks the Preacher.

Dale snatches the frozen turkey out of the Duelist's hands and puts it in mine. My wet hands stick to the ice crusted on the outside of the turkey, but I've never been happier to have my hands go numb.

Congratulations! Quest Completed: ***Head on Down to the Allmart…***

You have successfully completed your shopping list.

Rewards: 1,000XP

"The Thompsons are our new supplier of hunting gear, and we have graciously accepted their invitation to Thanksgiving," Dale says. He quickly gives them a glowing review of my products, from the uses of failed soap to the Camouflage Lotion, to the Wound Soap even at its weakest.

Revah elbows him.

"… and we're invited to celebrate Memaw's birthday on Saturday. I have been told gifts are not optional."

The group's attitude changes quickly, and they line up to place their orders with us.

Quest Granted: ***Back in Business!***

Make the following items for your new customers:

- *10 Bars of Improved Hunter's Soap*
- *10 Bottles of Camouflage Lotion*
- *5 Bottles of Caustic Water*
- *5 Bottles of Wound Wash*
- *5 Bottles of Wound Liniment*

Rewards: 10,000 Credits; 9,000 XP.

Inspiring Figures of Human History

I've been fascinated by certain inspiring figures in human history. People like Genghis Khan, "Weird" Al Yankovic, Charlie Chaplin, and Mulan seem to have inspired humanity even to this day. If you've got other stories of individuals who have taken inspirational figures into the apocalypse, I'd love to read about them.

- Roland_Not-Trolling89

CDeantheBeard887 – I… think you might want to look at what inspiring means.

Roland_Not-Trolling89 – I know what it means. I'm defining it broadly.

JoeDak_asp_DD – Very broadly.

Roland_Not-Trolling89 – If you're not going to be helpful, please stop replying.

10_Chat_Realms – There's a merchant who styled himself after "Honest Abe" working Mexico City. Look him up. Fascinating fellow.

OhCaptainmyCaptain_99SO – Captains Nemo and Blackbeard are the inspiration for a number of individuals in the Caribbean Merchant Navy. One even replaced their name.

Roland_Not-Trolling89 – Thank you!

MurdochMysteries411 – There's an investigator working for the Movana that has been hunting down thieves. Calls himself Holmes.

Daiyu_Frass-singer0991 – How about another teacher? Highly inspirational.

WWMRD?

By: Jason J. Willis

I'd like to blame the explosion for interrupting my class's lesson. But what really derailed things was Aul K'Unn Tek. It was always Aul. Even the porous walls shaking and crystal lights flickering would have been a relatively short delay, without his questions.

We were used to the ship being attacked; it had happened at least once a week since the voloids had landed. The four-armed, grey hexapods had practically guaranteed that when they'd landed their spaceship in a prime dungeon location. The only real threat had been when a pair of giant black bears with goat heads had tried to eat the thrusters. Even then, a blast of blazing rocket fuel to the face had persuaded them to find a less spicy meal.

As an early elementary teacher, the Squaw Lake Bird Watcher's Society had sounded like a great place to bring my class. So I had gone alone to scout it out as a potential field trip location, expecting to see some mallards and loons. As a vegetarian, I had been nearly as horrified by the antlered heads on display in the main lodge as I was by the announcement that it was about to become a post-apocalyptic dungeon.

I'd played enough RPGs and MMOs to know what a dungeon was, and I knew it was the last place I wanted to be standing during an apocalypse. Ignoring the rest of the messages, I'd run as fast as my couch-potato legs could carry me on a dirt road that still hid a few frozen spots, even in early April.

The white-tailed deer bounding into my field of vision by the time the countdown ended had made me smile. Distracted by its unusual size and fanged maw, I'd missed the spaceship behind the row of trees.

The voloid Matriarch, E'Kklon Vekk, had appeared like Predator from the movies, yanking me from the path of the deer monster and into the safety of her ship, where I had been her guest, or prisoner, ever since.

"Teacher, teach," she'd intoned with a high, resonant voice. Then she'd tossed me into a room with small children.

Other than attending a few rare hunts, that had been my job for the last two years while the rest of the world had gone to shit.

Even before the apocalypse, I'd prided myself on being able to handle disruptive students. Now, I had honest-to-God superpowers to up my game. None of that helped with Aul; he was my kryptonite. He was a genuinely curious child asking thought-provoking questions that entirely disrupted the lesson plan I'd laid out the night before.

"Caleb will not protect pack, is truth?" was the question Aul had asked me. His voice was deep and resonant.

More chirps, clicks, and buzzes flew at me from the rest of the class than they had for any other topic, with the possible exception of when he'd asked if I was a slave. I had answered with an honest, if uncertain, "Maybe."

"I will protect any sentients in danger," I said, "but I'm bad at fighting."

My Universal Translator Skill was amazing, but these beings were notoriously hard to translate, and my Skill's level wasn't fully up to snuff. With patience though, I thought we managed. It helped that Aul did most of the talking, no matter how much I tried to get the rest of the class to join in. Alone, the others would answer. When Aul was present, they deferred to him. I could speculate as to why, but I was a teacher, not an alienologist.

"Aul is confusion." His mandibles quivered slightly.

"You know I'm a vegetarian, right?"

He tilted his head in a way that my Skill told me meant agreement, though it still didn't feel right, even after all this time.

"Well, that's because I value life, especially sentient life. And it's damn near impossible to tell where to draw the line on what is and is not sentient. Because of that, I won't attack or kill anyone not attacking me or someone else. But I'm not a pacifist. I will attack those who attack others. I'm just not any good at it. My Class is Teacher. My points and Skills are spent to help me with that. And frankly, I'm too thoughtful for life-or-death reactions. I freeze up when a warrior needs to act without thinking.

"That's why I picked up Pavise here," I said, then reached over to knock on the metal head of the robot that had become the most reliable fixture of my life. He wasn't there. "Wherever he is. He's big and square and I hide behind him whenever we get attacked out there."

Pavise was the result of all of my Perks and a love of Star Wars and Medieval history. The System had him listed as a Shield Bot Protective Companion. I had upgraded his AI over time with about half of my Credits. He and my WWMRD necklace were my only prized possessions in this new world.

Where are you, buddy? I sent a questioning pulse through my neural link.

You left me in the hold again. And you've been ignoring your notifications. How am I supposed to protect you when you forcibly separate us?

The door closes automatically, I replied. *It's not my fault. If you're that worried about it, go first and make sure the path is safe.*

Alert me before departing and I will.

Aul's left mandible was twitching and I realized I'd been incredibly rude, ignoring his questions.

"Sorry, Aul. What were you asking?"

The ship is currently under attack. I should be with you.

They'll take care of it, they always do. Now hush. I quieted the alerts with a mental nudge.

"Pack hunt. Monsters attack pack. Caleb won't attack to protect pack? Only carry supplies and heal injured?"

"Yes."

"Caleb coward?"

"Not really," I answered. And I knew they knew I was telling the truth. One of my passive class skills, Ring of Truth, made it so that anyone I'd never intentionally deceived knew I wasn't lying. The skill didn't force me to tell them everything I knew, a fact that I had made sure to tell them as soon as I knew about it. Trust was essential if you wanted to be a teacher. And I'd never wanted to be anything else.

"How Caleb not coward?" He tapped low on the center of his chest plate, right underneath the bright red slash of color he alone shared with the Matriarch. I got a vague impression that this gesture was somehow meaningful.

It might be time to put one of my three remaining skill points into Universal Translator.

"If the pack was out exploring or gathering, I would fight to protect them, if badly. But the pack goes to where the monsters are to kill the monsters. Even if the monsters attack them first, that's not self-defense."

"Monsters attack pack. Monsters attack humans. Monsters attack everyone. Pack no hunt, monsters get stronger and stronger. Monsters kill everyone."

"Yes." This one word was weaker, almost trembling.

"Why not self-defense?"

My notifications were flashing, fast. I ignored them.

"I want to say that it's not self-defense because you can't know they will attack. And that's partly true." Being required to be completely honest was hard, but overall, it was amazing. It was good for the students, and it helped me to understand my own motivations. "But it does seem like almost all the monsters are hostile. Maybe all of them. And I want to say it's because it's not the monsters' fault. They didn't choose to be monsters. That might also be true. But killing other people because you're being forced to doesn't mean they don't have a right to defend themselves."

"Why not self-defense?" he said again. His upper hands were crossed now, in challenge.

"Levels," I finally told him. "Levels and loot."

He uncrossed his arms.

"The voloids did not come to Earth to help us. To stop the monsters. They came to Earth for Levels and loot. The voloids aren't protecting; they're attacking."

"Voloids kill monsters."

"They do," I agreed.

"Voloids good."

"Voloids are people," I replied. "They are good and bad."

He crossed both sets of his arms. "Matriarch's voloids good."

"Maybe," I answered. "The Matriarch saved me that first day. But she also kept me here. Sure, she pays me. She gives me Credits, orange Fanta, and veggie lovers pizza. She even gives me every book I ask for. But she never took me back to my people. She never asked if I wanted to stay. She even pretended not to understand when I asked if I was a prisoner." It had taken me nearly a year to realize that that hadn't been a difficulty in translation.

I kept quiet about the Skill I had picked up at level 31, called Class Trip. It was a teleportation Skill that I had planned to use to take myself to the nearest settlement. Temporarily or permanently, I had not decided. It had failed spectacularly, unfortunately, just two days prior. The System had informed me that it was not a self-only Skill. In retrospect, that should have been obvious. Because of that, I was as much of a prisoner as ever. I wasn't about to abduct a child to make my escape.

Emergency override, the shield bot's voice in my head grew very loud indeed. *The hull has been breached and enemies are entering the ship.*

I tried to stay calm.

"Matriarch no help owed."

"True."

"Matriarch good."

"Saving me was good."

"Matriarch good," he insisted. The System let me know that the way his mandible quivered meant he was not as certain as he sounded.

The attackers are human, Pavise told me, and the lesson became a lot less rhetorical.

"This ship is blocking the only real way to the best dungeon in the area," I said. "Look here."

I activated the first active Skill I had gained from the System—Show and Tell. Images from my trip to what was now the dungeon appeared in the air before the children. Some pictures were of the little town between the two lakes. Others were of the late winter austerity that would bloom into lush, dense greenery later in the year. There were log cabin style buildings, a large campfire, and a boathouse.

The image I expanded though was of the single-lane floating bridge. It crossed the deep marsh from the tiny, overgrown dirt road on one side to the equally overgrown dirt driveway that wound through the hardwoods and pines to the camp on the other. Their train-car-shaped spaceship was settled directly atop the rickety boards that were just wide enough to accommodate a single car tire on each side. The bridge had splintered around the ship and submerged when it couldn't take the weight.

"This is the one path to the dungeon that wasn't nearly impassible even before the world went crazy. Blocking that path was clearly the Matriarch's plan. She wanted the dungeon for her people, and she took it. It didn't matter to her that someone had owned this place before the System came. It didn't stop her that taking the dungeon would cost the humans in the area progress and wealth that they would need to survive this new reality. But the voloid hunters also keep the dungeon monsters from growing and escaping. That helps keep the human settlement safe. The voloids are good and bad."

Show me what's happening, I instructed my defender. I held up my hand to get Aul to stop. He didn't.

"Humans good and bad," he said. Even his tone said he was angry. That was a trait he had learned from me.

"Yes," I said. "Wait."

He didn't. "Caleb good and bad." He glared at me.

Then the connection finished, and I was seeing through the central camera that passed for the robot's eye. The five attackers were already engaged with the majority of the voloid warriors. The Matriarch was nowhere to be seen.

One of the attackers was an androgynous, short-haired Native American I labeled in my head as Slytherin, due to their snarl, spellcasting, and green robes. My second passive, Relatable, told me that their special interests included fantasy fiction, roleplaying games, and architecture. They tossed out glowing purple dust while they chanted.

Those voloids hit by the spell dropped their spears and blasters. They stood in apathy while a swarm of blade-legged, steel spiders shredded them like parmesan cheese.

I gagged but couldn't look away.

The one controlling the spiders was a young white woman. She was dressed in bulky, black leather armor with various tech components. Her chin-length blond hair was shaved on one side, where she had a much better neurological implant than mine. I knew that because it was the custom Dylo-Tek device I'd have bought if I had been able to scrounge together enough Credits.

Her special interests included anarchy, cybertech, and kitten videos. Because of her swarm, and the spikes and blades along her armor, in my mind I labeled her Edgelord.

The third, clearly the leader, was a rugged black man with skin even darker than mine. He had a shaved head, broad shoulders, and muscles a pro wrestler would've killed for. Plates and cybernetics that would look at home in a high-tech, dystopian hellscape covered him here and there.

He'd have been irresistible before the apocalypse. Now, he was terrifying.

His right leg had been replaced by a skinless prosthetic with flashing red lights. He drove a spike that extended down from it into the chest of one of the dying voloids, and it pulsed. His damaged cybernetic armor repaired itself as it did so.

His special interests included human independence, war, and high finance. I dubbed him Insurgent.

The last two, or one with a duplication power, looked like soldiers in full dress uniforms. Both had machine guns with under barrel launchers. They were too far away for my power to evaluate their interests. I dubbed them the Twins.

I could speak through my droid. I could have warned the humans about the extreme danger the Matriarch's absence posed. I'd learned about her disappearing act the day she'd saved my life and made me her prisoner.

The humans' faces were filled with rage. Their eyes were haunted by events I couldn't fathom. They were clearly not good people. They were also clearly the product of whatever had happened to them in this new world.

They might have been there to rescue me.

They might have been there to kill us all.

They might hurt the children.

My hesitation cost two of the humans their lives and it may have saved us all.

The Matriarch appeared from out of stealth, stabbing one of the Twins through the head with her two-handed spear and shooting the other with both of her blasters at point blank range. They dropped dead where they stood. Blood sizzled when the blasters hit the bodies. I was glad that my droid couldn't pass on any smells.

The Matriarch shrieked and clicked in rage, activating some sort of taunt Skill that pulled all of their attention to her. She must have activated some other last-ditch ability also, because the grey of all of the voloids paled. Even the ones in the classroom with me withered, for lack of a better word. The Matriarch and her spear doubled in size. Her blasters, too small for her new hands, clattered to the floor.

I thought about ordering my droid to shield her. She was the only thing that stood between me and potential rescuers. Or potential murderers. By the time I had processed the fact that they didn't look like saviors and did look like killers and it was better to err on the side of caution, it was already too late.

As powerful as she looked, as enhanced as she was, even the Matriarch's armor was cracking when faced with Edgelord's swarm and Insurgent's heavy blaster. Her spear was doing severe damage, but it was clearly not enough. And they were too close to us now for a shield wall to matter.

"You're right," I said to my students. "I am good and bad. I try to be good. Sometimes it can feel impossible to tell the difference." My voice sounded to my ears every bit as haunted as the faces of the attackers.

Aul must have noticed the change. Clever as he was, how could he not? "Aul…" He paused a long moment. "Will try to be good when Aul is Matriarch." Aul shuddered and the paling worsened. "If Aul lives to be Matriarch."

That blew my mind two ways. *Well shit*, I corrected my inner monologue, *she*.

"Good," I told her, pride and terror bringing tears to my eyes in equal measure.

"Caleb show-and-tell fight," Aul said.

She was right, I could show them exactly what I was seeing and hearing. It didn't even cost much mana.

"No," I said.

"Caleb show," Aul insisted, crossing her arms.

"You don't want to see this."

She uncrossed her arms.

I had never invested a better point than in my Ring of Truth Skill. Then and there, I dropped the three points I had been hoarding into it.

And that's when I remembered Class Trip. It had failed before, when I'd tried to use it to escape. But I wasn't alone now. And any ethical questions about taking the children with me were long since irrelevant. Best yet, even the basic version could get us all out of there. Only distance increased with a higher Skill Level.

I activated the Skill.

Skill attempt failed. Parental permission required.

Permission slips! Innocent children were going to be murdered because their slaughtered parents couldn't give me permission slips!

"Fucking System," I said out loud, though I had not intended to do so.

The ship's systems have sealed and hidden the doors. Given the Matriarch's level, it is likely that these beings have Advanced Classes, but even they should not be able to bypass the hologram.

Hope for the safety of the children surged in me as hope for the survival of the Matriarch died screaming right along with her. Unable to help and equally unable to look away, I watched as Insurgent claimed E'Kklon Vekk's spear. A device on Edgelord's wrist beeped.

I am sorry. It seems that I calculated correctly that the attackers would be unable to penetrate the holographic defenses. I failed to consider that the tech-classed cyborg could have a passive that would allow her to detect our communication channel and follow it back to its source. Again. I am sorry.

Sorry. It was sorry. This was all my fault. *No.* I told myself. *You have to hold yourself together for the children. This isn't over yet.*

Unable to spot the door to my classroom, Edgelord was using another device to melt through the wall as if by means of a lightsaber.

For the first time, I activated my level 30 Skill, Administrative Authority. "Try not to make any sudden movements, keep all of your hands where they can see them."

I wanted so desperately to lie and say, "They're not going to hurt you" or "I'll protect you." But my students weren't stupid, I wasn't a good liar, and my habit was to tell them the truth.

"I think they'll kill you if you give them any excuse," was the best I could manage, since my passive power didn't require me to include that I thought they'd probably kill all of us regardless, especially them.

I watched through the eyes of Pavise as the humans readied their assorted weapons.

Prepare to defend, I commanded my droid.

It is not my job to defend the children, it insisted.

No, it isn't. It's one of mine. Which is why you'd better be ready or be prepared to violate your contract.

For your safety, I must insist...

But whatever it was going to say came too late. As the area of the wall came down with a thud, the attackers opened fire blindly into our room and I dove between the attackers and the children.

A powerful blue wall of energy blocked and deflected the attacks, slightly inconveniencing but not particularly harming the high-level humans. What was left of the barrier flickered and sputtered, barely a trace of its power remaining.

I activated Administrative Authority and shouted, "Stop." Channeling my inner Chaucer from *A Knight's Tale*, I said, "Listen to me."

I was no Paul Bettany, but I prayed that the barrier, their surprise at seeing a human, and my Skill would buy me their attention at least long enough to give me a chance.

"You are not in any danger here. You've already won." When I saw the effects of shock and my power fading from their faces, I tried one last appeal. "You are about to murder innocent children."

Edgelord frowned. The Slytherin wannabe looked as if they had consumed spoiled milk.

The insurgent flinched as if he had been struck. "Wait," he commanded the others.

Edgelord's hand was still pointed toward me, and the spiders advanced again.

"I said wait, God damn it," Insurgent shouted. The force of whatever Skill he had activated staggered me.

The spiders stopped.

Insurgent turned that power, that presence, that deadly killing intent toward me as he met my gaze fully. "Why should I listen to you, traitor? And why should I, scratch that, why *do* I believe a single fucking word you say?"

"It's a passive Skill," I told him. "I'm a teacher. As long as I have never tried to deceive someone I'm trying to teach, they instinctively know that I'm not lying. It doesn't stop you from doing anything or make you do anything. It just means you know that you can trust me."

"Why would I trust a traitor? You're helping these aliens, these invaders."

"The Matriarch you killed in the other room. She saved my life during the fall. I've been here ever since. I would have died out there. They treated me well, but they would not take me to a human-run Safe Zone."

"You're telling me you were a prisoner? A slave?"

"It's complicated," I answered.

"It's Stock Market Syndrome. No. Stock something. I remember reading about that," Slytherin said. "It's on the tip of my tongue."

"Stockholm?" Edgelord asked.

"That's that one. You start liking or falling in love with your captors."

"You're saying it's not his fault?" Insurgent said.

They nodded reluctantly.

"Then he's not part of the quest," Edgelord said. "We just need to finish clearing out the aliens and we can take the ship.

"Quinn, you don't understand. The quest lists him," the leader said. "Unless there's another of these *things* left alive, the count is off. Why would the quest list you as a member of the crew?" He glared at me, his suspicion obviously returning.

"I'm their teacher." Because I knew he'd ask, I added, "When the Matriarch saved my life, she threw me in the room with them, and she must have seen my Class because she told me to teach. And so I did."

"Did you ever, even once, help them against humans or humanity in any way? And apparently, I'll know if you're lying to me, so don't bother."

"No," I said. I had considered it. I had been about to. But he didn't know that. And my Skill did not consider that deception.

He shut his eyes and sighed, then said to the others, "Then we failed the quest. We'll finish up here and head back to town with the loot from the aliens."

"But the ship," Edgelord, no Quinn, whined.

"Is his to claim, according to the System. He's already been here for two years, and he's got a legitimate claim. We're not thieves."

"Speak for yourself," she snapped back. She turned to Slytherin. If she was hoping for support, she didn't get it.

Slytherin looked utterly exhausted. Hell, as a powerful caster, they probably had endurance stats much closer to mine than their companions'.

Insurgent glared at Edgelord and she cowered, probably because a Skill was forcing her to. She didn't seem the type. "As long as we are grouped together, *we* are not thieves. *Is that clear*?"

"Yes, boss," she finally said, but there was fury in her eyes. If I didn't miss my guess, he'd pay for that, one way or the other.

He seemed to think so too. "You two can split my share of the loot, except for this spear. I'm keeping the spear."

"Fine. Let's kill these fuckers and get out of here." She seemed mollified, if only just.

"Not kill," I said, "murder."

The leader flinched again. "Why do you say that?" He let out a sigh that was louder and longer than the others. "And why is it true?"

"It doesn't have to be true," Edgelord said. "He just has to believe it's true."

"Good point," the leader said. "Why do you *think* it's true? We're at war, after all."

"You might be right that you're at war and everything you've done is justified."

He nodded, and I thought that he appreciated the acknowledgment of his position. Maybe I could build on that.

"Even if this is a war though, killing these children would be murder. They haven't done anything wrong."

"They're still invaders."

"No, they aren't."

He sighed again, which I realized was how he reacted to my passive skill. "Why not?"

"Because invaders invade. It's a verb. These children were brought here, through no decision or choice of their own."

He stood there for a long moment, and I watched in his eyes as his sanity flicked back and forth as he considered and finally started to break, probably forever. He was clearly making the wrong decision. His hand moved toward his weapon as his hatred slowly broke what was left of his decency.

And I had no power, no Skill, no spell or ability, no more arguments that could stop the atrocity that was about to happen. I could put my body in the way, but I'd die for nothing. In his mind, I was certain, that would be my fault—not his. He'd even finish his quest.

Whenever I had a student who was going through something so horrible that they acted out in ways I couldn't understand, or when I had students I couldn't seem to reach, I always asked myself the question that the acronym on my necklace stood for.

What would Mr. Rogers do?

It had become such an ingrained habit that it happened now, without me even trying.

The man had inspired me to be a teacher. To be a better man. And his lessons had never let me down. That one question had always been enough to shift my viewpoint when I needed it the most.

This time though, for the first time, it failed me. It failed me because I was already doing what I believed Mr. Rogers would have done.

And evil was still evil.

And I, being the kind of man I was, shaped by the man he had been, was simply not strong enough to do a single damn thing about it.

I cried then. For the last of my innocence. For the children. For the world, and for the loss of this man's sanity and humanity.

I cried, and he noticed. He noticed my sympathy. My pity. He saw that some of it was meant for him. And he asked me a single word. "Why?"

"Do you remember Mr. Rogers?" I thought about activating my Show and Tell Skill to make an image of the man, but some instinct held me back. Maybe because the Skill belonged in this world, and Mr. Rogers belonged in the one we had lost.

He stood there quietly, hurting, grieving for that world, if his eyes could be believed. In the end, he didn't speak, only nodded.

"That's why," I answered softly.

A bit of the hardness came back to his face, and the haunted expression came with it.

"His world is gone," Quinn, the Edgelord, said.

"Gone forever," Slytherin added, but they said it mournfully, not wickedly.

"We can never go back," Insurgent finished.

"You're right," I told him.

He nodded, and there was a dangerous shift in his stance. His grip tightened on the Matriarch's spear.

"But that doesn't mean we can't go forward," I said, and even I didn't know for sure that I truly believed it until he sighed.

Something dark took his expression, something that rode upon a pale horse. And that darkness fought with the inner child Mr. Rogers had touched, so long ago. This battle had nothing to do with me anymore, and everything to do with the remnants of his lost innocence.

The man who opened his eyes and met mine was still a monster, or someone capable of true monstrosity. But I would have said, and not lost my Skill by doing it, that he was not a man who would murder innocent children. His next words seemed to agree, but the bleeding edge of his tone sent chills of fear through my soul for the future of humanity.

"You have a spaceship," he said. "Get these aliens off my planet."

All I could do, all I dared to do, was nod.

He turned and walked away. Eventually, hesitantly, the other two followed him.

Quest alert: *You have been given a mandatory quest. Remove the children in your care from planet Earth and its surrounding area.*

Reward: 5,000 experience points and 50,000 Credits.

Additional reward: You will not be hunted down and exterminated by Commander Lee Greyson.

Time to failure: 1 week.

"Mr. Rogers good," Aul said. "Caleb good."

Relief for the children and fear for myself went to war inside me, but it was no real contest. My life as I had known it had ended two years prior. I had long since mourned it. Now, more than ever, it was clear to me that a dungeon world was not a place for a man like me.

Is there any place in this universe for a man like me? I thought with a shudder.

I shook my head. It didn't matter. I might not have a place, but I had a job to do. It wasn't the job I had signed up for and it wasn't a job I was qualified for. But it didn't matter if I was the right person for the job. I was the *only* person for the job.

My one priority now had to be the children. I would see them to safety, or I would die trying. It's what Mr. Rogers would have done.

About the Authors

D. J. Rezlaw is a rocket engineer building rocket engines in Rocket City. He's also a long-time avid reader who has been devouring progression fantasy books since he first discovered them, half a decade ago. When he isn't building rockets, reading, or writing, he's spending time with his wife, four kids, two cats, one dog, and a varying number of rabbits and chickens.

Follow D.J. here: www.facebook.com/DJRezlaw

InkWitch is a fan of LitRPG and of the System Apocalypse series. After reading (and loving) *Town Under*, she had to contribute a slice of New Zealand to the universe. She likes playing with non-traditional characters in her own LitRPG stories. You can read more from her on Royal Road.

Follow InkWitch here: www.royalroad.com/profile/172010

Craig Hamilton spends most of his day as a technical sales engineer, translating specifications and talking about IT infrastructure. While writing has been taking up most of his free time lately, Craig also appreciates playing tabletop RPGs or board games with friends. When his inner introvert demands a break from polite company, Craig can be found sprawled on a couch with a book or e-reader. Craig is the author of the spin off series *System Apocalypse – Relentless*.

Follow Craig here: www.facebook.com/AuthorCraigHamilton

Andrew Tarkin Coleman worked in finance for over a decade, then switched over to litigation support for another decade. He refused to sell his soul and they fired him. However, working with the damned drove him insane. He has developed a pathological hatred of social media, and quite frankly should not be allowed on the street without at least two beautiful women to always distract him.

He lives in New York City and is slowly turning himself into a cyborg version of Frankenstein's Monster. Andrew insists that the doctor was the real monster and Victor Frankenstein Jr. was merely the victim of child abuse - end flesh golem discrimination now!

Mike Parsons is a lifelong reader of fantasy/science fiction and a sporadic writer of sports articles, strategies for adopting advanced analytics, and compelling work emails.

Originally from Calgary, Alberta, Mike is a former Wall Street trader and ice hockey goaltender who played once for Canada and many times for New Zealand. He now lives in Auckland with his wife and three kids and is the head of data and artificial intelligence for Air New Zealand.

Nick Steele is the pseudonym of an author and ex-Lieutenant in the Royal Australian Navy Reserves. He lives with his wife and their young daughter in Brisbane, not too far from Garden City, the real-life location of the fortified shopping centre in *Town Under.*

The very first LitRPG Nick ever read was about a guy called John Lee in Kluane National Park. It is an absolute honor and thrill to now contribute to that ever-expanding universe.

Chelsea Luckritz developed a love of life early. As an army brat, she moved and met new people every few years, which allowed her the opportunity to see and experience a great deal. Perhaps it was all that adventure in her blood or perhaps she is simply contrary, but she has endeavored not to use her accounting degree. Instead, she has focused on her family and earned a living using skills other than math.

David R. Packer is the author of *The Anubis War* and the forthcoming *Salish Rift* series. He's been a full-time teacher of historical European swordplay, a high-tech wizard, and a security professional. For a few years he was a for-pay bad guy working in police training, which once had him on the run from the entire police force, across the whole city.

Aside from that, he lives a cozy life with two cats and a real-life she-hulk for a wife. He has many books and likes coffee far too much.

Follow David here: https://boxwrestlefence.com
www.facebook.com/randy.packer

Corwyn Callahan is a very new author, who thought that he should publish stories so others could see inside his head and wonder where did the normal side of his family go wrong with him.

E. C. Godhand is a LitRPG author by profession and nurse by trade. She is the author of the series *The Heartfire Series* based in the extended universe of *Viridian Gates Online*. She writes, runs a community garden, and fosters orphaned kittens. Her main character has always been a healer, whether in video games or real life, and loves game design, wordplay, and psychology.

All proceeds from book sales will go directly to supporting her habit of living so she can keep writing for you. She's been rumored to eat up to three times a day even. At the very least, the kittens need to be fed.

Don't buy the books for her though. Do it for the fun LitRPG stories about drunken priests, weird dream worlds, and characters' assured descent into madness. Do it for the kittens.

Follow E. C. Godhand here: www.facebook.com/groups/RatPackGodhand
Support E. C. Godhand here: www.patreon.com/GodhandAuthor

Jason J. Willis is a husband, father, geek, equalist, and lover of art. Gamelit, LitRPG and progression/cultivation fiction. Audiobooks especially are his addiction of choice. Due to a beloved day job that allows him to listen to anything he wants during his entire work shift, Jason spends more than full time consuming the above, plus podcasts, music, and the Great Courses series.

Follow Jason here: www.facebook.com/jason.j.willis
www.instagram.com/jasonjoneswillis

Tao Wong is a Canadian author based in Toronto who is best known for his *System Apocalypse* post-apocalyptic LitRPG series and *A Thousand Li*, a Chinese xianxia fantasy series. His work has been released in audio, paperback, hardcover and ebook formats and translated into German, Spanish, Portuguese, Russian and other languages. He was shortlisted for the UK Kindle Storyteller award in 2021 for his work, *A Thousand Li: the Second*

Sect. When he's not writing and working, he's practicing martial arts, reading and dreaming up new worlds.

Tao became a full-time author in 2019 and is a member of SF Canada, the Science Fiction and Fantasy Writers of America (SFWA) and ALLI.

If you'd like to support Tao directly, he has a Patreon page - benefits include previews of all his new books, full access to series short stories, and other exclusive perks. Tao Wong's Patreon. www.patreon.com/taowong

For updates on the series and his other books (and special one-shot stories), please visit the author's website: www.mylifemytao.com

Publisher's Note

Thank you for reading the second System Apocalypse Short Story Anthology. This is doubly true for those of you who backed our Kickstarter and helped raise additional funds for the authors involved. I hope you've enjoyed the stories within and seen another side of the System Apocalypse universe.

Short story anthologies in general do not sell well, both in the LitRPG world and the indie world. On the other hand, I truly enjoy short stories as an art form. It requires a different skill set to plot a short story, while at the same time, requiring many of the skills that make a writer good.

All these authors, in my view, have the ability to write fascinating works and if they wish, make a career as an author. I'm looking forward to seeing their future works and am grateful for the opportunity to aid them, in some small way, in progressing their craft.

As always, please do leave a review. Reviews and conversations about the work make a big difference in sales, which will be necessary here.

-- Tao

More Great Reading

For more great information about LitRPG series, check out the Facebook groups:

- GameLit Society
  www.facebook.com/groups/LitRPGsociety
- LitRPG Books
  www.facebook.com/groups/LitRPG.books

System Apocalypse – Relentless

Bail bondsman. Veteran. Survivor.

Hal Mason's still going to find surviving the System Apocalypse challenging.

While bringing in his latest fugitive, Hal's payday is interrupted by the translucent blue boxes that herald Earth's introduction to the System - a galaxy spanning wave of structured mystical energy that destroys all electronics and bestows game-like abilities upon mankind.

With society breaking down and mutating wildlife rampaging through the city of Pittsburgh, those who remain will sacrifice anything for a chance at earning their next Level. As bodies fall and civilization crumbles, Hal finds himself asking what price is his humanity. Are the Credits worth his hands being ever more stained with blood?

Or does he press on - relentless?

The System Apocalypse: Australia

What's worse than Australian wildlife? *Mutated* Australian wildlife.

The System Apocalypse has come to Australia, altering native organisms and importing even more menacing creatures to the most dangerous continent on Earth. For Kira Kent, plant biologist, the System arrives while she's pulling an all nighter at work with her pair of kids in tow.

Now, instead of mundane parental concerns like childcare and paying the bills, she's got to figure out how to survive a world where already deadly flora and fauna have grown even more perilous - all while dealing with the minutiae of the System's pesky blue screens and Levels and somehow putting together a community of survivors to forge a safe zone to shelter her son and daughter.

It almost makes her miss the PTA fundraising sales. *Almost.*

Read more of the System Apocalypse: Australia series

https://readerlinks.com/l/2316522

The System Apocalypse
Complete series

What happens when the apocalypse arrives, not via nuclear weapons or a comet but as Levels and monsters? What if you were camping in the Yukon when the world ended?

All John wanted to do was get away from his life in Kluane National Park for a weekend. Hike, camp and chill. Instead, the world comes to an end in a series of blue boxes. Animals start evolving, monsters start spawning and he has a character sheet and physics defying skills. Now, he has to survive the apocalypse, get back to civilisation and not lose his mind.

The System has arrived and with it, aliens, monsters and a reality that draws upon past legends and game-like reality. John will need to find new friends, deal with his ex and the slavering monsters that keep popping up.

Read more of The System Apocalypse series!
https://readerlinks.com/1/2440485

To learn more about LitRPG, talk to authors including myself, and just have an awesome time, please join the LitRPG Group!

www.facebook.com/groups/LitRPGGroup

www.ingramcontent.com/pod-product-compliance
Lightning Source LLC
Chambersburg PA
CBHW030622310726
48979CB00003B/844